PRAISE FOR *WINTER'S SECRET*

"Lyn Cote owes me a night's sleep . . . because I didn't get ANY until I'd finished this book. A special mix of romance, whodunit, and personal faith."

STEPHANIE GRACE WHITSON
Christy Award finalist and best-selling author of Heart of the Sandhills

"*Winter's Secret* by Lyn Cote has a hero guaranteed to make any woman's heart flutter and a mystery that will keep you guessing."

DEANNA JULIE DODSON
author of In Honor Bound, By Love Redeemed, *and* To Grace Surrendered

"Carefully plotted, filled with rich details, Lyn's writing is true to form, giving us an opportunity to uncover the secrets winter snows just can't hide. Bravo, Lyn! Great story, well told. I can hardly wait for the next book of this Northern Intrigue."

LOIS RICHER
author of Blessed Baby

"Lyn Cote has the ability to write about a snowstorm with such delicious description that I can get shivers in the middle of August. In *Winter's Secret,* she portrays a small Wisconsin town filled with characters of depth and substance, while leading us deeper into the mysteries of their collective past."

HANNAH ALEXANDER
author of Sacred Trust, Solemn Oath, *and* Silent Pledge

romance the way it's meant to be

HeartQuest brings you romantic fiction
with a foundation of biblical truth.
Adventure, mystery, intrigue, and suspense
mingle in these heartwarming stories of
men and women of faith striving to build
a love that will last a lifetime.

May HeartQuest books sweep you
into the arms of God, who longs for you
and pursues you always.

Visit Tyndale's exciting Web site at www.tyndale.com

Check out the latest about HeartQuest Books at www.heartquest.com

Edited by Diane Eble

Designed by Kelly Bennema

Library of Congress Cataloging-in-Publication Data

Cote, Lyn.
Winter's secret / Lyn Cote.
p. cm. — (Northern intrigue) (HeartQuest)
ISBN 0-8423-3556-0 (softcover)
1. Nurses—Fiction. 2. Sheriffs—Fiction. 3. Wisconsin—Fiction. I. Title. II. Series
PS3553.O76378 W56 2002
813.'54—dc21 2001005375

Printed in the United States of America

08 07 06 05 04 03 02
9 8 7 6 5 4 3 2 1

Northern Intrigue

WINTER'S *Secret*

LYN COTE

Romance fiction from
Tyndale House Publishers, Inc., Wheaton, Illinois
www.heartquest.com

To my great husband for taking me "up north"!

And to Marilyn LeClere, my critique partner.
Thanks for all those phone calls which start
"I've been thinking about your story . . ."

Many thanks to Harry Daugherty, chief of police of Marion, Iowa,
for his technical help with this book.

Trust in the Lord with all your heart;
do not depend on your own understanding.

PROVERBS 3:5, NLT

PROLOGUE

STANDING TO THE side of the battered door, Sheriff Rodd Durand eased out his gun.

"Police! Come out with your hands up!"

He expected no answer.

Still, he waited. Snow sifted down on him from the ragged edge of the overhanging porch roof. He tugged up his collar against the harsh wind while trying to detect any sound from inside. He nudged open the sagging door and looked in. Then he stepped inside and walked cautiously through the cold house.

This was the second time he'd been called out on a frigid morning to face a wrecked door of a farmhouse burglarized overnight. Fortunately, in both cases the owner had been away for the night, so no one had been hurt. Rodd had been on the job just over a month. This was the second unsolved burglary in three weeks. Two failures. What a way to start out as county sheriff.

Inside, Rodd found what he'd expected—broken knickknacks, slit cushions, dresser drawers dumped onto the floor. Everything about the crime scene shouted, "Careless, clumsy!" The only reason the perpetrator succeeded was that he chose his targets well—isolated, empty houses.

This low-life thief preyed on the most defenseless—the elderly who lived alone out in the country. Leo Schultz had spent last night in Steadfast's clinic-care center. The shock of coming home this morning and finding his home burglarized had taken its toll on Schultz. The old man had looked pale and shaky. So Old Doc Erickson, who lived nearby, had come to take Mr. Schultz back to the county's only clinic.

Righteous anger swept through Rodd like flames. He had a thief, a nasty little weasel to catch.

CHAPTER ONE

FIGHTING THE NOVEMBER gloom, Wendy Carey winked at the gray-haired woman who sat beside her in the front seat of Wendy's station wagon. "I saw Bruno Havlecek flirting with you—with my own eyes."

"What would I want with that old fool?" Ma Ukkonen snapped.

"I think he's cute, Ma," Wendy teased. Everyone loved this woman and called her "Ma."

As Wendy turned off Highway 27, the wagon fishtailed. *Oh, Lord, keep us safe*, she silently prayed. Easing off the accelerator, she hugged the middle of the slick Wisconsin county road. The windshield wipers flicked away tiny snowflakes. She glanced at Ma. Ma's blood pressure had certainly worried her yesterday. Ma still looked worn down. Another dreary, gray morning offered no cheer. Wendy decided to go on teasing till Ma smiled. "And I love those little bow ties he wears."

With a humph, Ma folded her arms over her generous middle, padded by an outmoded wool coat. "If you keep talking like that, I'll paddle you like I did when you was little."

The older woman's blustery answer pleased Wendy. She'd get Ma to laugh before she had to leave her this morning. "You never paddled me. You fed me pancakes and maple syrup!"

Ma chuckled. "You sure could put away my pancakes. Now why are you asking about me and Bruno? I want to know who you're sweet on."

Wendy shook her head, trying to ignore the flicker of irritation this question, a frequent one, always brought. She repeated her routine answer, "Nobody around here to date."

Ma wagged her finger. "If I was twenty-five and as good-looking as you, do you think I'd be wasting my days taking care of a bunch of sick people?"

Wendy picked up the new topic. "Nursing is all I've ever wanted to do."

"I know. When you was little, you read me that book—"

"Nurse Nancy." Wendy grinned with real pleasure at the memory.

"A million times. So now you're all grown up, Nurse Wendy. Time you find you a man."

Wendy shrugged. Back to that! *I should be used to this by now, but can't everyone just let it go?* But she kept her voice light. "I have plenty of time for that." She turned up Ma's rutted drive. "Now I want you to promise me you'll take your blood pressure medicine every day. High blood pressure is nothing to play around with."

Ahead was Ma's white farmhouse with its large bay window in the front. An image flashed in Wendy's memory—a little towheaded girl looking wistfully out the bay window, waiting for her tardy mother to come and pick her up—long after all the other children had been taken home. Remembering the loneliness jabbed Wendy like a dull needle.

Ma's voice interrupted Wendy's thoughts. "I hope Jiggs didn't miss me last night. He's getting too old to be left alone."

Wendy gave Ma a sly grin. "Jiggs is a sharp old dog. He probably entertained some old hounds he hadn't seen in a while."

Ma slapped Wendy's arm. "Hush."

Parking the car behind Ma's house, Wendy glanced at the back door and froze. The beaten-in door hung open on one hinge. Another burglary! Dear God!

"Oh no!" Ma gasped.

Protective fear rushed through Wendy. "Stay here. I'll—"

Heedless, Ma turned the handle and kicked open the car door. She lurched toward her house over the frozen ground.

"Ma! Wait!" Wendy raced after her. She caught up, took Ma's arm, trying to slow her.

Ma shook her off. "Jiggs! Jiggs!" She shoved against the splintered door.

Wendy crowded close behind her. Just inside on the scuffed linoleum, the black-and-white dog lay motionless, silent.

"Jiggs! No!" Ma staggered.

Wendy threw her arm around the older woman, who slumped weakly against Wendy. Supporting Ma, she guided her through the kitchen into the living room, where she eased her onto the sofa. Wendy didn't need her blood pressure cuff to see that Ma was in bad shape again. Her own heart quickened at the sight of the disarray around her. She took Ma's pulse—one hundred and fifty and threadlike. Worse than yesterday. Ma tried to speak, but her words came out garbled. Suddenly Wendy's fear became reality. Stroke!

Wendy pulled out her cell phone and ordered the ambulance. Then she quickly dialed the sheriff's number and tersely told dispatch about this third break-in. A sick feeling settled in her stomach. Finding Jiggs like that had been a shock. She knelt beside the sofa and chafed the old woman's icy hands. Poor Ma. Poor old Jiggs. Wendy blinked rapidly to ward off tears that wanted to fall. "Don't worry, Ma. We'll get you back to the clinic right away."

The mantel clock ticked loudly in the stillness. Ma moaned on and off. Praying for the ambulance to hurry, Wendy checked Ma's vitals and tested her limbs for weakness. All the while she tried to avoid looking at the mess that the thief had left behind. She would have gladly strangled the person responsible.

Finally she heard a siren coming up the lane. She rushed to the front door and peered out the frosted window. The sheriff's Jeep Cherokee swerved to a stop, scattering snow-crusted gravel against the steps. What? The sheriff? How did he beat the ambulance here?

As Sheriff Durand bounded up the steps, she threw wide the door. The cold made her gasp. He shouldered his way in, and she slammed the door behind him.

The sheriff's formidable presence drew her like shelter in a storm. She stepped near him—her cold hands clasped together. Where were the EMTs? "Did you pass the ambulance?"

He glanced around at the disarray, then laid a reassuring hand on her shoulder. "They radioed dispatch. They swerved to miss a buck." His deep voice wrapped itself around her raw nerves. "They slid off the road south of here, but no one was hurt. They're just waiting for the wrecker to pull them out." Nodding toward Ma, he murmured, "What's wrong with your patient?"

"I think she's having a stroke," Wendy whispered. "The shock . . ." She collected herself and led him back to Ma. "I just brought her back from spending a night at the clinic."

From the sofa, Ma reared up, her jumbled words sounding her distress. Wendy put an arm around her. "We've got to get her to the clinic for medication—right away!"

"I'll drive you in." The sheriff bent to lift Ma into his arms. "Get the door, please."

Wendy scrambled ahead of him, opening the front door, then outside, the car door. "I'll get in first. You lift her in and I'll cradle her head in my lap."

"Fine. Fasten your seat belt first." He eased Ma into the backseat with Wendy, then hurried to the driver's seat.

Wendy's heart beat a rat-a-tat. The roads into town were slick. The snow-splattered roadside weeds spun by the car window. Clutching Ma to her, Wendy remembered all the times Ma had wrapped her soft plump arms around her.

The sheriff glanced back at her, asking her wordlessly how Ma was doing. Her heart in her throat, Wendy looked into his ice blue eyes. Their depths—so clear and calm—steadied her. She nodded, telling him just to get them to the clinic. Ma would get the medication she needed there.

She gave Ma a gentle squeeze and prayed to get to Steadfast safely—without running into a patch of glazed ice or another buck. It was hunting season and the deer were on the move. *Lord, keep us safe.*

The miles flew past. At the outskirts of town, he radioed ahead to the clinic. At its entrance, a nurse wearing a heavy white sweater burst through the emergency-room doors, pushing a gurney ahead of her. The sheriff gently lifted Ma onto it.

Wendy slid across the seat to him. He lifted her out, too, as though she didn't weigh anything at all. His touch—or her worry—made her breathless. "Thanks, Sheriff," she managed. Then, her feet on the ground, she hurried after Ma. She felt his gaze follow her inside.

❋ ❋ ❋

SHERIFF RODD DURAND watched the automatic doors close behind Wendy. The young nurse's angelic, anxious face lingered in his mind. Keyed up, he felt drawn to follow her to see the end of the drama they'd just shared. Instead, he climbed into his Jeep. He had another burglary investigation to conduct and sick cattle at home.

Four miles out of town back at the Ukkonen property again, he bumped along its rutted road and pulled in, parking next to the nurse's dark station wagon. He radioed his location to dispatch, then got out.

Dread clumped in his midsection. Examining a crime scene here hit him harder than it had in Milwaukee. Here, the people who depended on him were individuals, not just the law-abiding public. As Steadfast's new sheriff, he'd expected drunkenness and disorderly conduct, petty theft, minor drug offenses, and the occasional drunk-driving case—stuff like that. He'd never expected a string of burglaries aimed at the most defenseless—the infirm, the elderly, the poor. Pathetically easy targets.

The thief—whom he'd nicknamed "the Weasel"—had used the same simple MO again—hitting the isolated house of an older person away from home.

Shivering in the brisk wind, Rodd paused next to the back door and glanced down at the footprints. The pretty nurse and her patient had trampled over the same brand-new, generic men's boot prints he'd seen twice before. The thief must have bought them just to use in the burglaries. They showed no unique wear patterns.

With his toe, he nudged the remnants of the door open and walked into the shadowy kitchen. He stopped short, the body of an aged black-and-white mixed-breed dog blocking his way. Out of habit, Rodd knelt and felt for a pulse. But the old dog had been gone for hours.

A picture from the past flashed into his mind—Bucky, his father's hunting dog and his own first pet. How many times had he wakened and found that Bucky had become his pillow for the night?

He ruffled the shaggy fur at the dog's neck. "Poor old fella."

A sudden spurt of anger whipped through him like the icy wind outside. An old widow living all alone and now her dog killed. And all for a few lousy bucks! Rodd felt himself steaming with the callousness of it.

Then Uncle George's words came: *"Ride your anger. Don't let it ride you."* Rodd sucked in air and rose. *You won't get away with this again, Weasel. I won't let you. This is your last job.*

With that pledge pulsing inside him, even and true, he began the first methodical examination of the crime scene, routine to him after more than ten years in law enforcement. Room by room, section by section, he viewed the upheaval—furniture upended with the bottoms slit open, old books dashed helter-skelter on the floor. Alongside the worthless bric-a-brac, expensive antiques lay shattered and scarred—one, a smashed, green-glass hurricane lamp over a hundred years old. A perp with brains might have taken this and fenced it successfully, but not the Weasel—a thief in a hurry, who took only cash. Rodd let out a sound of disgust and quit the house.

Outside, he scanned the snow-covered ground around the house and behind the precariously leaning barn looking for—there! Snowmobile tracks under the new snow.

The Weasel always traveled on a snowmobile. At the first two burglary scenes, Rodd had followed the machine's tracks, but each time the tracks had led him to a popular snowmobile trail where many snowmobiles had already crisscrossed. He'd lost the trail then, in the morass of tracks.

And using the cover of trees, this thief worked after dark. That explained the lack of leads. At night, a snowmobile was only a headlight and a roar—impossible to identify.

Icy wind whistling around his ears, Rodd stared at the bleak horizon. He went over the first two crime scenes in his mind and compared this one to them. Wearing snowmobiler's gear, complete with face mask, helmet, and gloves, meant that the thief left nothing—not even a hair—behind at the crime scenes. Rodd would supervise a couple of his new deputies in examining this latest crime scene and lifting a few latent prints, even if they wouldn't be the thief's. The experience would be good for them. He tromped back into the house.

In a kitchen drawer, he unearthed a used blue-gingham vinyl tablecloth. Kneeling, he gently wrapped the old dog inside its flannel backing, then carried him out to the barn. There, he carefully secured the long bundle up high across the open crossbeams, where it would be untouched until someone could come out and dig a grave in the frozen ground. He rested his gloved hand on the bundle. "Good-bye, old fellow," he whispered.

Back at the house, while he reinforced the splintered kitchen door to keep wild animals out, he thought of one constant that hadn't seemed significant to him until now: Wendy Carey, Harlan Carey's granddaughter. In only that scant time together, she'd caught his attention—as though he read her heart through her clear, honest eyes. He usually wasn't very attracted to women with such short hair, but her appealing face held a rare sweetness.

Suddenly his thinking cleared. He needed to talk to her, and she'd need a ride back to her car. As he headed back to town, he radioed the clinic and told them he was on his way to pick her up. He hoped she'd be able to tell him what he needed to know. But questioning a woman always put him on his guard. Raised by a father and a great-uncle, he considered women a mystery. He'd need Miss Carey's cooperation. Would he know how to get it?

* * *

WENDY WAVED GOOD-BYE to the clinic receptionist and stepped outside into subzero chill. She scurried down the snow-packed path to the waiting sheriff's car. Her head bent against the wind, she couldn't see him until after she opened the passenger door and jumped in.

Her breathing came quickly—not merely from running in the cold. Hearing that Sheriff Durand was coming back for her had set her all on edge. She avoided looking at him directly, afraid making eye contact would rattle her even more. "Thanks for coming to take me back to my car."

"No trouble. How is Mrs. Ukkonen?"

Taking strength from his matter-of-fact tone, she steadied her nerves. "We got her here in time. Thanks for arriving just when I needed you." A shiver shook her. Feeling the warmth blowing from the heater, she shook off her brown parka hood and braved a glance at him.

"Just part of my job."

Why was she feeling so fluttery all of a sudden? She never reacted like this to a man. Were her jitters due to all the anxiety over Ma? She tried to settle herself comfortably on the seat.

The sheriff started down the drive. "I need to ask you some questions."

She nodded, fighting her awareness of the long, lean man just inches from her. His presence filled the small space, making her breathing shallow. *What's gotten into me?* She drew in a calming breath. "You have me as long as it takes to reach my car, Sheriff."

Taking refuge in her role as nurse, she glanced at her watch. "I'm running behind. I've got quite a list of patients to visit today."

"I just need some details for my report. After paperwork, I have cattle to take care of myself." He drove out of the clinic parking lot.

Turning her head only slightly, Wendy studied the sheriff's profile, trying to analyze what was causing her unusual response to him. Sheriff Durand possessed good regular features, an honest face. Healthy skin and black hair. Vertical scar on his jaw. Looked like a deep one that had taken a lot of stitches to close.

Fighting the urge to trace the scar with her finger, she busied herself latching her seat belt. What was going on with her? From a distance, she'd seen him around in the few months since he'd moved up here to take over his great-uncle's place. Each Sunday she'd noticed him at the church, where he sat in the back and left immediately after the service ended. He just hadn't struck her as anything but what he was now—the county sheriff. Not a man she'd do more than notice.

But being alone with him now, she understood the buzz of interest he'd garnered among the unmarried women in the county. She wished them luck. Stiffening her resistance, she straightened her short hair by running her fingers through it.

The sheriff glanced sideways at her, catching her looking at him. "How many visits do you do a day?"

His catching her looking at him had warmed her cheeks, but she acted as though it hadn't. She unzipped her jacket and let out a long sigh. *Great. An easy question.* "It depends. Some visits are just med checks. Some take longer, like dressing changes."

The briefest of smiles touched his mouth. "You sound like the old-fashioned country doctor, Miss Carey."

Wendy let herself give him a cautious half smile. "Call me Wendy. Yes, Doc calls me his eyes, ears, and feet. In a rural county like ours, we're lucky to have Doc and his grandson. Without their clinic, we'd be driving more than an hour to get care."

She began to warm up. The uncommon flutters were calming down. Good. "Did you find any evidence at Ma's?" She relaxed against the seat, assessing him further from the corner of her eye.

He wore a khaki-and-brown, fleece-lined jacket over a starched khaki-and-brown shirt and matching slacks. A polished star on the jacket marked him as sheriff. But his self-assurance was just as evident. This was a man who took charge.

"You took Mrs. Ukkonen away from home last night?" His voice, unruffled and matter-of-fact, struck a note deep inside her, drawing her from her private observations.

She chose her words with care. "Ma's blood pressure was sky-high yesterday. Doc wanted to check her himself."

"So she'd been away for only one night?" he asked.

The mood in the Jeep altered. This ride to her car was more than just a courtesy. Wendy shifted in her seat. Outside the window, the snow flurries had picked up—showers of white flakes dashed themselves against the windshield as though committing mass suicide.

Uneasy, she tucked one leg under her. *Where is this leading, Sheriff?* "Yes," she said slowly. "Doc called me to take her home as my first stop today."

He nodded. "You called in the Leo Schultz burglary, too, right?"

The mention of the second of the three burglaries puzzled her. What was he getting at? "Yes, but Leo's nephew came to the clinic and drove him home himself that morning," she said, carefully spelling out each fact in order, the same way she reported vitals to Old Doc. "When they found the house burglarized, the nephew called me first because Mr. Schultz looked so pale and shaky. I told the nephew I'd call your office and report it for him."

"But you didn't come out to help Schultz? You didn't think he needed you?"

His question hit her wrong. What was he implying—that she'd let Mr. Schultz down? She sat up straighter. "Doc is his nearest neighbor—didn't you know that? And that morning Doc hadn't come into the clinic yet, so I called him to go over there. Doc could do more for Mr. Schultz's weak heart than I could." She lifted her chin.

"But you did take Schultz to the clinic the day before and had expected to drive him home?"

So? Is that a crime? "Yes," she replied, keeping her tone measured in spite of her growing tension, "and I'm visiting him later today to do another checkup."

He persisted. "You were also at Fletcher Cram's house when the burglary was discovered, right?" His unemotional tone unnerved her.

Why was he forcing her to go back over her patients' burglaries? Maybe they were just strangers to him, but not to her. She'd known them all her life! She blinked away tears. How could someone hurt old people like this? The crimes didn't just rob them of cash. They robbed them of their feeling of safety in their own homes! Worrying her lower lip, she gazed out at the snow-laden pines lining the highway. Emotion clogged her throat.

"You called that one in too," he prompted her. "But I didn't see you there."

Not trusting herself, she wouldn't look at him. "I couldn't stay. And Mr. Cram wasn't so ill that I couldn't leave him."

"But today you couldn't leave."

His question sounded like an accusation. It sparked her temper. "You saw Ma! Finding Jiggs like that . . ."

He nodded.

The roadside pines gave way to a harvested hayfield. Propping her arm by the window, Wendy faced away. She felt tears coming again. Poor old Jiggs. She murmured half to herself, "Only a sick person would kill a helpless old dog."

"Yes, a nasty, little weasel."

The unexpected but controlled anger in the sheriff's voice caught her up short. She glanced at him. A wary silence blossomed inside the police car.

"Miss Carey, you were the one who reported all three burglaries."

She twisted sideways and gave him a reproachful look.

"Before each burglary you took the patient to the clinic for the night; then the next morning you were supposed to be the one who brought the patient home."

He was connecting her to these crimes! How?

"I have to ask myself—why do burglaries happen only to patients you take to the clinic one day, then take home the next?"

His question stunned her. Of all the insults she'd taken over the years, this was the first time an accusation had stung her so personally. Just whom had the sheriff been listening to—Veda McCracken?

She'd reacted to this man in a way she hadn't reacted to anyone before, and now he was accusing her of hurting her own patients! "You think I take people to the clinic—" her voice shook—"rob their homes, then drive them back to see my handiwork?"

"No. I don't think you have anything to do with the burglaries, but your connection to these victims is my only lead." His police radio crackled. "Miss Carey, there's no reason to take this personally—"

"You connect me with three heartless crimes, and I'm not supposed to take it personally?" Outrage pulsed at her temples.

"I'm just following correct investigative procedure—"

"It's just a coincidence," she interrupted him.

"I don't admit to coincidence unless I'm forced to. Now think; did you tell anyone that you'd taken these patients in and when you would be bringing them home?"

"Of course not! I don't gossip about my patients. But this is a small town. Everyone has ears and a mouth, and they like to use them!" Unfortunately, Veda came to mind again.

He'd turned down the county road leading to Ma's property. Wendy zipped up her parka—she couldn't wait to get out of this car! Why had she thought the sheriff attractive? She wouldn't let him insult her anymore!

He pulled up beside her wagon.

She unhooked her seat belt and let herself out of the Jeep. The cold hit her like an ice wall. Slamming the door, she ran to her car.

The sheriff got out and called to her, "We need to talk!"

She didn't trust herself to look back. A tangle of emotions—hurt, anger, and fear—swirled inside her like snow flung about in a cross-current of winter wind.

He called after her, "I didn't mean to upset you. But I have to find out what the connection between you and the burglaries is."

The sheriff had stirred up the muddy depths of the past. And she didn't appreciate it.

She halted and spun around. "Sheriff, you're new here. Let me give you some words of advice. First, don't believe everything you hear. Second, you need to get to know folks before you go around asking loaded questions. We're not strangers here like the people you worked around in Milwaukee. Here it matters what you ask and whom you ask."

Her tone became gritty. "But most of all, you need to know some people around here never forgive . . . or forget."

CHAPTER TWO

SEETHING, WENDY JERKED open the creaky door of her wagon and jumped onto the driver's seat. She plunged the key into the ignition and twisted it. The big, old motor bellowed to life. Without glancing back, she drove away.

Mentally she shouted, Taking patients to and from the clinic is my job, Sheriff! I'm just doing my job. Her conscience whispered to her, *He's just doing his job.*

She gunned her motor and swung onto the county road, fishtailing slightly. She let up on the gas pedal. Just before she bit her fingernail, Wendy caught herself. She felt like slapping the hand away. Nail biting—how she hated it! Steering with her knees, she spread her hands over the wheel. Well-manicured nails, groomed cuticles, pale pink polish on oval nails. The kind of nails she'd always dreamed of having as a teen. She sighed. She'd come too far to let this aggravating man spoil her manicure.

Within minutes, she pulled into the yard in front of Bruno Havlecek's log cabin. She wanted Bruno to hear about Ma from her and get the facts straight. She switched off the motor but stayed in her car.

Internally, she still bubbled like a pot of boiling water. In the country winter quiet, she bent her head and prayed for a clear mind and a calm spirit. Her patients shouldn't suffer just because the new sheriff might have picked up on old rumors. Turning her agitation over to God, she waited with her eyes closed. *Those who wait on the Lord will find new strength.* She waited. She imagined she could hear the gentle *shush* of the falling snow on the windshield. The sound soothed her heart as though God were whispering, "Hush, my sweet child. Hush." She felt herself simmering down.

"Wendy! Are you all right?" A gruff voice shouted nearby.

Glancing up, she saw Bruno propped up on crutches, standing inside his open front door. She reached for her bag on the seat beside her, flipped up her hood, then braced herself to face the wind. As she hustled toward him, she scolded, "You shouldn't be standing in the cold! Get in!"

When she ducked past him into the house, he chuckled and closed the door behind her. "You're early, Wendy. I didn't expect you till around ten like you said."

"I'm sorry." She shed her jacket onto the back of a wooden kitchen chair.

"You look worried." Bruno, wearing a carefully pressed plaid shirt with a crisp red bow tie, handed her a mug of his special fresh-ground coffee, heavy on the cream.

Wendy breathed in the rich aroma.

Bruno lowered himself into the chair across from her at the spotless round table. "You've already had a rough day? This early?"

"Yes." Nothing would be served by hesitating. "Ma Ukkonen's place was robbed last night."

"Was Lou hurt?" Bruno asked, using Ma's first name.

"No, she'd just spent the night at the clinic. When I drove her home this morning, we found her back door broken open—"

"Blast this leg! Keeping me housebound." He slapped his injured leg. "Where is she now?"

"She's back in the clinic. I'm afraid the shock brought on a stroke."

"A stroke!" Bruno rubbed his forehead as though it pained him. "What did they take, for heaven's sake!"

"I don't know." Wendy lowered her eyes. "The thief killed Jiggs."

Bruno bent his head into his hand. "Will Lou be all right?"

Wendy touched his sleeve. "We got her to the clinic in time."

He looked up. "Did the sheriff come out?"

Her stomach clenched, but she kept her voice calm. "I'm sure he's doing his best."

"Well, he better be quick about it! This happened to Schultz and Cram, too. Three burglaries in less than a month! Nothing like this has ever happened around here. I figured a young sheriff with all that education and experience would have this all wrapped up by now."

Wendy gave Bruno a concerned look. She didn't envy the sheriff. But if kindhearted Bruno thought this, what were others thinking?

Bruno looked back at her sharply. "The sheriff didn't say anything . . . to you, did he? Perhaps he got the wrong idea . . . from somebody?"

Why had Bruno said that? What had he heard being said behind her back? Wendy's heart rate sped up to double time. Bruno meant his words as kindness, but they still hurt. She cleared her throat. "No, he didn't say anything against me." The sheriff had only intimated that she was somehow connected to the three burglaries. But how could that be?

"Lou needs help and I'm laid up with this cracked leg." He slapped his thigh again.

She turned her attention to him. "Let's look at your leg. Maybe it's time to change you to a walking cast."

"Would you?" Bruno gave her a shaky grin.

He is sweet on Ma. What a dear man. Wendy knelt beside him and began to examine the leg encased in a soft splint. When she was done, she nodded. "I'll take you in with me."

"I appreciate this, Wendy." He squeezed her arm. "I want to make sure for myself Lou's okay."

She nodded, then bundled herself into her parka. Bruno donned his black overcoat. While Bruno locked up, she hurried ahead to open the door and brush the light snow off her windshield. The routine medical visit had soothed her splintered nerves. But the sheriff's questions still burned like new salt in an old wound.

❖❖❖

WENDY DROVE THROUGH the early winter darkness that night. The closer she came to her destination, the more her spirits began to lift. Finally she passed the familiar back door and parked her car in the large machine shed. Without knocking, she walked in with a casserole in hand and shut the door with a backward kick. "It's me—Wendy!"

Her grandfather, Harlan Carey, got up from his worn recliner and opened his arms. Lady, his sheltie, stood up in front of the fireplace and barked a quick welcome.

Setting the casserole down in the kitchen, Wendy walked into the strong arms that had welcomed and hugged her all her life. She'd learned early that the circle of her grandfather's arms was her earthly sanctuary. After a moment, she sighed and stepped back. Then she bent to pet the aged tan-and-white sheltie who lived at Grandfather's side.

"Wendy, I didn't expect to see you tonight." His honest pleasure at her coming went straight to her heart, leaving her warmed.

"I didn't expect to see you either." She left unsaid, *But I needed to feel your love tonight.* First the break-in at Ma's, next the sheriff, and then her disagreement earlier this evening with her sister, Sage . . .

He reached over and snapped off the TV news. Lady settled down by the fire.

Wendy made her voice light, concealing her tension. "Sage made chicken casserole and I thought it would stretch for the two of us." Recalling the scolding she'd given Sage about having her boyfriend over every night before Wendy got home made her cringe with regret. *I'm sorry, Lord. I didn't mean to get on her case again.*

"My oven is all preheated." Grandfather led her into the neat blue-and-white kitchen. "I was just going to pop in a TV dinner. Couldn't Sage come, too?"

Wendy followed him, her spirits dragging. "No, she's ushering at the high school concert tonight."

"And I bet Trav's with her?" He turned to her.

"As usual." She couldn't keep the negativity out of her tone. Trav was a good kid, but she wanted more for her beautiful, intelligent sister!

"Now, just because Trav's Uncle Elroy has never gotten his life straight with the Lord doesn't have anything to do with Trav," Grandfather counseled. "Trav's been coming to church with Sage, and I have hope he's close to coming to the Lord."

"I know," she agreed, but with a frown.

"You have that sad look in your eyes tonight. Are you missing your mother?"

His genuine concern for her was like honey on a raw throat. Wendy took care putting the casserole into the hot oven to rewarm. After Sage and Trav had left for their high school, Wendy couldn't face eating alone in the old trailer where she and Sage lived. Ever since Mom had moved to Florida in the fall, their trailer had felt lifeless. Picturing her mother's full head of golden hair and bubbling laughter, she admitted, "Yes, I miss Mom, but I've had a long day, too."

He held up the coffeepot, asking without words if she wanted a cup. "I heard about the burglary. Bruno called me. How's Ma?"

She shook her head, saying no to the coffee. "I just saw her at the hospital before I went home." At least the news about Ma was good. "We got her there in time. The effect of the mild stroke was almost completely reversed, but she's going to stay at the care center for a few days."

Her grandfather set the pot back on its burner and put his arm around her. "That's good. I'll get a few men together from church to go over and fix up things for her before she gets home."

"She'll appreciate that. Ask Bruno to help. He'll want to." Wendy twined her arms around her grandfather's lean chest and rested her head there. Earlier, when she'd arrived at the trailer, she'd glimpsed old Miss Frantz spying on them from her parted curtains. The woman was their busybody neighbor who kept a hawkeye on Sage and Wendy. That's what had sparked Wendy to give Sage a hard time.

Grandfather touched her hair lightly. "What is it, pumpkin?"

The use of his pet name for her made her eyes moisten. She longed to pour out her frustration over gossip, her loneliness, her irritation with Sheriff Durand. But her grandfather was nearly eighty. He needed smiles, not her tears. "Just tired, Grandfather." She pulled away.

But he drew her back and hugged her close. "You're all I've got left in this wicked, old world. Remember that—always. I love your sister too, but she's not my blood. You are my only son's only child. My only blood relation left."

"I know." Why couldn't she ever get Sage to realize that because of their mother's wild youth, people measured both of them by a stricter standard? That alone had been enough to keep Wendy from dating in high school. Kept her from dating now. If she started dating, it would give people—Veda—a chance to rake up the past again. She couldn't bear that. How could Sage just ignore it? Wendy stayed within Grandfather's comforting embrace, letting go of her turmoil bit by bit. "I've always tried to do you proud."

With his head resting on the top of hers, he said simply, "You did me proud the day you were born."

She didn't know how he could say that, but she kissed his leathery cheek, then drew away.

The delicious aroma of baked chicken and sage dressing, which hadn't affected her at the trailer, was suddenly irresistible. "The chicken smells about ready. I'll set the table."

"That Sage is a great little cook."

In the midst of opening a kitchen drawer, Wendy halted. She gave him an arch look. "Is that a backhanded way of telling me my cooking lacks something?"

"Pumpkin, you're real good at opening a can of soup, and your toast is dee-licious." Scraping back a kitchen chair, he sat down, looking pleased with himself.

"Well, just keep that in mind." She quickly laid out a new cloth on the small oval table in the kitchen. As she finished setting the places, she thought she heard a motor outside.

"You set a pretty table, Wendy. Just like your grandma."

Wendy never knew what to say to her grandfather when he mentioned his late wife, a woman who had been better at hating than at loving Wendy. With quilted pot holders in hand, she opened the oven. Heat warmed her face.

A knock sounded on the back door.

"Now who could that be?" Her grandfather opened the door. "Well, I'll be. Come in. Come in."

When Wendy heard the voice answering her grandfather, she almost dropped the casserole dish. She turned slowly.

Sheriff Rodd Durand stood within feet of her. A shock like electricity shot through her from her toes to her scalp. A blush warmed her cheeks, and she hoped she could blame it on the heat from the oven.

"Miss Carey, I didn't see another car," he said, eyeing her like a man watching a geyser ready to spout.

"Call me Wendy, Sheriff. I always park in the machine shed." Shaking inside, she made herself walk casually to the table and set down the dish. She wanted to ask, *What are you doing here?* Had he followed her?

Suppressing her mounting paranoia, she paused by the table. Though averting her face, she forced a friendly tone. "We were just sitting down to supper. What can we do for you, Sheriff?"

"I had to go down to Eagle Station for medicine for my cattle." The sheriff sounded subdued, wary. "I stopped at the Old Brown Jug and picked up some of their ribs. Thought I'd share them."

Her grandfather rubbed his hands together. "Chicken and ribs and two young people to keep me company. And I thought I'd be eating a frozen dinner alone tonight. Wendy, set a third place, please. And get out that fresh bakery bread and bring over the coffeepot. Rodd, give me your jacket and hat."

At this, Wendy stared at the sheriff, wondering how he'd come to be on a first-name basis with her grandfather so soon. She'd been under the impression Rodd had stuck to himself pretty much. She worked at masking the chaos this man's appearance had stirred up within her.

Then the scent of barbecued ribs distracted her. Suddenly, she was more than hungry; she was ravenous.

She quickly set a place for the sheriff and prayed that neither she nor Durand would let anything about their earlier encounter slip out.

Her grandfather seated her formally at the table, nodded to Rodd to sit down across from her, then sat down himself. "Rodd, won't you say grace for us tonight?"

"I'd rather have you say it—if you don't mind."

Wendy wasn't surprised. Instinctively she thought, *I'll bet it would be hard for him to ask for anything*. Then his strong profile captured her attention, making her take a deep breath. Her grandfather cleared his throat, and she hastily looked down at her folded hands.

Grandfather's voice rumbled in the quiet kitchen, "Father God, we thank you for this day, the beautiful snow, and the sharp, clean air. Thank you that Lou wasn't home when her house was broken into. We ask that Rodd will bring this wrongdoer to justice and that you will bring this sinner to repentance—a miserable man he must be. I thank you for bringing me welcome company and good food tonight. In Christ's name, amen."

Listening to her grandfather's simple, sincere prayer went right to Wendy's heart. The blended aromas of chicken and tangy smoked ribs made her empty stomach growl.

Her grandfather chuckled. "We'd better feed her quick."

Blushing, she received the food from Grandfather and passed it on to Rodd. She tried in vain to think of some safe topic to introduce, but her wits had scattered like snow in the wind. She'd known that Rodd's great-uncle George and her grandfather had been lifelong friends. Why hadn't she guessed that Rodd dropped in on her grandfather like this?

After a few bites of food, her grandfather paused. "I'm glad you two finally got to meet. I should have had you both over before now, but you're so busy."

"We met this morning." Rodd took a sip of coffee.

Wendy looked up, suddenly alert, his words freezing her in place.

Grandfather looked at her expectantly.

She forced her mouth to work. "After Ma and I discovered the door smashed in at her place, I called to report it. The sheriff got there before the ambulance." The words left her feeling wobbly.

Her grandfather patted her arm. "Wendy, you must be more careful. What if the thief had still been there? Don't you think she should have waited outside, Rodd?"

Over the rim of his cup, Rodd's eyes gazed at hers. "With a home invasion, that's usually the best advice. But in this case, the perpetrator has chosen only homes he knows to be vacant."

Wendy held her breath, hoping the sheriff wouldn't bring up that she was always the one who drove the victim to the clinic for the night. The thought blazed in her mind. Suddenly she realized she had definitely overreacted this morning. *The sheriff's right! I am the one link.*

The idea chilled her.

She looked at Rodd, wishing she could explain that his questions had touched her tender spot. She lowered her gaze. Looking into this man's blue eyes held danger for her. Maybe if they hadn't met the first time under such dramatic circumstances . . . but they had, and what could she do about it now?

Harlan spoke up. "I think I'll ask the pastor to bring this up at the next prayer meeting. We should pray for this culprit to be caught quickly. I don't want him scaring or hurting my friends. At our time of life, we have enough to worry about."

Trying to behave naturally, Wendy relaxed the tenseness in her shoulders and picked up her fork.

Rodd nodded, but Wendy sensed a resistance in him.

The sheriff cleared his throat. "You know God helps those who help themselves. And it's my job to find this thief."

Harlan replied simply, "But prayer helps everything."

❧ ❧ ❧

"I'LL HAVE HARRY from the garage send someone out to change the flat in the morning," Wendy told her grandfather before stepping outside his back door. She found Rodd parked by the stoop, waiting for her.

She hesitated, conflicted. On the one hand, she was glad that Rodd had not gone off and left before she'd discovered the flat tire. He had waited to see that she drove safely off. Rodd's likeness to his Uncle George was more than physical. Rodd possessed the same gentlemanly manner and sincere regard that had characterized his great-uncle. But she dreaded having to admit to him that she'd overreacted this morning.

The below-zero windchill finally pushed her into the passenger seat. Shivering, she slammed the door behind her. Alone with the sheriff, she kept herself busy hooking and adjusting her seat belt. "Thanks again for the ride home. I can't believe my tire went flat while we were eating."

"No problem. As long as you don't mind stopping at my place first. I need to check on a couple of sick cows."

"No problem." Being alone with him like this presented the perfect opportunity to show she regretted overreacting this morning. But how could she broach it—with her nerves jumping so?

She squeezed her eyes shut. As her grandfather had taught her as a child, she began to pray, *Father God, I'm all shook up about these burglaries . . . and everything. It doesn't matter what this sheriff or anyone else thinks. I know you love me and I didn't do anything wrong.*

"Aren't you feeling well?"

Wendy's eyes snapped open. "No, I . . . I wanted to say I'm sorry we didn't get off to a better start today."

"I hope you didn't think that I thought you were implicated—"

"I know you didn't." The words had all rushed out. She halted, not knowing how to go on.

He gazed forward. "Someone is probably watching you, keeping track of your movements. It's the kind of thing an honest person doesn't notice."

An honest person. Hearing those heartening words steadied her. She let her back touch the seat, feeling her tension ease. The night closed in around them as they drove through the country darkness.

He glanced at her. "I'd like you to think over each of the incidents—both on the day when you took your patient into the clinic and the next day when you learned a burglary had been committed. Maybe you'll come up with something, someone."

The silvery moonlight cast his face into an arresting pattern of planes and curves. Again, her fingers itched to trace those contours. Why did this man pique her interest? After her disastrous first and only love in college, she'd gone back to avoiding men. So what was so special about Rodd Durand?

With effort, she dragged her mind back to the matter at hand. The three burglaries and consequences like Ma's stroke crystallized her fears. These burglaries had to be stopped. She inhaled deeply. "I'll give it some thought."

"Good."

Glancing out the darkened window, she recognized the short road leading to Rodd's family farm. She hadn't noticed the distance over the back road. "It's been a while since I've been here," she murmured.

"My great-uncle was one of your home-health patients?"

She nodded, then smiled. "Yes, I was pleased that you came to be with him at the end." George Durand had been one of her favorite patients.

"I wish I'd come back sooner, but somehow I always thought we'd have more time than we did."

She felt him withdraw from her. Her sympathy was stirred. She stopped herself from touching him. "That isn't uncommon. I do so much work with the elderly that I see it every day. My patients make the same mistake themselves. They will put off doing things—taking trips, doing home improvements, forgiving old wrongs—until they are physically unable."

She turned to face him, wanting to comfort him. "You shouldn't feel you came too late. You came when your uncle needed you. That's what counts."

"Uncle George stood by my dad and me when we needed him. After my mother left, he always invited me to spend summers and Christmas and Easter vacations up here. My dad was a cop in Milwaukee, and police don't get holidays off. I couldn't let Uncle George down."

Wendy glanced at him. She hadn't thought about it before, but this man had never known his mother. She had never known her father. "Nurses don't get holidays off either," she said wryly. "Your uncle was a fine gentleman. Everyone knew that. Your family has always been respected in the county." *Unlike mine.*

Rodd stopped his Jeep in front of his classic red barn. His family homestead was a centennial farm, one that had been worked by the same family for a hundred years or more.

"Do you want to come in or wait—"

"I'll come in." She wasn't surprised when Rodd motioned for her to wait till he opened the door for her. He certainly was a gentleman, just like his uncle. The traditional act of courtesy gave her a lift.

As he held the side door of the barn open, she walked past, just a breath from him. The change of atmosphere was instant—from brittle cold wind to moist warmth. She automatically unzipped her parka and pushed back her hood. She inhaled the distinctive, pleasant smell of a well-kept cattle barn, the rich aromas of cured hay, feed, and cattle. She heard the clatter of hooves against the old cobbled floor, the unmistakable sound of bovine jaws and teeth chewing methodically, then the subtle lowing of a cow.

The quaint setting made her feel at ease—even near this handsome man. If only her father hadn't died before she was born and that hadn't sent her mother into a tailspin, Wendy wouldn't feel this gulf between Rodd and her. The only scandal that had ever touched the Durands was Rodd's mother taking off when Rodd was a toddler. Rodd's mother hadn't been from the county and had been quickly forgotten. But until she died, Wendy's grandmother had kept gossip stirred up against Wendy's mom.

Wendy walked beside Rodd to a few stalls toward the rear of the barn. "How many head do you have?" she asked, filling up the silence.

"Not many, only a dozen for breeding dairy cattle. They're not much work till calving next year." He grinned suddenly. "As soon as I learn what I'm doing, I'll be adding more."

She smiled back. Though still too physically aware of him, she was seeing another facet of the man. He might be maddening, a very take-charge sheriff, but he was Uncle George's great-nephew. He was a Durand.

That was why the county residents had asked him to run for sheriff and had accepted him easily into their midst. He might be from Milwaukee, but his father's family's long-established reputation for integrity worked in his favor, while all her life, her family's reputation had worked against her. She'd have to be careful and not be seen much with the sheriff, or they'd become a topic of nasty gossip—Veda would see to that.

She glanced up. Rodd was looking at her. The intensity of his gaze rattled her, and her cheeks warmed with a sudden blush.

One of the cows in front of them lowed. Rodd reached over and patted the broad, white-faced holstein. "The medicine looks like it's doing its job. Let me get you home, Wendy." With his other hand on her shoulder, he turned her back toward the door. His hand rode on her back once again, sparking her awareness of him. Why couldn't she just slip out of his touch? She couldn't. He turned out the lights and closed the door behind them.

Inside the Jeep again, she shivered and said, "Brrrr!" But her inner glow warred with the cold winter night.

"Everyone tells me this is really cold for early November." He made a wide U-turn and headed down the road to the highway.

"The temperatures do feel more like January. But every year is weird in its own way." She shrugged as though she weren't bemused by him.

He chuckled softly.

The sound skittered up her spine. "You know what I mean," she chattered. "Every year the weather has something unusual about it. People complain about so much snow so early, but if we were warm and dry, they'd be worried about the snowshoeing and the snowmobiling season not making money."

Then she regretted her reference to snowmobiles. By the dash light, she saw his hands tighten on the wheel. "I'm sure you'll catch the thief," she said.

His dash radio crackled to life. He picked up. The voice on the radio barked, "Sheriff, you there? Disturbance. Respond to Flanagan's Bar. Code three."

"I copy that." He snapped it off and the siren blared. "Sorry. I guess we'll have to make one more stop before I get you home."

Wendy felt as though the air had been knocked out of her. As they sped down the road, her pleasant evening dissolved. *Not Flanagan's! Why did it have to be Flanagan's?* Her hand went to her mouth. But when she felt her nail touch her lip, she sat on her hands—hoping against hope that this wouldn't be what she feared. *Surely not.*

Within minutes, they surged over a rise and saw the garish, green neon sign with a shamrock that emblazoned the night sky with "Flanagan's." Then, with sinking spirits, Wendy anticipated her worst nightmare.

CHAPTER THREE

AN UNRULY GATHERING filled the road in front of the bar. At its center, two middle-aged men—one with short dark hair and one with long white blond hair pulled back into a straggly ponytail—yelled curses at each other. They circled each other with menace. Their anger must have been hot because they'd come out of the bar into the bitter cold without jackets or hats.

Wendy recognized both men instantly—Dutch and Elroy, Trav's uncle—just as she'd feared. Flanagan's, the most notorious bar in the county, had always been their favorite place to fight. The loud voices, the raucous music from inside the tavern, the rotating red light on top of the police car lent the scene an unearthly quality. She wanted to shrink down in the seat. Her temples throbbed.

Reporting his arrival on the radio, Rodd parked the Jeep and jumped out. He strode forward to the center of the crowd. But before he could do or say anything, Dutch swung at Elroy. Wendy watched in alarm as Rodd stepped between the two.

Dutch pulled his punch. The fight ended.

The onlookers drew back toward the entrance of the bar but waited outside, not wishing to miss any of the evening's "entertainment." Wendy pressed her fingers to her temples. Dutch's blond hair, which had earned him his nickname, shone in the dim light. Dutch talked loudly to Rodd, gesticulating toward Elroy, who was backing away with his hands in front of him. It was like a scene from some TV cop show.

Dutch glanced at the sheriff's Jeep; then ignoring both Elroy and the sheriff, he walked quickly toward Wendy.

Wendy felt something in her mouth. She spit out one of her pale pink nails. *Oh, great!*

Rodd trailed behind Dutch, but she watched the sheriff's face. Did he know? As Dutch came closer, he shouted in a drunken slur, "Hey, Wendy girl! Sheriff, why's Wendy in your car? Hi, Wendy!"

Wendy sat up straight and met the sheriff's questioning gaze head-on. Family was family. "Hi, Uncle Dutch."

❋ ❋ ❋

THE NEXT MORNING, the opening prayer ended, and Rodd sat down in the very last pew to listen to church announcements. But his mind wasn't on a potluck supper or church cleanup day. He'd come to a decision about how to proceed with his investigation, and he'd act on it today. But what had happened last night might interfere with his plan.

After ending the fight outside Flanagan's, he'd been taken completely by surprise. He was still surprised. How could he have known that Dutch Rieker, a county resident with a long list of priors—charges of drunk and disorderly behavior, petty theft, vandalism—was Wendy's uncle?

Now he understood some previous comments people had made to him about how Wendy favored her father's family, not her mother's. Dutch must be her mother's brother. He'd never bothered to look into it, dismissing it as unimportant gossip. If he'd only realized her connection with Dutch, he'd have tried to save her from embarrassment. Every family had its black sheep.

The song leader motioned the congregation to rise and Rodd followed suit. The organist began to play. Rodd sang along with the old hymn: "'Under His wings I am safely abiding; though the night deepens . . .'"

With his superior height, Rodd scanned the congregation until he located Wendy's short-cropped, golden brown head. When he'd entered church this morning, he'd found himself looking for her—as if he'd planned to sit with her. But he always sat alone in church. Wendy shared a hymnal with Harlan. Beside her stood a young man and an attractive brunette teenage girl. She must be Wendy's sister and the boyfriend Harlan had told him about last night.

The music swelled: "'Still I can trust Him. . . . He has redeemed me and I am His child.'"

His eyes slid over the brunette and settled again on Wendy. She stood straight, her squared shoulders giving witness to her strength. He could tell she was used to carrying a lot of responsibility on those slender shoulders. He admired that. Above the other voices, he heard her strong soprano: "'Under His wings, under His wings, who from His love can sever?'"

Then she glanced up at her grandfather and smiled with such sweetness. Rodd's own voice caught in his throat. It was easy to believe that Wendy belonged to Harlan. Did she think Rodd thought she was like her uncle he'd met last night? Had this been what prompted Wendy's angry reaction to his initial questions and her comment that folks around here didn't forget or forgive? An unwelcome thought.

Again, his sympathy stirred for Wendy while he joined in on the end of the chorus: "'Under His wings my soul shall abide, safely abide forever.'" The hymn ended and he sank back into his pew. Around him, songbooks snapped shut. Everyone settled in, ready to listen to the sermon.

Rodd recognized a large woman from the back of her gray head. This unfriendly woman always sat alone off to Rodd's right a few pews ahead of him. He'd seen her every Sunday, but she never sang, never spoke to anyone or smiled. Now she turned her head left, toward Wendy. Even from her profile, he could see that she gave Wendy a scathing look—one so full of malice that it made Rodd uneasy. What could have caused that? Did Wendy have an enemy? He was learning he had to be aware of small-town feuds. Late last night the dispatcher had filled him in on the longtime Elroy Dietz–Dutch Rieker feud and its causes. The two men were notorious troublemakers. Could either one have any connection to the burglaries?

Pastor Bruce Weaver, a younger man with sandy-colored hair, glanced to the back of the church where Rodd sat. "Elder Carey has requested a special Wednesday night prayer meeting. We are very concerned about the burglaries taking place in our county. And we want to ask God to help our sheriff catch the culprit. Is that all right with you, Sheriff?"

Rodd stood up. He hadn't done his job, and his county was losing respect for him already. But what was he supposed to say—no? He nodded stiffly and sat back down.

"Let's pray about it right now," the pastor began.

As the pastor prayed, Rodd wrestled with his reaction to it. He'd attended church all his life, but he never felt comfortable asking God to help him do a job—something that was his responsibility and within his power to do. *Just give me a chance! I'll do my job!*

The prayer ended and Rodd tried to concentrate, but instead he gazed at the back of Wendy's head, the gold in her hair shining under the church lights. Why did she wear her hair in such a short severe style? She was so feminine in every other way. He remembered lifting her from his Jeep yesterday at the clinic. His hands had nearly circled her slender waist.

Pastor Weaver opened the large Bible on the pulpit amid the sound of people turning pages in their own Bibles. He read the morning Scripture aloud, Ecclesiastes 4:9-12:

"'Two people can accomplish more than twice as much as one; they get a better return for their labor. If one person falls, the other can reach out and help. But people who are alone when they fall are in real trouble. . . . A person standing alone can be attacked and defeated, but two can stand back-to-back and conquer. Three are even better, for a triple-braided cord is not easily broken.'"

As the pastor began his sermon about working together, Rodd kept his attention on it. He'd come to appreciate the quality of the pastor's sermons, straightforward and caring. And today the Scripture paralleled uncannily the direction of his own thoughts.

Still, Rodd didn't completely agree with the message. In his profession, a smart officer depended primarily on himself. Even a good partner could let you down badly—and at the most critical moments. An image from the past flashed in his mind, and the old anger at himself burned inside him. He pushed it away. This was now and he had a thief to catch. That meant—

Without warning, a very small boy wedged himself in the tight space between Rodd's hip and the side of the wooden pew. Startled, Rodd looked down into a cheerful, freckled face. Rodd couldn't recall which family the boy belonged to. He leaned down and whispered, "Young man, do you need anything?"

The little boy, blond and brown-eyed, shook his head and pressed his index finger to his lips. He motioned for Rodd to lean down again. When Rodd did, the boy whispered, "You aren't supposed to talk in church."

Rodd suppressed a grin and nodded solemnly. The sensation of being so close to a little child brought him an unexpected nostalgia. As he listened to the sermon about helping one another, one of his earliest memories flashed in his mind—Uncle George and he sitting side by side on the old sofa in front of a winter fire. Uncle George said, "Now this is what I call cozy." *Cozy.* Without planning to, Rodd grinned down at the boy. The child grinned back at him, then pressed his finger to his lips as a reminder. Rodd nodded, then looked back to the pastor.

But as much as he tried to keep his mind on the pastor's words, his mind kept drifting to the investigation. His next move was so simple; it was like reading from a law-enforcement textbook. But it all depended on Wendy. What answer would she give him today? Talking to women had never been his strong suit.

Also he couldn't approach her the way he would in the city. Here she wasn't just a source. She was Harlan Carey's granddaughter, a woman who obviously felt her own reputation had been tainted by her mother's family. Did she think he didn't know how having a less-than-perfect family felt? His mother had run off when he was only two, leaving his dad struggling to raise Rodd alone. His father had never spoken much about Rodd's mother, but it must have made him leery of women. He hadn't started dating again until Rodd was in his teens. Raised without a mother or a sister, Rodd always felt uncertain around women. He turned his gaze to Wendy again. Would he say the wrong thing and hurt her? offend her?

But he had to ask.

In the midst of his unruly thoughts the sermon ended, and the congregation rose to sing the closing hymn, "Blest Be the Tie That Binds." The boy climbed up on the pew to stand beside Rodd. Sharing his hymnal with the little guy, they sang, "'The fellowship of kindred minds is like to that above.'" The final prayer was offered, and the organist began playing the postlude. Everyone relaxed, gathering their belongings and chatting as they started to exit.

"Hi. I'm Zak!" the little boy announced and stuck out his hand.

Rodd shook the small hand. "Hi, I—"

"You're the sheriff! I seen you in your police car. It's really neat."

Rodd nodded, then glanced toward the aisle in time to see Harlan and Wendy coming toward them. Suddenly the large, mannish woman Rodd had noticed before deliberately stepped in front of them, pointedly turning her back to them. How odd. Rodd recalled the final hymn. Evidently, it hadn't touched every heart here. This cold heart hadn't let itself be bound by Christian love.

As the grim, rude woman stalked past Rodd, Zak shouted, "Mr. Carey, hi! See me! I sitted quiet all the way through my daddy's sermon! I didn't talk once. Did I, Sheriff?"

Rodd nodded with a smile. So this was the pastor's son.

Harlan stepped closer to them to let others walk by. Zak launched himself upward, and Harlan caught and hugged the child. "When are you going to come out and visit me again, Zak?"

"Mom!" Zak twisted around, looking in one direction, then the other. "Mom!"

"Yes, Zachary." Penny Weaver, pretty and plump, bustled up the aisle. She leaned down and tapped her son's nose. "Why did you come up from the nursery, young man?"

"The nursery is for *babies!*" Zak declared from Harlan's arms. "Daddy said I could get out of the nursery when I could sit still for the whole sermon." Zak twisted toward Rodd. "Sheriff, I didn't talk even *once,* did I?"

Rodd laughed and shook his head.

Harlan intervened. "Rodd, you've met Wendy, but you haven't met my other granddaughter, Sage, and her friend Trav Dietz."

The introductions took place. Rodd found himself near the center of attention as everyone chatted with Zak, congratulating him on his success at sitting quietly. Wendy stood just in front of Rodd, wearing a soft red dress of some kind of knit. He had to keep his hand down at his side to keep from touching her shoulder to feel its softness under his palm.

Steeling himself against this, he tried several times to catch Wendy's eye, but she never quite made eye contact with him. Finally, they all moved up the aisle to greet the pastor, Wendy just to Rodd's right.

During more friendly greetings and chatter, Rodd eased closer to Wendy. He whispered in her ear, "I need a favor."

She looked up, startled. "What?"

He read caution in her eyes. "Walk with me a ways." He motioned toward the church entrance.

She hesitated.

But Harlan must have overheard him because he nodded at them, then turned back to Zak. In the church foyer, beside the long coatrack, they paused. As Rodd helped her don a long, blue, down coat, he breathed in her light fragrance, something like fresh strawberries. She appeared uncomfortable with his help—or was it just him? She led him outside into bright, freezing sunshine.

"What favor do you need, Sheriff?"

Last night in his barn, he had been "Rodd," not "Sheriff." He tried to think of something to say that would bring back that casual friendliness he'd enjoyed with her before seeing her uncle at Flanagan's. Maybe the direct approach would be best. "I need your help with the investigation."

She looked down. "What do you need?"

Good. She believed in the direct approach too. What a relief. He started, "First of all, have you mentioned your connection to the burglaries to anyone?"

She folded her arms and eyed him. "You probably haven't thought about it, but my profession is very similar to yours. I have to keep a great deal of information confidential."

He grinned, hoping to put her at ease. He lowered his voice. "I want you to call me the next time you take another patient into the clinic for a night of observation."

She stared up into his eyes. "You think there will be another burglary?"

He wished they could be talking about anything else, anything to ease her defensive posture. But he had to concentrate on the crimes, which had pulled them together. His tone was grim. "I'm sure there will be. Thieves don't give up until they're caught."

"I was hoping . . ." She gave a little shake of her head, as though wishing away the trouble they had to confront. "I just hate to think of this happening again." Her voice caught with raw distress. "Isn't there anything else I could do to help you?"

He cupped her shoulders with his hands, reassuring her. "No, just leave everything else to me." He left unsaid his worry that the thief could guess that his MO had been figured out and adopt a new one.

She gave him a tremulous smile.

He found himself looking at her face, examining its oval contour, the soft pale skin. He tightened his hold on her and smiled, encouraging her.

The church doors behind them burst open. "Hey!" Zak shouted as he rushed up to them. "We're going for pizza. Wanna come?"

Rodd dropped his hands and turned. From the corner of his eye, he noted Wendy's cheeks turn pink.

In a wink, Harlan, Sage, Trav, the pastor, and his wife surrounded Rodd and Wendy. Before Rodd could make an excuse and leave, he found himself walking the few blocks to the local pizzeria along with the rest. He willed his eyes not to keep shifting to where Wendy walked beside him. Finally, he gave up and let his gaze linger on her winsome profile.

"I like pepperoni." Zak tugged at his sleeve.

"What?" Rodd looked down; then he took the red-mittened hand Zak offered him. The small hand in his felt good.

"I like pepperoni; do you?" Zak gave a jump, then a hop on the sidewalk packed with a layer of frozen gray snow.

"Sure, I like pepperoni." He glanced over to Wendy. "Do you like pepperoni, Wendy?" he asked in a conspiratorial murmur.

"Not alone." She gave a determined shake of her head. "I'm definitely a deluxe-pizza woman."

"Deluxe pizza! Yuck!" Zak declared. "Daddy calls that garbage pizza!"

This outburst was so unexpected and comical, Rodd couldn't keep from laughing out loud.

Wendy chuckled too. He liked the soft feminine timbre of her laugh. It took the sharp edge off the heavy burden he'd been carrying since yesterday when he'd examined the crime scene at Ma Ukkonen's. He'd intended to go to his office immediately after church, but now he was glad he had come along. Wendy and Zak lifted his spirits. Besides, a man had to eat.

Zak saw the pizzeria ahead. He yelped happily. "I'm cold! Let's run!" Zak tugged on Rodd's hand and started forward.

Rodd automatically reached for Wendy's hand, and the three of them ran together. Zak squealed and Rodd grinned, liking the feel of Wendy's gloved hand in his.

⁂

WENDY STOOD AT the wall phone in the care-center side of the clinic lobby. Behind her, Olie Olson grumbled loudly at the day nurse admitting him. Wendy punched in the sheriff's number while her nerves did funny little hops and jumps inside her.

"Durand speaking."

Hearing Rodd's voice made the little hops and jumps spike like the readings on a heart monitor. Wendy cleared her dry throat. "Hi, it's Wendy."

"Wendy?" The sudden hope in his voice was unmistakable.

"This is the call you've been waiting for, Sheriff." *And the one I've been dreading to make.*

"You've brought a patient to the clinic?"

"Yes, Olie Olson from out on Winneshiek Road."

"He'll be in for the night?"

She fiddled with the twisted phone cord, trying to untangle it along with her hope and fear. "Yes, I brought him in for observation for heart arrhythmia."

"Have you told anyone else?"

"No one." She gave up and let the knotted phone cord drop.

"Good. Has anyone seen you bring him in, Wendy?"

She pictured the sheriff's face, how eager it must be. Still, her mood was as tangled as the phone cord. Would this put Rodd in danger?

"Wendy?"

"I don't know. You didn't tell me to try to hide—"

"Right. You followed your regular routine then?"

"Exactly as always, Sheriff." *Except that I feel like I'm going to jump out of my skin!*

"Good."

"Good?" How could Rodd stay so calm? Another burglary might happen tonight. "What do I do now?"

"What would you normally do after bringing a patient in?"

"I'd get him settled and go on with my calls." Out of the corner of her eye, she noticed Olie eluding the nurse's attempts to get him to sit in the wheelchair. *Olie, not now.*

"Then do that."

"Is that all you want me to do?" Let down, she thought he'd have another duty for her to carry out.

"I want you to act as normal as you can."

His words spoken so seriously hit her sense of humor. What had he expected her to do—start toting her grandfather's rifle? break into song? She grinned and said in an exaggerated tone, "Well, Sheriff, I'll do my best."

There was a pause. "Sorry." His voice sounded sheepish. "I didn't think about how that sounded."

"That's all right." Her grin waned. Even in the midst of her anxiety, she wished she didn't feel so inadequate around this man who kept creeping into her thoughts regardless of her intent to put him from her mind. Just the sound of his voice shredded her resistance. "Isn't there anything else I can do?"

"I'll take it from here. Just act—"

"I know, act normal. Okay." The nurse was waving for her. "I'll let you go, Sheriff, but I expect you to call me tomorrow." She found herself almost shaking her finger at the phone. "And I mean it."

"I will."

"I'll be praying for you."

"Good-bye and thanks."

Act like nothing is going to happen—how can I do that? What if someone gets hurt tonight? She hung up and hurried over to help the agitated nurse.

"Mr. Olson, please!" the nurse said, still trying to corral Olie into the wheelchair.

"I don't need any wheelchair. I can walk, lady." Olie sidestepped the nurse again.

"Olie Olson!" Wendy barked. "Sit down."

The grizzled gray-haired man paused.

"Now!" Wendy finished.

The old man, still grumbling and frowning furiously, sat down.

Wendy reached his side and bent to adjust his foot supports on the chair. "If you didn't need to be here, I wouldn't have brought you in."

"My heart may not be ticking just right, but I'm not crippled, Wendy."

"No one said you were. Why are you complaining? The complimentary wheelchair ride is just part of our blue-ribbon service." Wendy winked at the nurse over Olie's head. "Now I'm going to wheel you to your room." She pushed the chair down the hall toward the patients' wing. "Should we call your son at home or at work?"

"Ted's sleeping. They switched him to nights at the truck stop. Don't call him till 4 P.M. That's when he gets up."

"I'll have to give that pleasure to you, Olie. At four, I'll be about done for the day and heading home." *About that time the sheriff might be setting up his trap.* A shard of fear sliced through her. *Don't take any chances, Rodd.*

Olie glanced up at her, his bravado slipping. "Stop back by here then. I'll be ready to leave this place. Old Doc will send me home. You wait and see. You youngsters think you know best, but I know better."

"Old Doc will have you taking tests," Wendy said wryly. She entered his room and stopped beside his bed. "Now put on your hospital gown. I expect you to follow doctor's orders."

Olie stood up and straightened slowly, painfully. "I'll follow *doctor's* orders, but you tell that woman to steer clear of me." He pointed a finger at the nurse who had followed them.

"The nurse will be following doctor's orders too, so don't you give her any guff." Wendy shook her finger at him. "The sooner you do what you're told, the sooner you get home."

The grumpy man gave her a glum look.

It caught her heart. When she was a child, she'd often spent after-school hours doing homework at the Black Bear Café, where her mother had been a waitress. Every time Olie had come into the café, he had given Wendy red-and-white-striped mints. She softened her voice. "Promise?"

He hitched up one shoulder. "I ain't makin' any promises."

She leaned over and kissed his deeply lined cheek, then turned to the nurse. "His bark is worse than his bite."

The nurse grimaced. "Better tell him my bark and bite are equally bad."

Wendy shook her head. "You two will have to work it out between you. I've got to go." *Besides, I don't have any patience today. How can I wait until tomorrow to hear if the sheriff's plan worked? Oh, God, calm my spirit and help Rodd catch the thief.*

❋ ❋ ❋

RODD QUIETLY DROVE his Jeep into the deep cover of a stand of pines behind the Olson garage. About three hours earlier, dark had fallen on the mid-November night. He had stayed in his office doing paperwork until he left at his customary time. He had done nothing out of the ordinary that might be observed. This wasn't the big city. Here people noticed things.

That had been proved already. Someone in the county had noticed Wendy's movements and used them for larcenous purposes. Someone could be watching him too, though that didn't seem to fit the Weasel. But Rodd couldn't take any chances. Three burglaries were three too many. So at the end of his day, he'd driven home as usual, checked on his cattle, and gotten his mail while the moonless night advanced.

Finally, he'd left his home and taken a circuitous route to Winneshiek Road. Then he had turned off his headlights and trusted his luck to get off the road onto Olson's property without being noticed by the distant neighbors. Now he backed his Jeep into a rough but cleared area hidden by the tall pines. The patch of ground looked as if farm machinery had been parked there in the past.

He had planned carefully. Earlier in the daylight, to make sure he would know right where to drive and wouldn't fumble around in the dark, he had driven by and glimpsed this stakeout position. The layout of the property was so perfect for a stakeout and arrest that he'd felt like singing—if he were a man who sang. But the elation still tried to tug his mouth into a grin. The trap had been set and baited.

Ever since Wendy had called him this morning with her news, he'd felt the buzz of adrenaline. Tonight he'd do what he'd promised when he took his oath of office. He'd protect the community. The string of snowmobile burglaries would end—tonight.

If the thief nibbled the bait.

All Rodd had to do was wait. He checked to make certain nothing would beep or ring when he opened his car door; then he sat inside and waited.

Tonight had to succeed—because tonight's stakeout would reveal that he'd figured out the Weasel's MO. If he didn't get the perp tonight, he might not get such a clear-cut chance again. And he wanted to catch the Weasel red-handed, not just scare him out of business.

Only the distant whine of an occasional motor driving by on the two-lane highway disturbed the deathly silence of the winter night. Minutes crawled by . . . one by one . . . by one. He fought the chill by sipping black coffee from his thermos. Fortunately, tonight was still. Falling temperatures to endure, but no windchill. He'd dressed in layers, but the fizzing excitement in his blood did the most to keep him alert.

Wendy's soft voice spoke in his memory: *"I'll be praying for you." Wendy, all I need are your prayers to keep me awake. Everything's in place.* He'd taken Pastor Bruce's advice and let Wendy help him set up the trap. But now it was all up to him. He didn't need God to do the stake-out for him. He could handle that much himself.

At last, when the luminous dial on Rodd's watch registered 11:37 P.M., he heard the distant roar of an engine coming closer. His cold-dulled senses snapped alive. A headlight flickered far back on Olson's property, then disappeared. Moments later an unlighted snowmobile slid into the dark area just beyond the glowing back-door light. Something . . . a rock? . . . hit the side of the house. And again.

Then with the tinkling sound of shattering glass, that light went out. *Okay. Make your move. Leave your snowmobile. Get out in the open.* In the almost total darkness, Rodd detected nothing further until he heard the battering of the door. The sweet sound he'd been waiting for.

CHAPTER FOUR

RODD OPENED THE Jeep door and slid out. He ran lightly over the snow, grateful that the snow-packed ground muffled the sound of his boots breaking a path through dry snow.

With his gun drawn, he paused at the edge of the garage. He waited, making certain the perpetrator entered. Legally and logistically, it would be better to make the arrest just inside the door—before the thief got his bearings.

He's in. Rodd left the cover of the garage and ran toward the house.

Without warning, a pickup truck barreled off the county road. Its high-beam lights blinded Rodd, who was caught between the house and the garage. Still running forward blindly, Rodd sped up, trying to reach the thief before he could escape the house.

"Hey! What's going on?" a voice boomed from behind the truck's lights.

Rodd heard footsteps both in front of and behind him. When he detected a flicker of movement in front of him, he lunged forward, but the slippery material of snowmobile gear slid through his grasp.

"Hey!" the voice behind him boomed once more.

Rodd shouted, "Stop! Police!" His eyes adjusted to the light. The thief in a dark snowmobile suit, helmet, and mask slithered away to his snowmobile. Rodd raised his gun to squeeze off a warning shot. "Stop! Po—"

The intruder from behind tackled Rodd. As Rodd went down, his gun fired into the air.

The snowmobile roared into action. Rodd tried to get up, but the huge man who'd tackled him held him down. Rodd shouted, "I'm the sheriff! Didn't you hear me? Let me up!"

"The sheriff? Really? Who was the guy on the snowmobile?"

"The thief who's getting away! Let me up!"

Giant arms released Rodd. He staggered to his feet. Staring into the blackness beyond the circle of light, Rodd could detect no sight of the snowmobile, only its distant roar. *And my Jeep can't follow a snowmobile cross-country.* Rodd swallowed a curse.

Vaguely aware that lights in the house had just come on, Rodd faced his attacker. "Who are you? Don't you know the penalty for interfering with a police officer?"

"I'm Ted Olson. I don't hear so good," the huge man with a boyish face explained. "They said my dad—"

"Reach for the sky!" an aged voice shouted.

Automatically obeying, they both spun around to face a shotgun.

"Dad! It's me, Ted!"

Behind the shotgun, an old man wearing pajamas glared at them. "What're you doin' here? And who's shootin'?"

Ted answered, "Dad, it's the sheriff—"

"The sheriff! What's he doin' out here?"

With a groan, Rodd let his arms drop. The old man must be Olson, but why was he here? Why had this stakeout turned into a slapstick comedy? Another vehicle turned in off the highway and up the short road.

Now who? Rodd fought his fury.

The familiar station wagon pulled up. He couldn't believe his eyes. "Wendy! What are you doing here?"

"I just found out Olie went home." She hustled into the glow of Ted's headlights. "Olie, what are you doing home? You're not well enough to leave the care center!"

"I didn't make you no promise, girl. That nurse wouldn't stop bothering . . ." Olie's voice gave out. Clutching his chest, he began to sink to his knees.

"Dad!" Ted hustled forward and caught his father.

Rodd jogged beside Wendy as she ran to the doorway. She leaned down and spoke into the old man's face. "Olie, where are your nitro pills?"

"Bedside," he gasped, shifting his weight in an attempt to rise. Then he slumped against Wendy. Rodd knelt beside her to help support Olson.

Wendy shouted, "Quick, Ted, get his pills!"

The younger man squeezed by them. His thundering footsteps echoed in the stillness.

Rodd asked, "What is it? Shouldn't we move him in?"

"Yes, this bitter cold is the worst thing for his heart and lungs."

Rodd carried the man into the house and laid him on the couch in the cluttered living room.

Wendy pulled a frayed afghan from the sofa back and put it over Olie. "Once I slip the nitro under his tongue, it will work almost immediately. It's his heart. Call for the ambulance, will you?" Holding Olie's wrist and gazing at her watch, she explained, concern plain in her voice. "When I found out Olie would be here . . . that's why I had to come out. I was afraid of this. You didn't know . . . I'm so sorry."

"You did what you had to do." He pulled his cell phone from his belt and speed-dialed dispatch. What else could he say? Besides, she hadn't caused this farce. It was his fault. It had never occurred to him that Olson would turn around and come home early. *I should have called the clinic and made sure!*

He couldn't stop himself from questioning Wendy. "But why'd you wait so late to come? Why didn't you call me? let me know?"

"I was on a call; then the woman's neighbor went into early labor. I delivered the baby, then took them into the clinic afterward. That's when I found out Olie had called a friend to drive him home. I came right out—"

Rodd pushed all the what-ifs behind him. The old man was as white as the snow outside.

Wendy glanced at the nearby staircase and called, "Ted, what's taking you so long?"

Rodd hovered close to her, ready to help her any way she needed him.

Finally appearing with a bottle of pills in his hand, the son crowded close to them. Wendy quickly took one and slipped the tablet under Olie's tongue.

Rodd wondered if he should offer to speed them to the clinic as he had Mrs. Ukkonen. "Will he be all right?"

"This should help. But I want the ambulance with their equipment to take him back in. I don't want to take any chances. Ted, put that shotgun away. We don't want it just lying around here."

The big man left to do the chore he'd been given.

"Thanks, Rodd." Wendy looked up at him. "I'm so sorry. This ruined everything, didn't it?"

Hours of quiet, then total chaos had turned him inside out. *I almost had him!* But the anguish in Wendy's eyes made him speak of hope. "There will be another chance. There always is." He touched her arm. "Do you need me?"

Wendy rose and drew Rodd a step away. In a low voice, she said, "His color is coming back and he's beginning to breathe better, but I'll feel safer when we get him back to the clinic."

Breathing in the last trace of her sweet scent, he nodded.

"I agree and I won't leave until the ambulance gets here." He didn't remind her that the ambulance hadn't made it to Mrs. Ukkonen's. "I'm certified for CPR so I could help."

"I still feel awful about all this, Rodd."

He felt the urge to draw her close but ignored it. She had her duty and he had his.

"You had to come. This isn't your fault." She looked so apologetic. He squeezed her shoulder. "It'll be fine. Don't worry. I have some other tricks up my sleeve." He forced a grin. He wanted to reassure her more but knew she would continue to feel responsible. She was that kind of woman. Not like his mother—who had walked away and never looked back.

Wendy nodded, then turned back to her patient.

Turning away reluctantly, Rodd walked past the big man in the kitchen and out into the night. Outside, he stood for a moment. The events of the bungled stakeout ran through his mind like a crazy video. Then he turned and began to push and pull the damaged door back into some semblance of its original shape to keep out the cold and little animals seeking a warm place to nest for the night.

He thought of how he should be examining the area just outside the door for evidence. But Ted, Wendy, and he had trampled the area because of the medical emergency. The only evidence this stakeout had turned up was that this time he'd actually glimpsed the suspect in dark anonymous snowmobile gear, which masked his identity from head to toe. All Rodd knew was that the thief was of average height, perhaps a bit under six feet. The thief had slipped in and out of the yard like a shadow, leaving nothing to follow up, nothing to link up. Rodd was left with only the sensation of slippery fabric sliding through his gloved hands. He gave a final savage push and the derelict door stood propped up but leaning.

He took a step, then paused. Trying to remember something that had happened in the excitement, he went back over the sights and sounds of the incident. He heard it again. A whack. He'd heard the snowmobile hit something—maybe a tree trunk? Had the burglar broken a headlight? Would there be some physical evidence at last?

Pulling a flashlight out of his pocket, he ran to the trees, following the machine's retreating track. Then he saw it. A fresh scar near the base of an old maple. Rodd examined the area painstakingly, hoping to find pieces of a shattered headlight.

Nothing. He'd already taken a cast of the snowmobile tread at the first burglary. Fresh irritation vibrated through him. The Weasel's snowmobile would probably have a fresh dent on its front end. But he couldn't arrest everyone in the county with a dented snowmobile. Still, he'd cord this section off and examine it by daylight.

Giving up for now, he walked over to Olie's son's truck and Wendy's wagon. He switched off their headlights and motors. He almost removed the keys, but then he remembered where he was and left them dangling from the ignitions. *This isn't Milwaukee. There when you set up a stakeout, it doesn't turn into a clown act.*

He waited for the ambulance to arrive. Wendy might still need him. The wind rattled the icicles on the garage. Rodd halted. He scanned the stark landscape. The glittering stars overhead gave just enough illumination so he could glimpse the spearlike tops of statuesque pines that surrounded him. He glanced higher.

The sight above him made him pause. Overhead, wispy veils of shimmering white and pale green light undulated like ghosts dancing a ballet. Northern lights. The first he'd seen this year.

Silent moments passed as he drank in the ethereal beauty. It lifted him from the mundane facts of a botched stakeout. Lifted him from the frustration of coming so close, yet failing. Lifted him from himself. *Your ways are higher than our ways, oh God.*

When he finally heard the ambulance approaching, he moved toward his Jeep to get out the yellow tape to cord off the snowmobile path. First, he'd meet the EMTs and try to help them get Olie without destroying every possible bit of evidence on their way in and out.

This stakeout had been his best chance for a quick end to the burglaries. His plan had seemed flawless, and he would have carried it out successfully—if there had been no interference. *God, just keep everybody out of my way next time. That's all I'll need.*

Later, as he drove away behind the ambulance, he made a promise: *I'm not done with you yet, Weasel. You won't slip through my fingers next time.*

⁂

FLETCHER CRAM STALKED toward Rodd, where he sat at the counter in the Black Bear Café on Steadfast's Main Street. "So, Sheriff, heard you had quite a time last night?" Cram, an older man shaped like a telephone pole, was the local newspaper editor and the Weasel's first victim.

The newspaperman's disagreeable tone set Rodd's teeth on edge, but he couldn't blame the man for not being happy with him. It had been weeks since Cram's house had been burglarized, and Rodd hadn't been able to close the case or the subsequent ones, which Cram had titled "The Snowmobile Burglaries" in his weekly paper, *The Steadfast Times*. Rodd lowered his brown stoneware mug. "Can I buy you a cup of coffee?" he asked, trying to buy time.

Was it his imagination, or had every other conversation in the café quieted? Wendy had called him at dawn and asked him to meet her here for breakfast. Why had she insisted on meeting him in such a public place?

Cram glared at Rodd, his bushy white brows squeezed together. "Got all the coffee I want back at the office. Saw your Jeep outside and came over to find out what the hullabaloo at Olie Olson's last night was about."

Still fatigued from lack of sleep, Rodd lifted his cup and took a long swallow. The rich, hot brew braced him to face last night's debacle in the morning light. Too many people had converged on Olson's property last night for it to go unnoticed.

"Well?" Cram leaned forward.

Rodd kept his mug at mouth level, hiding his chagrin behind it. "Olson had to go back to the clinic."

"Did Olie have another heart attack?" The tall, twenty-something, red-haired waitress paused behind the counter with a coffeepot in hand.

Relieved his misdirection had worked, Rodd nodded. If Cram had his way, everyone in the county would soon know that Rodd's stakeout had turned into a bad joke.

Ushering in a blast of frigid air, Wendy—looking surprisingly fresh after her long stressful night—entered and came up beside Cram.

Telegraphing his discomfort to her with a guarded look, Rodd rose and nodded to her, wishing Cram would disappear. Wendy didn't need all this stress first thing in the morning. He'd followed the ambulance to the clinic, but who knew how long she'd had to stay there with Olson? Rodd took a step closer to her.

"I was listening to the police band on my radio," Cram said. Insistently he added, "I want to know why you let that snowmobile thief get away."

All conversation around Rodd, Wendy, and Cram cut off.

Wendy's cheerful voice filled the listening silence. "Hi, Sheriff. Sorry I kept you waiting." With a quick brush of her small hand, she pushed back her parka hood.

Ignoring Wendy, Cram leaned closer to Rodd. "Well, Sheriff?"

Wendy slid between the two men, facing the editor.

Her blocking movement goaded Rodd. He didn't need her to run interference for him. "I—"

"Mr. Cram, how are you going to stay in business?" Wendy cocked her head to one side.

"What?" Cram looked down at her.

Silently, Rodd repeated the man's question.

Wendy grinned as she straightened the editor's rumpled shirt collar. "If the sheriff tells you everything about last night in front of everyone here, who will want to buy your paper to read about it?"

A few eavesdropping customers chuckled.

Rodd noticed the large, mannish-looking woman he'd seen at church staring at him from a rear booth where she sat alone. Who was she? And why were he and Wendy objects of her frowning?

"I'm asking about this as a concerned citizen," Cram blustered. "These burglaries must be stopped."

"They will be." Rodd felt himself literally getting hot under his collar. He glanced at the last booth by the back door of the café. The couple in it rose and walked to the front to pay at the cash register. *Great.* He touched Wendy's arm and inclined his head toward the vacated booth.

"Why didn't you catch him last night then?" Cram hung on like a pit bull.

Wendy began leading Rodd away but spoke over her shoulder, "All right, Mr. Cram, if you insist on hearing everything here. How could Rodd—with Ted Olson tackling him right when he had the thief in sight?"

"Ted?" the waitress exclaimed. "What was he doing out there?"

"Checking on his dad before he went home from work." Wendy paused, still looking back. She addressed the waitress by name. "Ginger, you know how Ted doesn't hear well. He didn't hear the sheriff declare himself, so Ted tackled him."

Rodd hated this. Wendy was forcing him to stand in the middle of the café, filled with locals and out-of-town hunters all dressed in blaze orange, listening to her explain why his plan had gone awry. And the old woman in the back watched him like a hungry hawk. Didn't Wendy realize talking like this about last night was the last thing he wanted to do at breakfast?

"So Ted's to blame?" Cram folded his arms and looked suspicious.

Rodd noted the big woman alone in the booth glare at Wendy. But Wendy didn't even glance her way. As he trailed after Wendy, honesty forced him to concede, "If I saw a stranger with a gun running toward my father's door in the middle of the night, I'd probably do the same thing." The newspaper editor was only doing his job. Rodd wished he could say the same about himself. If everyone had stayed where they were supposed to, he'd have had the thief in jail this morning!

"But how did you know the thief was out at Olson's?" Cram stood his ground by the counter.

A very good question, sir, but it's not one I'll be answering today. "Just proper investigative procedures." As Rodd helped Wendy take off her jacket, his knuckles brushed her shoulders—so slender. He recalled her rushing to Olson's aid—still on duty after midnight. A woman, so young, so slight to carry such heavy responsibilities. His irritation melted.

Wendy slid into the high-back bench. She surprised Rodd by saying—with a proprietary air as though she wanted to get rid of Cram so they could be alone, "Rodd, why don't you stop by after breakfast and give Mr. Cram all the details?"

Rodd kept his back to Cram so the editor wouldn't see his raised eyebrows. What was Wendy up to? He had nothing he wanted to tell Cram, period!

"Do that." Cram pulled his worn gray overcoat closed and let the café door bang behind him.

Rodd sat down across from Wendy. Before he could say anything to her, the young waitress came over and handed them paper menus. The waitress left with an odd expression on her face, like something was amusing. He'd also noticed curious glances and knowing smiles cast in their direction. But the atmosphere of tension that Cram had created lightened. The sound of general conversation resumed.

Rodd glanced at Wendy, her face lifted toward his. Her gaze searched his, and he stopped his hand from reaching across for hers. She'd smoothed matters over for the time being, but he could have done without this attention. How could he phrase that without offending her?

"You should relax," Wendy said in an undertone.

"What?" he murmured, puzzled by her suggestion.

"Relax. People are watching you."

The waitress returned to wipe the table and serve Wendy a cup of coffee. His discomfort was his own fault. He should have suggested they meet some place else, *any* place else.

When the waitress left, Rodd said only for Wendy to hear, "I don't want to talk to Cram. You don't understand—I wanted to keep a lid on this."

"That's why we're here. And that's why you should stop later and answer Mr. Cram's questions." Wendy looked him directly in the eye.

"What?" Rodd stared at her, her mahogany eyes capturing his attention, distracting him. "That doesn't—"

"Sheriff, there's no way we could keep the Olie Olson episode a secret. That's why I asked you to meet me here." She leaned forward, keeping her voice low. "Too many people were at Olson's, and Ted Olson couldn't keep quiet to save his life. It's much better to answer questions here in the open, right away. In a small town, the more you try to hide something, the more talk you get." Wendy lifted the mug to her lips.

Understanding dawned. Rodd had to give Wendy credit. He hadn't considered taking this direct approach to controlling the fallout from last night. Obviously, she knew her town and how to handle it. She'd pointed out again that rural law enforcement differed from Milwaukee's. His estimation of her as an ally increased again. He took a deep breath and caught a trace of her sweet fragrance. "I suppose you're right."

"So we've given out a few facts about last night—the same ones Cram can get from Ted and probably will. But we've concealed the thief's MO. That's what you wanted, isn't it? If you're going to try to catch the thief again, right?" Wendy looked at him with hope in her eyes.

"Right." He gazed back at her, enjoying the lift in his mood that she gave him. Her ivory skin glowed against the dark wood of the booth. Fine gold loops dangled from her ears. The collar of the brown sweater she wore accented the paleness of her neck. How would her translucent skin feel to the touch?

Wendy interrupted his thoughts. "I'm really sorry about last night—"

"You're sorry? You didn't do anything wrong!" Rodd couldn't think how she could deem herself to blame.

She shook her head. "I knew Olie didn't want to be at the care center overnight. I should have warned you that he is unpredictable—"

"Stop." How could she hold herself responsible? "I'm the one who should have checked to see that he stayed at the clinic. But the idea that Olie might go home never occurred to me."

Ginger returned to jot down their order on her green pad and to ask if Wendy and she were still on for the movies Saturday night—unless Wendy got a better offer. As Ginger spoke, a strange expression came over her face and she winked at Wendy. Rodd couldn't figure out why Ginger was behaving so strangely. Did she know something about last night? Then a glance showed him that Wendy was blushing. Was she embarrassed because of the waitress's marked attention to them?

"Heard from your mom, Wendy?" Ginger asked. "Does she still like Florida?"

"She's fine. No problems," Wendy answered quickly.

To Rodd, Wendy's reply sounded as though she were covering something up. What was going on with her mother?

Ginger looked like she wanted to say more, but left them instead.

When they were alone again, Wendy traced the rim of the mug with her forefinger. "So where do we go from here?"

Watching her slender hand, he wished he had an answer to her innocent question. And he had to impress on Wendy that while he needed her cooperation, solving the crimes was a job for a professional. "I'd appreciate your cooperation," he said guardedly. She lifted her cup, her slender wrists looking too delicate for the heavy mug.

"What can I do to help you, Sheriff?" she asked with a tilt of her head.

Her earnest tone touched him. He observed her take a sip, then focused on her question. "You can call me again the next time you take another patient to spend the night at the care center. We can't assume the burglar won't still be watching you." *But I'm going to have to come up with a surefire way to draw the burglar out. He'd have to find an easy target and set another trap.*

Concern showed in her expressive eyes. "Is that all? The targets are my patients—"

"I need your information, but you are busy enough as it is," Rodd interrupted. A thought came to him. The disaster last night showed him that he really needed something more to catch the Weasel—next time. He studied Wendy. Maybe he should—

"Hey! Sheriff!" Zak, in a bright blue snowsuit, burst into the café and ran straight back to their booth. "I seen your Jeep outside!"

"Hi." Smiling, Penny followed her son in. "I'm here to put up another flyer about the Senior Bazaar at the VFW next month. Ginger called me and said the one I put here had fallen down—"

"It got stepped on," Zak finished for her.

Rodd grinned. "I didn't know little guys like you were big on bazaars."

"They make peanut brittle. That's my favorite." Zak climbed up next to Rodd. "We need help too. You're strong, Sheriff. You can help!"

Rodd half rose and motioned for Penny to sit with them. "What kind of help do you need?"

Penny shook her head but smiled. "Since you asked, we need a few people to set up the tables and chairs."

"And sample peanut brittle?" Wendy teased. "That sounds like a job for a man."

She made him grin. "With or without peanut brittle," Rodd told Zak, "I'll be glad to help."

"Great!" Zak threw his arms around the sheriff's neck and gave him a quick hug.

Rodd smiled. What a great little guy.

Wendy asked softly, "How have you been feeling, Penny?"

"Fine. I'm just fine." Penny brushed the question aside.

Rodd wondered why Wendy was concerned about Penny. Was her health in question?

Ginger set a platter of scrambled eggs and bacon in front of Rodd, plopped a heavy cereal bowl and small pitcher of milk in front of Wendy, and handed her a small box of Raisin Bran. "Sheriff, I bet you didn't know that our Wendy always helps with the Senior Bazaar. . . ."

Rodd wondered what the waitress was getting at.

Ginger grinned. "Wendy was the only girl in our high school class who failed cooking class. She helps by not baking anything."

Wendy's face turned rosy pink. "So my cakes always fall. Is that my fault?"

Grinning, Penny said, "Of course it isn't, Wendy! We have to go, Zak, and let them eat breakfast." She tugged a reluctant Zak away. Ginger followed them to the front to help position the new flyer.

Rodd waved good-bye, then breathed in the heartening aroma of bacon and began enjoying his breakfast.

❋❋❋

WENDY SPENT A few moments fixing her bowl of cereal, pouring the milk, sprinkling sugar over the flakes. Rodd's presence was a blessing and a bane. She hoped she'd helped him and the investigation here this morning. But Veda was here and she'd seen Wendy with Rodd. What would happen now?

The slim appetite Wendy had come in with deserted her when she'd seen Veda. Whenever she came to the Black Bear, the only café in town, and found Veda McCracken here, she thought of the verse in the Twenty-third Psalm: *"Thou preparest a table before me in the presence of mine enemies."* Rodd had no way of knowing that Veda would react to their being seen together. Wendy's stomach clenched.

Ginger's bringing up Mom hadn't helped Wendy's digestion either. Her mother had been weeping the last time she called. What was going on with Mom and her new husband?

Wendy sighed. Would seeing Wendy with Rodd give the old woman more grist for the rumor mill? No wonder Wendy had given up any idea of dating or romance when she'd come home after college. Maybe if her first love hadn't turned out to be a big mistake, she might have come back with someone. But she had come home single, and as she'd expected, Veda did everything she could to cause trouble and embarrassment for any man that showed even a passing interest in Wendy. And after all the years of verbal abuse, Wendy couldn't willingly invite any more of the same.

She forced these thoughts from her mind and prayed, *Lord, bless this meal and don't let that woman sour my stomach or any part of my life.* In spite of the woman sitting just a booth away, she forced herself to begin eating. *Lord, please don't let her use me to give the sheriff a hard time. Bless our breakfast. Amen.*

The bell on the front door jingled as Penny and Zak left the café. Penny had looked pale and tired to Wendy. Was Penny still run-down from her miscarriage last summer? Should she talk to Penny about that or keep her peace? Rodd asked her a question about Harlan and she smiled as she answered.

When Wendy and the sheriff were almost done eating, out of the corner of her eye, Wendy glimpsed Veda leave her booth and turn toward them. Wendy braced herself.

CHAPTER FIVE

"SO, SHERIFF, YOU were called out to Flanagan's the other night?" The grim-faced older woman stared at him, pointedly ignoring Wendy.

Wendy forced herself to go on chewing as though she hadn't heard anything. Ignoring Veda had evolved over the years as Wendy's only successful way of handling the argumentative woman.

Rodd rose politely. "I'm sorry; we haven't met."

"I'm Veda McCracken," the woman replied stiffly. "How come you didn't arrest Dutch Rieker and Elroy Dietz? And you let the burglar get away last night!" Without waiting for a reply, Veda plunged on. "You don't arrest deadbeats for being drunk and disorderly. . . ."

Wendy regretted making Rodd a target for Veda by having breakfast with him here. But then Veda never needed an excuse for being rude—to anyone.

Rodd interrupted Veda's diatribe. "Ma'am, do you know firsthand of any information about criminal activity by either Rieker or Dietz?"

Wendy heard the coldness in Rodd's tone. Apparently, he didn't appreciate being put on the spot. Well, that never stopped Veda.

"I don't need to have any firsthand information. Everyone in the county heard about that brawl the other night. Just because you're trying to get on the good side of Rieker's good-for-nothing niece—"

Veda glared at Wendy—"doesn't mean you should let trash like Dutch and Elroy off with just a slap on the wrist."

Rodd bristled. "You still haven't told me anything to the point—"

The café's door opened. Wendy glanced around to see Ma and Bruno walk in, and Wendy braced herself again. Ma never suffered Veda in silence.

The two women faced each other. Ma stared hard at Veda.

Wendy held her breath.

Veda sneered at Ma and Bruno. "Well, if it isn't love's young dream? Or are you just two old, nearsighted fools?"

Bruno tried to move forward toward Veda.

Ma lifted her chin. "Veda McCracken, you're just jealous because even if you walked down Main Street stark naked, no man would look at you twice—"

Veda's face turned red. "If Bruno knew what kind of woman you really are, would he want you?"

"I know what kind of woman Ma is and yes, I would," Bruno replied quietly. "Why don't you turn around and walk out that door? No one here is interested in anything you have to say, Veda."

With the sheriff, Bruno, and Ma staring her down, Veda humphed, turned, and walked toward the front. Wendy kept her eyes down until the door closed behind the ill-tempered woman.

"Good morning, Wendy, Sheriff." Bruno greeted them as though he hadn't even seen Veda. "As you can see, Doc just took my cast off! So Ma and I came to celebrate with a sticky roll and a good cup of coffee!"

Wendy smiled. "Wonderful!" She stood up and hugged Ma. She whispered into Ma's ear, "I'm so glad to see you looking so well. You had me scared a couple of weeks ago."

Ma hugged her back and whispered, "And I'm glad to see you sitting with a handsome man."

Grimacing, Wendy shook her head. She didn't need Ma's reminder. The way Ginger had been acting showed she also assumed something had started between the sheriff and Wendy. She'd have to set her straight before sweet but talkative Ginger could spread it countywide. Wendy was already too aware of the sheriff's appeal. And eminently more to the point, the fact that she'd better work at ignoring it.

Veda's attack had proved Wendy right. She'd have to keep her distance from the sheriff—or Veda would aim her harassment toward Rodd as well as Wendy. No one knew better than Wendy the kind of unpleasantness Veda could engineer. Wendy couldn't risk going through again what she had as a child and as a teen. Veda knew no shame or kindness.

Grinning, Ginger came over and cleaned off the table while Rodd helped Wendy on with her parka. He insisted on paying the check. As he walked Wendy out, everyone turned to watch them go.

Beside her station wagon, she glanced up at the long lean man gazing down at her. She cleared her tight throat. "You look like you have something on your mind."

"Are you a mind reader too?" He grinned.

She shook her head, unable to look away. "I won't badger you, but remember, I'll do anything I can to help you stop these burglaries."

He opened her door for her. "When's your next day off?"

Sliding past him and trying not to touch him, she got in, then glanced up. He looked like his question wasn't an idle one. "Day after tomorrow."

"Keep it open—please?" He leaned closer. "I have something to think over. You might be able to help me out." He paused, leaving only inches between them.

"Fine." Finally, she eased the door shut, forcing herself to break away. But she couldn't stop herself from watching him walk toward Cram's newspaper office.

Sheriff Rodd Durand was tall, handsome, and smart. But would he succeed? Some matters only God could handle. Did the sheriff realize that? *Oh, Lord, please give this fine man the opportunity to catch the thief—soon.*

❧ ❧ ❧

TWO DAYS LATER, Rodd walked into Harlan's kitchen. He smiled at Wendy sitting at the table. Morning sunshine glinted in her gold brown hair, and her pleasing face lifted in welcome. How could he tell her that her smile boosted his spirits? He couldn't, so he smiled in return, hoping she understood.

Grinning as though reading Rodd's thoughts, Harlan stood up, Lady at his side, wagging her tail. "Morning, Rodd. Hear you're going on a snowmobile shopping trip to Duluth."

"Yes. Thanks for letting us meet here." Suddenly restless, Rodd reached for Wendy's parka, which hung on the back of a kitchen chair, and held it open for her. Now that he was here he wanted them to be off. This was just the first step in his next move against the Weasel. And he wanted Wendy alone for the day. He had a lot of questions and she'd have the answers he needed.

Turning her back to him, she slipped her arms into the sleeves. "Has it started snowing again?"

Intensely aware of her sweet strawberry fragrance, Rodd covered this by glancing out the window. Snow was the furthest thing from his mind. "Frankly, it's snowed so much already this year I just expected it to snow today."

Harlan nodded toward the muted TV in the corner. "You're right. We've only had one snowless day since late October, but a front is moving in from the west."

"A front moves in from the west every day." Rodd shrugged. Spending a day away from the county with an interesting woman like Wendy—while getting started again on solving the burglaries—was worth a little slippery driving.

"Well, they say it's just a weak one," Harlan conceded. Then, grinning, he shook his finger at Rodd. "If it weren't, I'd make you two postpone this trip. Winter driving is nothing to take for granted."

Rodd took a step toward the door, but Wendy hung back.

She patted Harlan's shoulder. "Don't worry, Grandfather. I have everything I need for a winter emergency in the old wagon."

"We'll be back before nightfall, safe and sound." Rodd touched Wendy's delicate shoulder, pointing toward the door. He wanted her sitting beside him in the station wagon, putting miles between them and Steadfast.

Finally, after kissing his granddaughter, Harlan waved them on. "Okay! Have fun, kids!"

Outside, Rodd helped Wendy into her station wagon, which had Harlan's empty trailer hitched to its rear. As Rodd drove away, she waved good-bye to Harlan while snowflakes drifted against the windshield. She drew her legs up under her and turned toward him with an eager grin. "I feel like we're escaping!"

Happy to see her relaxing, he smiled and cocked his head toward her. "I couldn't agree more."

"Yes." She sighed a happy sigh. "I did feel funny asking Grandfather to let us leave from his place. It felt like we were sneaking out of town."

Recalling the confrontations with Cram and Veda McCracken at the café, he'd decided that leaving from Harlan's—so far out of town—would be best. "There's no reason for us to advertise what we're doing."

Wendy agreed. "And I told only Grandfather that this new snowmobile is really for you, not me. But since it would be natural for me to keep it at Grandfather's place, we'll let everyone else assume it's mine."

"Thanks. It probably is a good idea." Rodd shook his head over the necessary deception. With a snowmobile of his own, he wouldn't be left standing in the perp's dust again! "If there's any chance after the Olson stakeout that the burglar will try again, I can't afford to let him find out I'm buying a snowmobile right now. I want him to think he still has that edge."

Wendy nodded. "The sheriff's old 'bile was wrecked before he passed away. Your department needs a new one."

Her understanding bolstered his mood and gave him a confidence he hadn't felt lately. "That's what I want everyone to think—that the department snowmobile is still out of commission."

"Do you think the burglar will try again after he saw you at Olie's?"

Noting the snowfall intensifying, Rodd gripped the wheel, mastering his lingering reluctance. Under ordinary circumstances, he'd never discuss ongoing investigations with a civilian. But Wendy had become enmeshed in this one. And she knew the county better than he did. He needed her information in order to catch the thief. "My biggest problem has been the lack of witnesses and no physical evidence to link anyone to the burglaries—no fingerprints, nothing left at the scenes." The criminal's snowmobile's tread he'd cast had no distinctive differences from a dozen others he had examined, and the nick on the tree trunk had led him nowhere.

"The first four burglaries appeared to me to be the work of an opportunist. Someone saw an easy, safe way to pick up quick cash."

EYEING THE HEAVY snow clouds, Wendy nodded, a lump lodged in her throat. Her unknowing role in the string of crimes still depressed her.

"When an opportunist's easy way is detected, he usually comes up with a new MO. Or quits."

She watched the play of emotion over the sheriff's rugged face. The desire to trace the hard line of his jaw shook her. She clasped her unruly hands in her lap. "So we just have to wait and see what he does next?"

He shook his head. "I drew up a list of suspects—"

"I didn't know you had one." Wendy's stomach tightened. The snow fell steadily now. The increasing wind swayed the roadside maples' naked branches. Even the tips of the tall evergreens bowed in the west wind.

"It wasn't easy to come up with one. Late Sheriff Capshaw didn't bring any new blood into the Sheriff's Department for a long time."

Every fact he shared with her heartened her. The sheriff did trust her. That felt wonderful. Unable and unwilling to express this, Wendy remarked, "Grandfather said the county should have seen that they needed a few young deputies coming in."

He dismissed this with a lift of his shoulders. "My dispatcher has worked for the department for over ten years. She gave me a rundown of the most likely suspects in the county; then I pinpointed which ones had means, motive, and opportunity." He spoke with cool authority.

Sliding her freshly manicured hands under her, Wendy didn't want to ask who was on the list. She had to assume her uncle and Trav's uncle were both on it. Both had been arrested before.

Rodd slowed as he negotiated a narrow curve. The empty trailer rattled behind them. The wind buffeted the station wagon.

Wendy decided to broach her fears. "Trav's uncle Elroy Dietz is on that list and my Uncle Dutch too, right?"

Rodd hesitated.

His regard for her feelings warmed her, straight through, top to bottom. She was able to go on. "Both have snowmobiles, both are out of work, and both could have kept an eye on me without my being aware of it." What would he say?

"Yes, on all three counts. But it fits many others too. That's what's so maddening about this perp. He's come up with a way to pick up easy money and get away with it—so far."

The wiper blades batted the wet snow, while a layer of slush piled up at the bottom of the windshield. Ignoring the worsening weather, she paused, dragging her mind back to the burglaries and the danger they brought. "Should I warn my patients to not keep cash on hand?"

He let out air. "I was surprised that some of them have had way more than a hundred dollars in the house."

Her grandfather's caution came back to her mind: *"A front is moving in."* Though distracted, she went on. "Remember, most of my clients were children in the Depression. They like to deal in cash. They definitely aren't the plastic generation."

He nodded.

She studied his determined expression from the corner of her eye. She shivered once—for the burglar. "You really think he's going to steal again?" She watched for Rodd's reaction.

"I can only assume he will." The sheriff sounded matter-of-fact. "My task now is to make him strike where I want him to."

Wendy glanced at him sideways. "How do you do that—make him come to you?"

He thought for a moment. "I have to make someone a really attractive target."

She didn't like the sound of that. "What do you mean?"

"The burglar wants cash. I need to find someone with a lot of it who will cooperate with me in setting a trap."

"Not too many of my patients have more than a spare hundred or two."

"Zak's mentioning the Senior Bazaar and Bake Sale at the café made me think that whoever takes the proceeds home from a fund-raiser might tempt the burglar."

"The bazaar will bring in around three hundred—"

"Is there another fund-raiser that would bring in a larger sum?"

Wendy worried her lower lip. "The only other one I can think of in the near future is the Bingo Fund-raiser at the VFW in LaFollette."

"Our thief hasn't gone that far from Steadfast."

"Yes, but the one who'd have the money from Sunday till Monday would be Gus Feeney. Gus is an old army friend of my grandfather's. And he lives out in the country closer to Steadfast than LaFollette."

"How much money are we talking about?"

"At least six hundred dollars or more."

"That's a lot of bingo!"

"It's a big deal—a meal is served, snacks, drinks. People line up to get good seats and play six cards at a time. It's like a noon to midnight shindig. People from all over the county go."

"You said Gus lives out in the country—is his place isolated like the other victims'?"

"Yes."

"Then I guess I better talk to Gus Feeney."

Wendy turned over in her mind the three burglaries and the one attempted. "I wish I could be of more help." *And I wish the snowfall wasn't getting worse each mile we drive west into the front.*

Rodd grinned suddenly. "Just help me get a good deal on a snowmobile. And I could use a great late lunch. I'm counting on you to make this easier for me. I know Milwaukee—"

"And I know Duluth." She grinned, enjoying the moment of being a valued confidante. And since they'd left without anyone but her grandfather knowing, she wouldn't have to worry about Veda trashing her reputation or Rodd's. A day with Rodd without anyone trying to make something out of it—priceless! After all, what was another snowstorm?

❋ ❋ ❋

RODD BOUGHT HIS snowmobile at the third dealership they shopped at. By then, the snow—heavy moist clumps of flakes—pelted the showroom windows.

Wendy stared out at the leaden sky. "I thought the front coming in was supposed to be a weak one." Her tone carried worry.

Rodd glanced over at her as the salesman handed him the sales slip and the key to the new snowmobile, which was being loaded onto the trailer outside the door. "Lake-effect snow. The front has passed and its winds changed direction. They're blowing off Superior right onto us. Ten miles from here, it probably isn't snowing at all," the salesman reassured them. "It's early yet for a real storm, but you people drive carefully anyway, okay?"

Rodd bid him a polite farewell. Leading Wendy through the thick veil of snow, he opened the car door for her and blocked the wind while she climbed in. Behind the wheel, Rodd threaded his way through the congested city streets onto the highway out of town. Feeling the wind blow against the car, he had a feeling that the lake-effect snow might be with them for more than ten miles.

He was right. Though he'd left the city traffic well behind, he slowed the wagon and trailer to a crawl on the snow-slick highway. Cars turned off at small towns for the night while the 18-wheelers sped on, sticking to their schedules.

A semi barreled around them as though it were a hot day in July. Its white wake blotted out the road, the horizon, everything. Rodd tensed, trying to stay on the road. *I feel like I'm driving by Braille.*

"About now, I wish we had your Jeep and its four-wheel drive," Wendy murmured.

Rodd leaned forward over the steering wheel, peering into the white night. "I can't disagree with you. I'm afraid we're going to be getting home quite late."

"What's that?" Wendy suddenly pointed forward.

Flashing blue lights and rotating red lights loomed out of the whiteness. Nothing more could be seen.

"It's an accident. We have to stop. Brace yourself." Rodd began pumping the brakes. Pump. The trailer fishtailed, skidded. Pump. Pump. The rear of the wagon swerved to the right.

His heart pounding in his chest, he steered into the skid. The wagon and trailer slid left and rocked to a halt. Just yards ahead, a jackknifed semi lay across the road—a beached whale in a whiteout snowstorm.

Feeling the weight of fatigue settling over him, Rodd stared ahead into the swirling wet snow. He had to get out and identify himself and offer assistance to the law officers already at the scene. They probably wouldn't need him, but they could tell him how long the two-lane highway would be blocked. He just wanted to get both Wendy and himself home safely for a good night's sleep.

"I'll come with you. Someone may need medical attention," Wendy said.

Mechanically, he zipped up his jacket and turned up its collar. "No, I'll go and let you know if you're—"

"No, I'm coming." She dragged on her outerwear too.

Under the circumstances, he appreciated her gallantry. Since they'd left Duluth, she'd been watching the dashboard clock. Obviously, she dreaded getting home late, afraid of possibly sparking more gossip about the two of them. He'd been told by his dispatcher that already people were speculating about him and Wendy being a couple. The dispatcher had also warned him against Veda McCracken. Evidently the woman's venom knew no bounds where Wendy Carey was concerned. He didn't want to open Wendy up to any mean-spirited talk, but he couldn't control the weather. *I should have paid attention to Harlan's weather forecast and postponed this trip.*

Insisting Wendy wait for him, he opened his door, got out, and walked around to her door. Soggy snow pelted him, leaking down the back of his neck while wind buffeted him. He opened Wendy's door and, guiding her by the arm, picked his way through the snow sweeping across the pavement. Reaching into his pocket, he got out his wallet with his badge tucked into it. He approached the first officer and held it out. "Hi, I'm Sheriff Durand. This is Miss Wendy Carey, a nurse. Do you need our assistance?" Drawing in cold air with his words pulled the chill deep inside him.

The state policeman glanced at Rodd's ID and Wendy's face. He touched his hat brim politely to her. "No one is injured, miss. We've radioed for a wrecker, Sheriff. We're closing down a ten-mile section of this highway."

Raw arctic wind swooped around Rodd. His spirits dropped. "That bad, huh?"

"The front has stalled over Superior and this is the worst stretch." The bitter wind slashed at their unprotected faces. The officer lowered his chin, trying to protect face. "We're going to get dumped on all night. If we shut down the highway, we think we'll save more truckers from ending up in the ditch like this one."

Resigning himself, Rodd glanced around at the snow-shrouded forest that edged the road. Not a place he wanted Wendy stranded. She shivered beside him. He angled himself in front of her to shield her from the wind. "Is there a motel anywhere near here?" He folded his arms, trying to hold in his body heat.

"No, but a public shelter has been opened." The trooper motioned behind Rodd. "Cross over and go back to that frontage road." The gale carried away the man's words. He shouted to be heard. "We've put it out on citizens band that the road is blocked and is shutting down."

A public shelter, not separate rooms in a motel. No hot shower. Rodd snatched breath from the whirlwind and shouted, "Where exactly is the shelter?"

"A little town, Good Hope. They're setting up at the community church there." Then the man began backing into the wind toward his own vehicle.

Rodd waved his thanks. With Wendy sheltered under his arm, he headed into the sharp wind back to the station wagon. Inside the warm car again, he opened his jacket and wiped his wet face with his hands. "Well, I guess we better turn around."

"Right." The howling wind muffled Wendy's subdued voice.

Rodd didn't blame her for a lack of enthusiasm. He'd have to think of a way to shield her from wagging tongues—but later. Now he had to get them safely out of the storm. Conscious of the trailer, he eased the car into reverse, backed up, and carefully turned onto the other lane. "We don't have much choice. Why don't you call your grandfather?"

❋❋❋

WENDY HAD NOTICED that Rodd was upset about their not arriving home as they'd planned. She refused to think about possible repercussions from their being stranded overnight together. God was still in control. They'd bought the snowmobile, and now God was sending them to a safe harbor in this dangerous storm. *Thank you, Father.* Using the dash light, she punched her grandfather's number into her cell phone. The musical tones sounded.

Harlan picked up on the first ring. "Where are you?"

Grandfather sounded worried. She was glad Rodd couldn't hear him. "Grandfather, the highway's been closed because of lake-effect snow. We're being held up by a storm, so we're headed for a public shelter in Good Hope."

"Certainly." Grandfather's voice came through loud and clear, trying to sound cheerful. He went on. "Don't you worry. I'll let Sage know you're all right. Tell Rodd I'll feed and water his stock before supper. It's not even snowing here, but that's lake effect for you. We'll probably get some of it later."

"Thanks, Grandfather. We'll see you tomorrow." Snapping the phone shut, she looked to Rodd. "Grandfather says he'll take care of your cattle." She pursed her lips. "I didn't consider the possibility we wouldn't be back tonight. I have calls scheduled at seven-thirty tomorrow morning."

Rodd nodded. "Not much we can do about a closed highway. Call the clinic and tell them to reschedule your morning appointments."

She did as he suggested, while he fought the wind to stay on the road. Wendy said another prayer for their safety. The elements pounded the windows, drawing her closer to Rodd's silent strength. Weather like this could become even nastier—and without warning.

Finally, Rodd turned off onto the frontage road. The town's sign, plastered with snow, read "ood Hop." "We're going to spend the night in 'ood Hop,'" he teased.

Wendy rewarded his effort to lighten the mood with a half smile. The chill in the wagon was gaining on the old heater. She had to force herself not to inch nearer Rodd.

He negotiated the snow-packed road into the tiny town, which turned out to have a tavern and one church. Two SUVs were parked along the road in front of the small, white frame church. He parked beside the church and turned to Wendy. "I'm sorry—"

"I know." With swift jerks, she adjusted her hat and gloves and gathered up her purse. "Let's get inside." Without waiting for him, she yanked open her door.

He met her at the back of the station wagon and grasped her arm at the bend of her elbow. The wind whipped the power lines overhead, jangling them like bracelets. The force of the storm made her glad for the sheriff's support. With her head down, she leaned into the shelter he provided as he piloted her through the snowdrifts to the faint light over the church door. He tried the knob and it opened. He drew her inside.

She was winded but tried to hide it. The dark foyer didn't feel very warm. She pointed toward a dimly lighted stairwell. "Let's go downstairs. That's probably where they're setting up." He let her precede him. She heard voices from below and called out, "Hello, you've got company!"

"Come down," an older male voice replied. "We're about to fire up the old woodstove down here. We'll be warm before you know it."

After stomping the snow off their boots, Wendy and Rodd shuffled down the steps and found an elderly couple bundled up to their chins in an assortment of mismatched coats, hats, and mufflers, waiting to greet them at the bottom.

"Hello! We're the Learys. I'm Tiny and here's my wife, Lolly." The small, wizened man offered Rodd his hand. The sheriff shook hands and introduced Wendy and himself.

"So you're the sheriff one county over?" the older lady asked.

Rodd nodded.

"Can we help?" Wendy shivered in spite of herself.

"Oh, after Tiny gets the woodstove hot, I'm going to open the cupboards and get some food going." Lolly beamed at them as though they were the answer to a prayer.

"It's really nice of you to set up a shelter for us." Wendy tried to stop shivering.

"Don't think a thing of it," Tiny assured them. "We only live a few doors down. The pastor lives out of town, so we always open up the church. Been members here since we were little kids. We'd have you in our home, but it's only a one-bedroom. Just big enough for us. This isn't the first time we've done this. One time we had people here for four days. That was back in the seventies!"

Knowing that tonight would be added to Tiny's collection of winter tales to tell, Wendy grinned. Rodd caught her eye, a mischievous glint in his. Her grin widened as she shared their private joke.

With arms loaded with wood, two large men clumped inside, stomping off snow. "Here are our other guests." Tiny introduced them to the two out-of-state hunters who'd been sidelined by the storm.

Rodd took a step closer to her. Wendy wondered why. Was he protecting her? Rodd asked, "Do you need more wood? I can go out and bring in a load."

"No, this should be enough for the night." Tiny shook his head. "We keep the gas furnace set real low to save money. This is an old woodstove, but a good one. It burns good and steady. This whole basement will be warm before you know it."

In the kitchen, Wendy helped Lolly inspect the church cupboards and fire up the propane stove. She listened as Rodd helped the men load the stove with wood and kindling, then began to unpack musty cots and blankets from a storage room. She wasn't surprised when Rodd took charge and the other men followed him. She didn't think it was because he was a sheriff. He was just a man who commanded respect naturally.

Within an hour, it was warm enough to hang up their jackets. Within the next hour, everyone—including two more travelers, a husband and wife—sat down to a supper of a surprisingly tasty tuna-noodle casserole in the church kitchen. As they sat around the table, Tiny recounted storms from the past. Wendy began to relax, chatting with Lolly and the stranded wife.

Rodd had settled into the company too. His deep assuring voice soothed her, overriding the constant bluster of the storm. Her gaze kept straying to him until she noticed Lolly watching her.

All of a sudden the lights went out.

"Oh! More excitement!" Tiny chuckled. "Everyone stay where you are so I don't step on you. I set the oil lamp right here on the counter."

Wendy heard Tiny's footsteps and his fumbling in the darkness for the oil lamp and matches on the counter. A grating, then the golden flare of a match. In the glow, Tiny lit the wick. He settled the glass globe over the flame and placed the hurricane lamp in the center of the table. "Some people put these on shelves and call 'em antiques. My grandmother bought this lamp at the Good Hope Mercantile. That's been years ago. . . ." Tiny rambled on.

Wendy realized then that she'd reached for Rodd's hand. Feeling foolish, she tried to let go. For a moment, he gripped her hand, then released it.

Feeling her face warm, she was grateful for the low light. What had she been thinking? One look at her Uncle Dutch and anyone would know that the daughter of a Rieker—even one who'd married a

Carey—and a Durand didn't go together. But what would it feel like to hold Rodd's hand and know he sought her touch?

❄❄❄

IN THE MIDDLE of the night, Wendy woke up, slid off her cot, and tiptoed up the steps. She stood by the doors, looking out at the swirling snow under the scant moonlight. The snow had stopped falling, but it still obeyed the wind, which blew it in broad sweeps. The beauty of its savage wildness touched something deep inside her; even in its harshness the power of the wind and snow could awe her. The Creator had given everything a beauty of its own.

But she hadn't gotten up to stand in the chilly entryway just to contemplate the snow. The question she'd gone to sleep with had wakened her, insisting on an answer. What was going on between her and the sheriff? Was anything going on between them? Could she stop it . . . ?

A shadow behind her . . . a tingling raced up her spine.

CHAPTER SIX

"CAN'T SLEEP?" RODD had come up behind her. The creaking of the old church and the swish of the wind against the glass must have masked his footsteps.

Stifling a gasp, she glanced at him warily. "I just wanted to see how the weather was. The snow's stopped, but it's drifting." She gestured toward the blue-shadowed snow cliffs and shallows around vehicles slumped all along the empty street. "God took care of us—well." Her voice sounded funny to her.

Rodd made a sound of nominal agreement. "We should have taken off earlier; then I could have beaten the storm home."

His lukewarm tone worried her. Did he believe what she'd said? Didn't he believe that God could and would take care of them? "You can't think of everything. God knew where we'd be and what we'd face."

"If the wind stops," he went on without commenting on her observation, "they should be able to clear the highway, and we can get home in the morning." His low voice rumbled close to her ear.

So close, she felt him breathing. His nearness brought her senses to life, and her own breathing became shallow. In her life, she rarely found herself alone with a single man under the age of seventy. But the larger truth was that Rodd Durand made her feel different than any other man ever had, much different than during her brief, unhappy romance in college. What was she going to do about this? That was the question that had wakened her.

Here, far from Steadfast, it was too easy to forget she was her mother's daughter. Her mother's notorious reputation had kept Wendy from dating in high school. Too many guys had expected her to be like her mother. Wendy shook herself. She couldn't forget Veda's watchful eyes and her sharp tongue. That woman would have a heyday making this innocent trip and snowbound night something it wasn't!

"I know you're worrying, but don't."

The sheriff's softened voice curled itself around her like an embrace. She looked straight ahead. "I'm trying not to."

Rodd rested his hands on her shoulders.

She stilled, her heart thumping out of control. His touch was just a common gesture. Meant to be reassuring. But she fought her own reaction—her desire to rest her cheek upon one of his warm, strong hands. Did he feel a similar pull toward her?

"Don't worry about what people will say." His voice rumbled so near again, making her neck prickle in response. "The unreasonable people or the ones who have their own guilty consciences will think the worst. The good people will give us the benefit of the doubt."

His understanding caught her off guard. Alive to his warm breath against her nape, she nodded. "I know. I just . . . hate it . . . when people talk." Had he heard any of the lies Veda was spreading? He must have. This alone twisted her heart. *It isn't fair, Lord.*

"Everything will be okay," he murmured. His lips grazed the skin just below her ear.

A kiss? Her breath caught. Had he kissed her? Probably not. Just a chance touch, but if she turned her face toward him, would he? Her face turned of its own accord. The air between them became warm, charged. She couldn't breathe.

Rodd tightened his grip on her shoulders, then rested his cheek against hers.

His unshaven skin, roughened from the late hour, sent shivers of awareness coursing through her.

"I'll get you home safely tomorrow; don't you worry," he murmured, tickling her ear with his breath.

She struggled with herself. He had come up here to ease her worries—that was all. They weren't doing anything wrong. In spite of her elemental reaction to him, she wouldn't let anything mislead him into thinking she wanted more than friendship. Love was too dangerous a venture for her to contemplate—with anyone. She just wanted to help him catch the thief who preyed on her patients. That was all she wanted, wasn't it?

"Let's go back downstairs." She forced herself to step away from his touch. "No use losing sleep over what we can't help." *And no use getting accustomed to being near you.*

IN THE HUSH of morning over a week later on Thanksgiving Day, fine snow fell like crushed diamonds. As Rodd walked beside Wendy over the freshly plowed church parking lot, he watched snowflakes frost her hair.

When Rodd had stopped at church to see how the Thanksgiving Outreach Dinner was going, Harlan had asked him to help Wendy deliver meals to church members who couldn't come to the church and to nonmembers who had signed up but didn't want to come out on the snowy roads. He'd been more than happy to oblige.

"I'm so sorry you got hooked into this." Wendy passed in front of him and slid into the passenger side of his Jeep.

Wendy's abashed tone surprised him. Didn't she want him along? He got in the driver's side. "Did you have a reason for me not to deliver the Thanksgiving dinners with you?"

"Of course not." With both her small hands, she began ruffling the fresh snow from her short hair. "You're welcome to help, but I could have done it by myself." She lowered her eyelashes and her voice. "I just don't like it when Grandfather tries to . . . matchmake."

He chuckled. "Don't let it bother you." Even as he spoke the words, his mind munched on the concept of matchmaking. "For myself, I was glad to be asked." It had been a long time since any friend had tried to fix him up, mainly because most of his friends' marriages had failed. Unfortunately, he'd seen too many cop marriages collapse under the unique pressures of being a law officer.

He cleared his throat. "I felt like I haven't been able to do anything to help with the Outreach meal today. This gives me a chance to do more than invite people." He'd have to watch his emotions around Wendy. Somehow she'd found a tiny chink in his bachelor armor and had slipped inside, warming him with her golden presence.

She sighed, sounding relieved. "Okay. Why don't you just head toward Highway 27 while I check the list?" She glanced down at the handwritten list with its many scribbled notes and fell silent beside him.

And that was just like her—she never tried to catch his attention. She was more dangerous than that. She caught his notice without even trying.

Looking out his window to keep his eyes away from Wendy, he drove through Steadfast. Seeing Carl and Patsy's Grill on Main Street again redirected his memory to earlier that morning. In the quiet, he let his mind drift away from Wendy back to today's first hint of the trouble brewing.

Earlier, as he'd driven through the deserted, snow-blanketed village, he'd experienced a time-travel sensation, as though a century had slipped away and he should be riding a horse through the empty streets. The hush of deep winter had crept inside him, giving him a profound peace.

But whether he'd been a sheriff a century ago or today, one of his duties was to remind everyone that the law hadn't taken the holiday off. Though it seemed ironic, holidays often triggered an increase in police work, with domestic disputes and people overdoing what they called "holiday cheer." So he'd pulled up in front of the only business open on Main Street, Carl and Patsy's. Through the chilly morning snowfall, he'd walked inside the darkened interior.

"Hello, Sheriff!" Carl, a stocky, white-haired man well over retirement age, had called out from behind the bar. "Come on in. I'll buy you a Thanksgiving brew!"

Rodd had waved his greeting and sat down on a barstool. A few old men were already at the bar, but they were drinking coffee and watching a muted Christmas parade on the small TV above the bar. Carl and Patsy's place usually gave him no problem. The average age of their customers must hover in the sixties. Carl's was more of a senior center than a bar, completely different from Flanagan's. "Make it a root beer, Carl, and I'll accept."

Carl chuckled. "One sarsaparilla coming up." He served Rodd a foaming mug. "Feel like we're in an old Western on TV. I'm the friendly old barkeep and you're the teetotaling young sheriff."

Rodd grinned. "And I just rode through the ghost town."

Carl nodded.

Rodd sipped his foam-topped root beer. "Just wanted to say Happy Thanksgiving and I'll be hanging around town if you need me. I'm wearing my pager. Later I plan to stop by the church for Thanksgiving dinner. If you hear of anyone who wants to get together for a meal, send him there, would you?"

"Will do. But my Patsy roasted two thirty-pound birds and stirred up a vat of cranberry sauce last night. We'll be serving turkey sandwiches all day to customers."

"Sounds like a plan." Then into Rodd's peace, the day's first disturbing note had sounded.

Wiping the bar, Carl leaned close with his head down. "Sheriff, I heard a rumor. Maybe it's something, maybe not. Kids may be planning a kegger tonight. That useless Elroy Dietz might be getting paid by high school kids to set one up."

Rodd had given the barest nod, stood up, and put a dollar down. He'd waved good-bye to the men sitting at the bar and left. Then he'd driven around town once more before he parked by the church. All the while, he turned the word *kegger* over in his mind. A teen drinking party out somewhere isolated was a prescription for disaster. It would take some handling—if it proved to be more than a rumor.

Now leaving Steadfast behind and with Wendy beside him, Rodd concentrated on his driving. The snow- and ice-packed roads and all the dishes of food boxed and stowed carefully in the rear of his Jeep made him negotiate the curves and hills more cautiously. He readily understood why some seniors had decided not to drive in for the Thanksgiving Outreach Dinner. But the thought of the possible kegger irritated him like a painful speck in his eye.

Wendy interrupted his thoughts. "We're nearly at our turnoff. The Barnes place is just a mile from here."

Rodd glanced at her. She'd opened her parka, partially revealing her dress, a fine corduroy, reddish brown like oak leaves in the fall. It made her hair look richer, more golden. Was she letting it grow? It looked longer than it had been that first day they'd met at Ma's. Sun glinted in her tiny golden earrings shaped like fall leaves. The same kind of leaf dangled on a gold chain around her neck.

He wished he were the kind of man who could say casually, "You look pretty today." But would she welcome a compliment or retreat from him? She'd pulled away from him that early morning in Good Hope. . . .

Wendy wasn't like any of the women he'd dated in the past. He liked women with long hair, classy women who wore makeup and perfume, women who made him want to don a suit for a date. But none of them had kept his interest like Wendy Carey had. Ever since their trip to Duluth, her angelic face had popped into his mind at will. He halted this line of thought. It had no future. He'd decided years ago he wasn't the marrying kind, and no woman had ever shaken this belief. Uncle George had never married. Some men just weren't cut out for it—especially cops. That was one of the reasons that his father had delayed remarrying until he'd retired early from the Milwaukee PD.

"Here's the turn." She pointed the way.

Soon, he parked in front of an old house with peeling yellow paint. Snowflakes blew around as though tired, aimless. In the sharp air he helped Wendy get out the covered tray from the box in the back. He was about to carry it in when his cell phone rang.

"I'll take it in." Wendy lifted the tray from his hands and walked up the short flight of steps to where an old man in a worn green sweater held open the door for her.

Watching her go, Rodd opened his cell phone and climbed back inside his Jeep.

"Hello, Sheriff." The voice of the dispatcher sounded perturbed. "Mrs. Beltziger out on Casey Road wants to talk to you."

"Mrs. Beltziger? What does she want?"

"I'm not important enough for her to tell," the dispatcher said with a sardonic twist. "You have to call."

"Okay." He gave dispatch his location and hung up. Since anyone could own a radio with a police band and many county residents had them, he'd decided that he and all his deputies should be equipped with cell phones and pagers for privacy. Digital cellular messages couldn't be picked up by others unless they had high-powered electronic equipment. The fact that dispatch contacted him via cell phone, not radio, said that Mrs. Beltziger wanted her communication with him kept private. He punched in the Beltziger number and identified himself.

A woman with a forceful voice spoke in quick even beats. "We need you to come out here. It's that Dietz bunch. They're always up to something."

Instinctively, Rodd didn't appreciate the woman's complaining busybody tone. He didn't think he'd like her as a neighbor any more than the Dietzes probably did.

She went on, "I think some of the younger ones are planning a kegger over in that old barn way back on their property."

So the kegger, that speck in his eye, rubbed and stung him more. "Why do you think that, ma'am?"

"It's happened before on holidays, and late last night I seen that Elroy Dietz drive by our house, then off the road to the old barn. Ain't any reason for him to be out there. And this morning, I seen several young boys—teens—snowmobile out that way."

"Is that unusual?"

"On Thanksgiving Day it is. I'll bet you anything that Elroy bought a keg or two of beer for his nephews and their friends for tonight. Though where he got the money, I don't know. Now I don't want a bunch of liquored-up kids driving snowmobiles onto thin ice on the Tamarack Lake over here or smashing into trees," she insisted.

"I don't either, ma'am. I'll get right on it."

"Well, I hope so, but don't you let on to them Dietzes it was me that called. They're an ornery bunch, especially that sneaky Elroy. He's just as bad as the Riekers. I hear you're making up to Wendy Carey. Did you know she's a Rieker on her mother's side—"

Rodd cut her off. "Don't worry, ma'am. This conversation is confidential."

"Good. Now don't mess this up like you did that business at Olson's. Good-bye." *Click.*

Rodd strangled the receiver in his hand. Listening to the dial tone start, he hung up. Mrs. Beltziger needed to reread her copy of *How to Win Friends and Influence People*. Her comment about Wendy had come close to making him hang up on her. Who cared who Wendy was related to? Then the unpleasant woman had put into words how he'd already assessed the fiasco at Olson's. That had been his best shot so far at catching the Weasel red-handed. In the weeks since, the snowmobile thief had lain low. Rodd had planned on letting Wendy know how far he'd gotten in setting a new trap.

Now a kegger might be on today's agenda. Rodd called dispatch to find the location of another deputy. He was on the other side of the county busy enforcing a no-contact order. Rodd told dispatch to have the deputy contact him as soon as he could.

When Wendy let herself back in, cold air rushed inside the Jeep. She eyed him. "Can you go on, or do you need to be off on a call?"

"I've got time," he said, keeping his tone light. A sharp woman, Wendy had already picked up on his preoccupation. He drove back onto the highway. "I contacted Gus Feeney in LaFollette."

"What did he say?" Her quick interest showed in her voice.

"He said he'd think about it. He seemed to think that I should keep the thief in Steadfast."

"That sounds like someone from LaFollette, not Gus. Maybe it's because you're new in the county."

"Why would someone in LaFollette—"

"It's just an old feud between the two towns. But my grandfather and Gus served together in World War II, and vets from any war are welcome at the VFW for bingo. You just have to ask him again."

"I will. The big bingo night fund-raiser is still two weeks away. I want to have time to really build up how successful the event will be so Gus will become a target. Or should I say his house?"

"How will you do that?"

He grinned. "My deputies and I will prime the gossip pump, and I'll ask Old Doc to really promote it and Gus in Cram's paper. Then Gus will have to be overcome with the excitement—his heartbeat becoming irregular—and be taken into the clinic. I've driven past Gus's house, and an ambulance would have to go past Flanagan's both ways. I'm certain the thief, whoever he is, will be there and want to find out who is in the ambulance. And if the thief doesn't nibble the bait, Old Doc could keep Gus over a second night."

"Sounds good. I'll pray about it."

He made no reply. They reached the next stop.

Wendy glanced at him, a worried look on her face.

He paused. Something was bothering her. He looked at the house, then back at Wendy. "Why don't I deliver this one?"

"No, I don't think you'll . . ." She confessed, "This is Veda McCracken's house—"

"Then I'm definitely delivering this one—"

"No, I—"

Rodd climbed out and went to the back. The least he could do today was protect Wendy from the woman who counted Wendy her enemy.

"I—" Wendy tried to object again.

"I'll be right back." With tray in hand, he trotted up the rickety steps and knocked on the door.

Veda opened the door, scowled at him, took the tray, and closed the door.

"Happy Thanksgiving to you too, Miss McCracken!" he said to the door. Back in the car, he cleared his throat. "Would you mind telling me what that woman has against the world?"

Wendy lowered her gaze. "Veda is my father's aunt."

"Your aunt?" This close relationship between Veda and Wendy hadn't occurred to him, but again he had overheard comments, which now became clearer to him. "I won't hold you responsible for that! Why is she angry all the time?"

Wendy tried to smile. "My grandfather tried to answer that for me once. He showed me a picture of my grandmother, his late wife, who was Veda's older sister. She was blonde, petite, and very pretty—and popular, he said. She was everything that Veda never was. Grandfather said Veda was jealous of her older sister from the cradle. It made her spiteful when people went on and on about how pretty and sweet her older sister was. He thinks that's why she first became so nasty. But . . ."

"But?" Rodd prompted.

"But my mother always says that Veda just enjoys being mean. She likes people to shy away from her, be afraid of her. It must make her feel powerful or something. I don't get it myself."

Rodd let the unpleasant topic drop. Why spoil Thanksgiving with thoughts about Veda McCracken? Only God knew what made a woman turn so bitter.

Wendy and he made five more quick stops, and then Wendy asked him to drive to Flanagan's.

"Flanagan's?" He'd already intended to stop there after Thanksgiving dinner in his official capacity in an attempt to daunt its rowdier customers from making trouble.

"I think my Uncle Dutch will be there." Wendy sounded stung by Rodd's disparaging tone; her voice stiffened and a faint blush colored her cheeks.

Guilt over embarrassing her made his face warm. Here she was showing true Christian charity. And he was coming off as a holierthan-thou hypocrite. He hadn't meant to. After all, Jesus had eaten with the publicans and sinners.

She went on in a subdued tone, "I need to drop a dinner off for him. I promised Mom."

"Fine." While more snowflakes landed on his windshield, he drove over the empty roads to the bar. Wendy stirred his compassion. First Dutch Rieker, now Veda McCracken—Wendy had a fine set of relatives.

Though only noon, several cars and trucks were already parked around Flanagan's under its garish green shamrock sign. Loud country music blasted from inside.

He parked and glanced at her. He just couldn't see this young woman of character going into a dive like Flanagan's. "I'd be glad to take it in for you."

She turned to him and smiled with her head cocked slightly. "No, I think I should do this myself." Her gaze slid down from his face to her lap. "I haven't been to Flanagan's since . . . well, for a very long time. I hate to go in, but I think this is what I should do. Uncle Dutch, no matter what his faults, is still my mother's brother."

Her words only strengthened Rodd's high opinion of Wendy Carey. He got out and walked to her side and helped her out. He had seen people wear WWJD, What Would Jesus Do? bracelets, but how many of them would walk into a bar to show God's love?

Helping her walk over the packed-down gray snow on the gravel parking lot, Rodd escorted Wendy inside with quiet pride. He paused just inside the door to let his eyes adjust to the murky interior. All eyes turned toward him, the usual response he received when entering Flanagan's. Over the haze of cigarette smoke, he picked out Dutch's white blond hair. Wendy must have seen it too, because she made a beeline for the man.

Rodd also located Elroy Dietz at the end of the bar, playing a pinball machine. Elroy hit the jackpot and did an odd little hand-pumping gesture and peculiar hooting laugh. Would he be arresting Dietz tonight? The odor of stale beer and cigarettes hung in the sluggish air, a sickening mix. To Rodd, Wendy glowed like a pure white candle against the shoddy background. Didn't anyone else notice it?

"Wendy girl!" Holding a cue, Dutch straightened up from the pool table. The blaring jukebox fell suddenly silent, letting the other sounds surface—the crack of balls hitting each other at the break, the swish of water as the bartender washed glasses, and the low rumble of voices.

Walking behind Wendy, Rodd met each glance with a hard stare, letting everyone know they'd better be on their best behavior.

"Happy Thanksgiving, Uncle Dutch." She let the scruffy man hug her with one arm and kiss her cheek.

"Same to you, honey. What's that in your hand?"

"Since you wouldn't join Sage and me at the church, I brought you a plate of dinner."

"Well, thank you. I miss your mother this year. She can sure cook a turkey."

Rodd noted the sincerity in Dutch's voice. How did Wendy Carey and Dutch Rieker fit in the same family? It made him wonder about Wendy's mother . . . about Harlan's late son, too. How could a Rieker have married a Carey?

Wendy replied softly, "I miss Mom too."

Dutch received the plate from Wendy. "But I'm happy for her. She snagged herself a good man this time. She finally got her happy ending."

Wendy smiled. "I think so."

Dutch eyed the sheriff and gave him a cocky grin. "I been hearing you're sweet on my niece."

A few men around the pool table sniggered at this. The fierce urge to shut their mouths arced through Rodd. But a law against being a jerk hadn't been passed yet. Dutch should have sheltered his niece, but he just stood there, grinning.

As though he hadn't heard the sniggering, Rodd kept his voice neutral. "Happy Thanksgiving, Rieker."

"Well," Wendy, blushing, stammered, "we'll be going."

Dutch pulled Wendy into another brief, one-armed embrace and kissed her cheek. "Bye, Wendy girl. Bye, Sheriff. Happy Thanksgiving!"

Wendy looked troubled but gave her uncle another hug, then turned and led Rodd outside to the Jeep.

Relieved to be done with Flanagan's, he drove away, heading back to town for their dinner at church.

Staring straight ahead, Wendy said in an odd tone, "Uncle Dutch whispered something to me. He said I should tell you there's going to be a kegger out at Dietz's tonight."

The urge to slam on the brakes hit Rodd. Three separate sources clinched it. Later, he'd be dealing with a kegger. Outwardly calm, he asked, "Why would he think that?"

* * *

WENDY GATHERED HER pride around her. She'd faced a lifetime living down the Rieker reputation, but it still stung fresh every time something like this happened to stir it up again. Every time she let herself hope that this might change, she found out things like this never did. "Uncle Dutch and Elroy Dietz are enemies. In fact, the Dietz and Rieker families haven't gotten along for two, maybe three, generations." Wendy considered bringing up the fact that Sage and Trav had defied this feud but decided it wasn't the time.

"Why are your uncle and Elroy Dietz enemies?"

Wendy hated to bring up the past. "I don't know the whole story. It has something to do with my mom when she was young." The sheriff didn't need to hear that story.

"I see." Rodd fell silent.

Uneasy, Wendy squirmed in her seat. She'd have given anything not to have been forced to bring up this disreputable side of her family again. But reality was reality. She wouldn't disown her mother's family. They had loved and accepted her, especially Uncle Dutch, who had helped support her when her "God-fearing" father's mother had refused to admit she existed. And Veda had done everything possible to make Wendy's mother's life miserable.

"How would your uncle know about what Dietz is up to?"

Wendy sighed and smoothed the skirt of her dress with both hands. "He makes it his business to know."

"I see."

Wendy didn't like the sheriff's professional but disapproving tone. She pushed it aside. The meals were all delivered. Thanksgiving dinner awaited them at the church. She couldn't change her uncle or the feud with the Dietzes. She just wished she weren't so aware of Rodd sitting next to her.

Ever since those few moments alone with him that night in Good Hope, she'd had to fight her growing attraction to the sheriff. The more she tried to avoid him, the more they were thrown together. At least it seemed that way to her. As if with a will of their own, her eyes turned to him. His freshly shaven jaw with the small white scar drew her attention. Her unruly mind brought back the sensation of his lips grazing her sensitive nape that night at the church.

With determination, she turned her gaze to the familiar scenes passing by the window on the way back to town. The sheriff seemed preoccupied. Her thoughts jumped ahead to dinner. Today, she'd spend the first Thanksgiving without her mother. That fact kept trying to drag her emotions into the minus column. But she, Sage, and Trav would have Thanksgiving with her grandfather at church. *I'm not alone. Lord, bless my mom today. This can be a good day; make it so. And please help Mom and Jim adjust to their move.*

Once again, her disobedient mind brought Rodd into her thoughts. Having him near gave her emotions more power over her. Why couldn't she stay neutral toward him?

Rodd broke the silence. "As long as you know about the kegger anyway," he said, "can I ask you for some more information?"

"Sure." She felt for him, having to spend his holiday dealing with this.

"Have these keggers taken place at Dietzes' before?"

"Yes. Sometimes at Dietzes', but other places too." She gazed at his resolute profile. His hard jaw showed his intensity. The sheriff certainly never took life lightly. She liked his seriousness. "What are you going to do?"

"Not much I can do right now. Having a keg or two of beer on your property isn't against the law."

She frowned. "That means another stakeout?"

He nodded. "The trick is letting the kegger get started, then moving in before everyone gets there. A bunch of drunk kids are a danger to themselves and to others. One of them could simply wander outside, pass out, and freeze to death by morning."

"I know. I won't mention it to anyone," she assured him.

He smiled at her. "I didn't think you would."

His quick approval lifted her spirits. She liked Rodd. If only she could control her attraction to him!

He drove them into town and parked near the church. When he opened her door, she heard the lively voices from inside. She led the sheriff down the handicapped ramp to the lower-level doors. Inside, a chorus of cheerful hellos greeted them.

Wendy glanced around the freshly painted basement fellowship hall decorated with pumpkins and fall leaves. She noted the pastor's family, her grandfather, and many others who had come. But what was holding up Sage? Wendy walked over to her grandfather, who looked distinguished in a new gray suit. "Hi! Where's my sister? I thought she'd be here by now."

Her grandfather tugged her close to his side. "Now, pumpkin, don't let this upset you. She and Trav stopped by to tell us that his grandmother had relented and they were invited out to the Dietzes' for Thanksgiving. Sage wasn't too pleased, but I told her to give Mrs. Dietz the benefit of the doubt."

An unwelcome jolt crackled through Wendy. She didn't want her sister or Trav anywhere near the Dietz property today!

She let her eyes drift to the sheriff. He appeared deep in thought. If he'd overheard her grandfather, he'd connect the dots. Her sister had gone with her boyfriend, a Dietz, out to where a kegger might take place later. Would he think Sage and Trav had gone because of the kegger? Well, why wouldn't he? He'd just exchanged greetings with her uncle at Flanagan's!

Any suggestion that she and the sheriff could ever share anything more than friendship would always be spiked by her mother's family's reputation. At times like this, Wendy's family burdened her like a heavy yoke around her neck.

If she'd been here when Sage and Trav had stopped in, she'd have tried to persuade them to stay at church today. Sage and Trav were good kids, but even good kids made mistakes in judgment. Closing her eyes, she sent up a prayer: *Dear God, stay with them and keep them from making poor choices.*

But Wendy's holiday peace lay around her feet in jagged pieces like shattered icicles. *Oh, Sage, please come home early tonight. And bring Trav with you!*

CHAPTER SEVEN

WENDY FELT HER grandfather's attention on her. Not wanting to worry him, she put a smile on her face.

Another couple walked through the basement door and Wendy exclaimed, "You came!" Tears moistened her eyes.

Ma, leaning on Bruno's arm, looked gratified, but answered gruffly, "Sure, I came. I'm not one to pass up a free meal."

Wendy didn't reply that Ma had passed up these Thanksgiving meals for the past four years. Having Ma here was like having a favorite grandmother come for the holiday. She took a deep breath, calming her runaway emotions.

Bruno solicitously helped Ma off with her coat while she grumbled unconvincingly about his not fussing over her. Ma wore a new navy blue polyester dress. Wendy couldn't remember the last time Ma had bought a new dress.

Penny, wearing a pretty blouse embroidered with fall leaves under a blue denim jumper, came out of the kitchen. Zak bounded up to her. "Is it ready yet, Mama? Is the turkeys cooked?"

Penny dried her hands on her holiday apron. "Yes, Zak. Everyone, please find a place. We'll bring the platters out to the tables now."

After the pastor's kind voice thanked God for the early hay harvest, the warmth of friendship, and the bounty of God's love, a happy rumble of voices swelled around Wendy. But missing her mother, worrying over Sage . . .

Rodd held her chair for her. Wendy hid a frown. Her grandfather had struck again. He'd placed all the name cards and had put her between Rodd and him. Feeling on display, she sat down. Embarrassment over her grandfather's not-very-subtle matchmaking made her too aware of herself.

As Rodd passed her the platter of turkey, his hand brushed hers. A current raced up her arm. She faltered, and the large fork clattered to the floor. Her face burned red.

"No problem!" Penny called out. "I brought extra serving pieces to the table."

Still blushing, Wendy accepted the new fork, which had been passed to Rodd.

"Don't drop the turkey," Zak prompted, perched on his knees on his chair across from Rodd.

Penny made him sit back down. "Now mind your manners, young man."

Wendy served herself a small slice of breast and passed the platter on to her grandfather.

"That's not enough!" Zak perched on his knees again. "You gotta have proteem or your bones won't grow."

Wendy laughed out loud. "I'll take seconds later, Zak. Promise."

Penny shushed Zak and sat him back on his seat again.

Rodd glanced down at Wendy. His smile warmed her, head to toe. She ducked her face, trying to hide the overwhelming smile Rodd had sparked. *Lord, why are you letting me have these feelings for this man? I'm afraid I'll make a fool of myself or Rodd by letting them show!*

"Since it's the day for saying thanks . . ." Ma drew herself up as though facing a challenge. "I want to thank this church. You came out and helped me after Jiggs . . ." Obviously fighting tears, she stopped speaking.

"We were glad to help, Lou," Harlan said in his kind voice. "And it won't be long before the sheriff here has these burglaries all sewn up."

"That's right!" Zak in his exuberance stood up on his chair. "The sheriff's going to get the bad guys! Aren't ya, Sheriff?"

Wendy sensed Rodd flinch. She observed the rigid angle of his jaw, the steely expression in his blue eyes.

Rodd motioned Zak to sit back down. "I'm doing my best."

"I know you are," Ma said testily. "I told that Cram to get off your back. He ought to know a Durand won't come up short."

A murmur of agreement sounded around Wendy. However, she could tell by the stiff way Rodd folded his arms over his chest that he didn't appreciate this discussion of his criminal investigation.

Personally, she wouldn't want to be on the wrong side of the law where Rodd Durand was sheriff. Sitting so close to him made her intensely aware of the man's energy, the restrained power in him. She thought again of the kegger. How would the sheriff handle it? Sad, unpleasant scenes of her mother's drinking and spoiled Thanksgivings from the past spun through her mind.

From the corner of her eye, Wendy saw Ma and Bruno touch hands. Ma blushed. Wendy turned this over in her mind. What had brought Ma and Bruno together now? They'd known each other for years. Their respective spouses had been gone for many years, too. No one would have tried to match them together. Ma was abrupt, overweight, and blowsy. Bruno was dapper, slim, and precise to a pin. Why had they grown closer in just the past few months? What drew a man to a woman and vice versa?

Wendy glanced at the sheriff. Their gazes met. For one wonderful moment, she knew that he shared the same thoughts as she. She looked away first, breaking their connection.

The dinner, which had taken hours to prepare, lasted only an hour. Still, everyone lingered at the table, sipping coffee or fresh cider. Finally Rodd pushed his chair back and stood up. "I'm sorry to have to leave so soon, but I've got to get back on duty."

"Thank you for coming, Sheriff," Penny said warmly.

"My pleasure." Rodd picked up Zak, tossed him once in the air.

Zak squealed. When Rodd put him down, the boy ran to his father's lap and climbed up.

Worried about the kegger, Wendy popped up. "I'll walk you out to the Jeep. I think I left something in the back."

Outside, with her jacket over her shoulders, Wendy hurried beside Rodd.

"What did you leave in my car?" Rodd asked, unlocking the door.

His deep voice snared her, making it doubly hard for her to speak. She shivered under her open coat.

He closed the gap between them, cupped his hands around her shoulders, shielding her from the cutting wind.

His nearness scattered her thoughts. How could she say, "Please watch out for Sage and Trav and if they're at the kegger, please bring them home"? So she replied, "I . . . nothing. I . . ." She shrugged and then shivered more violently. "I guess . . . be careful." Pulling away from his wonderful touch, she ran back to the church.

His understanding voice followed her. "Keep warm and don't worry!"

❋❋❋

THROUGH THE DEEP nightfall, Rodd drove north. Everything was in place. Right after Thanksgiving dinner, he'd driven through town, then out around the county, past Flanagan's again, keeping an eye on it. Then he'd casually driven by the Dietz property. He'd noted he couldn't hide his vehicle anywhere near the solitary barn, but he'd located where he thought the teens would park and walk through the straggle of pines to the barn. Next he'd stopped in his office to go through the procedure to get a warrant to proceed against the kegger. Finally he'd alerted all his deputies and explained his plan to the two who would work with him on this.

He remembered a particularly nasty party near Marquette University in Milwaukee. Girls had been given GHB, the rape drug. He hadn't heard of any of that being passed around here, but keggers were always unpredictable.

The regular dispatcher had come to replace the relief dispatcher for the night. Mentally Rodd had made a neat list about handling the kegger, and he'd checked each point off with increasing satisfaction. So while one of his deputies remained on duty for other calls, he and two others would bust the Dietz kegger at just the right moment. Warrant in hand, he'd stopped at home after dark to dress for the long, cold stakeout, and feed and water his breeding stock for the night.

Now in the darkness, Rodd parked his Jeep off the road behind a line of tall, snow-flocked evergreens. He slogged silently to the spot in the woods he'd chosen earlier, which must be on Beltziger property. A clump of pines and a few old leafless maples gave him meager cover. With grim humor, he hoped Mrs. Beltziger wouldn't shoot him as a trespasser.

One deputy would park a mile down the road in a stand of pines and walk to a spot near the anticipated parking area. The deputy would await the sheriff's flashlight signal—two flashes—then on foot they'd close in for the bust. The other deputy would cover the rear-access road.

A few moments later, Rodd felt the pager in his pocket vibrate. He illuminated the message. "Number two in place." That meant the officer nearest the parking area had arrived. Rodd flashed his pocket light once in that direction as prearranged. Before long, he received the second pager message alerting him of the other deputy's arrival. Rodd flashed his light once toward the road behind the Dietz property. The half-moon shed an eerie sheen on the surrounding grazing pasture studded with high, rolled hay mounds shrouded in black plastic.

Then the serious waiting began. The frosty cold of night moved in. Even through layers of clothing, insulated socks, boots, and gloves, the near-zero temperature began its silent assault. Rodd wore a knitted ski mask over his face. Soon he felt each little hole in each little knitted stitch as a pinprick of ice. The insidious, persistent cold wrapped itself around him—an icy boa constrictor squeezing the life, the warmth out of him.

Fighting the yawns, which seemed a surrender to the numbing

cold, Rodd tried to go over in his mind the events of the day. But Wendy's face imposed itself over everything. The way she'd stood out—pure and untouched in the murky light of Flanagan's. Her golden glow in the oak red dress. Her smiles over Ma's coming and Zak's chatter. But most of all, her restraint when she walked him out to the car.

He'd caught the fact that Trav and Sage had gone to the Dietz house. When Wendy had walked out to the car with him, he'd thought she'd say something about her sister and boyfriend. In the end, she'd only told him to take care. She hadn't asked the favor he'd feared she would ask. She hadn't asked him to shield Sage and Trav if they turned up at the kegger. He hoped they wouldn't turn up—

The roar of a snowmobile.

Rodd hunched down. The snowmobile's light went straight to the area Rodd had predicted and parked. Silence. Then a glimpse of a bobbing light. Someone with a flashlight was heading for the barn. Elroy Dietz?

The scraping of metal against old wood, a fumbling of a door catch. The dry night air transported the sound, crisp and clear. A noisy truck rattled down the nearby road, masking any other auditory clues. After a deadly quiet lasting several minutes, a clanging sounded, followed by sparks out of a half-tumbled-down chimney on top of the barn. Someone had come to start a fire in what—an old iron stove? So it was to be a heated winter kegger. This arrival bolstered Rodd. He hadn't been able to shake the suspicion that after the Olson stakeout, this might be another wasted effort.

Out of the still darkness, two more snowmobiles barreled over the snow and swerved into the parking area, and then three more snowmobile-suited bodies vanished into the barn. They'd start drinking soon. He could move in anytime now. The two deputies would follow him and make sure no one got away. While one deputy stayed to pick up stragglers, he and the second deputy would cuff the half dozen, take them in and book them, and then call sleeping parents out of bed to come claim their errant offspring. He drew in a deep breath. A fun evening for all.

His pager vibrated. He glanced at it: "Deputy Four responding to a disturbance at Flanagan's. Code three." So the other deputy was keeping busy too.

Time for action. Rodd flashed the light twice to his counterparts and then ran straight for the entrance to the barn. Exhilaration banished the cold. He reached the shadowed corner of the barn when the sound of another snowmobile sped up, then halted. A long shadow betrayed another figure hustling into the barn.

His pulse throbbing in his ears, Rodd waited tense moments, then moved around to the side door everyone else had used. He shoved the door open and flashed his large lantern flashlight inside. Seven shocked faces stared back at him. There was a rush toward him. He stepped in and slammed the door behind him. "Freeze! I'm the sheriff. This kegger is over!" The deputies were right behind him.

Two of the teens put up their hands as though Rodd had a gun in his hand instead of a flashlight. Rodd flashed the beam of light from face to startled face, then around the interior. "Where's the keg? Which one of you is standing in front of it? Don't waste my time."

"There isn't any keg," a young male voice squeaked and cracked. "We were just figuring out that somebody played a joke on us."

"Everybody against the wall there." They obeyed him. Rodd played his light carefully over every part of the old, cavernous barn.

"Somebody played a joke on us, Sheriff," the same voice apologized in a tone that begged for leniency.

Somebody fooled me too.

Not revealing his inner chagrin, Rodd spoke in his sternest voice, letting everyone know he wasn't letting anyone off. "Then you're fortunate. That means you're only guilty of trespassing. Put your hands on your heads and walk outside single file." The teens followed his order. Outside, his deputies took over.

Sour defeat choked him. Someone had played him for a fool.

His pager vibrated again. He read the message: "Breaking and entering" followed by an address on the other side of the county near Flanagan's. Another dose of adrenaline shot through him.

A terrible premonition twisted his stomach. "Take care of this! I've got another call!" Rodd broke into a run. He jogged steadily, breaking through the dry snow, sliding and skidding over patches of ice. Reaching his Jeep in seconds, he turned onto the road, his siren blaring, his lights flashing. His foot on the gas pedal pushing the needle on the speedometer to near sixty, he lifted his cell phone to his mouth. "Give me the details."

❋ ❋ ❋

IN HER TRAILER, Wendy paced the small rectangle of the living room. The sky outside the small windows showed black satin night and golden streetlamp glow. She'd changed out of her holiday dress in the afternoon intending to take a nap. She'd been on call for the clinic last night and hadn't slept well. Exhausted, she still hadn't been able to relax and take a much-needed nap. She couldn't forget the kegger.

She had no doubt the sheriff would handle things well. She felt sorry for the foolish kids who would be picked up at the kegger and for their embarrassed parents. But mostly she agonized over why Trav hadn't arrived home with Sage by now. She glanced at the old half-melted, mushroom-shaped clock over the stove. Nearly 11:30 P.M. Where could they be? Sage would not go to the kegger, Wendy insisted to herself.

She stopped in front of the telephone for the thousandth time. She could dial the Dietz number. But what would she say? What would she do if Sage and Trav weren't still there? What if Trav's old truck had broken down or failed to start in this cold?

The phone rang. She picked up the receiver.

"Wendy, is that you?"

Her mother's voice brought moisture to Wendy's eyes. "Mom, hi. Happy Thanksgiving."

"Same to you, dear. How did the dinner at church go?"

"Fine."

"Is Sage there?"

"No, she's out with Trav." Wendy wouldn't worry her mother.

"Oh." A pause. "We went out for dinner. Jim didn't want me to cook."

"That's nice."

"I missed you girls today."

"We missed you too, Mom." She thought she heard tears in her mother's voice.

"I didn't know . . . it's so . . . hard being . . . away from you girls and from Dutch—"

"Mom, it takes time to adjust; you know that." Fear shot through Wendy like an icy wind. Would this stress cause her mother to begin drinking again?

"Don't worry. I didn't call to worry you. And I'm going to AA every week down here. Jim goes with me."

"I'm glad." But not completely reassured. Mom would say she was going. *Oh, Lord . . .*

"Well, it's late. I'll talk to you soon. Give my love to Sage and your grandfather."

"I will, Mom." Wendy slowly put the receiver back.

Worry over her mother falling off the wagon shifted to frustration. *Mother, you should be here. I need you.* The thought hollowed her out, taking her back seventeen years. She remembered the winter afternoon her mother, Doreen, had brought Sage, only three days old, home from the hospital. Ma Ukkonen, who had kept Wendy while Doreen was in the hospital, had brought her home to straighten up the trailer for the new baby's homecoming. When her mother had come in, little Sage had been put into Wendy's arms. The thrill of having a sister washed through her. After Ma had left, her mother had taught Wendy how to diaper Sage and make her a bottle. Then leaving Wendy to take care of a newborn, Doreen had fled to Flanagan's.

After all these years, Wendy experienced that same fear now, the same feeling of being deserted, of being left with responsibility too large, too heavy for her. Over the past couple of years, she'd watched with some trepidation as Sage and Trav drew closer. It wasn't the family feud that concerned her. It was the fear that Sage might make the same mistake their mother had made—marrying too young. Wendy wanted college for Sage, then perhaps marriage. This worry increased now, weighing on her, pressing in on her, making it hard to breathe.

"Oh, Father," Wendy prayed aloud, "I'm only twenty-six, too young to take care of a teenager. I'm not Sage's mother. I'm just her sister! What do I do? Do I call? Do I wait?" Wendy slumped down at the tiny table and bent her head into her hands. "Am I worried over nothing? Tell me what to do."

As she'd always done, she combed her memory, bringing up Bible verses she'd repeated over and over when she'd felt afraid. *"I will be a father to the fatherless. . . . I am your Rock and salvation. . . . I lift my eyes to the hills from whence my help comes. . . . Thy rod and thy staff they comfort me. . . . Surely goodness and mercy shall follow me all the days of my life: and I will dwell in the house of the Lord for ever."*

Her heart slowed to normal. God, her Father, had never forsaken her. She felt his reassurance, his love. She calmed. His strong arms wrapped around her.

Then she heard the distinctive rattle of Trav's beater truck as it pulled up beside the trailer. The last trace of Wendy's fear vanished, leaving her with relief.

Sage and Trav surged inside, laughing and shivering. "Wendy, hi!" Sage greeted her.

Thank you, Father! "Where have you been?" Wendy asked, concealing her worry with effort. "Did you have car trouble?"

"Didn't you see my note?" Sage asked, looking around the small kitchen area. "Oh, here it is." Sage plucked a piece of paper that had slid under the table, half behind the counter. "It must have blown off when we slammed the door." Sage read aloud, "'Wendy, we drove to the movies in Iron Lake. Home after midnight.'"

Wendy closed her eyes. With all the stress gone, she felt faint. "You went to the movies?"

"Sure. Where did you think we went?"

Wendy hoped her sister would never know the answer to that question. "I didn't know what to think."

The phone rang. She reached for it.

"Wendy, is that you?" Dr. Doug's familiar voice came over the phone. "We're swamped at the clinic. Can you come in?"

"I'll be right there." Wendy hung up and grabbed for her coat. What had happened at the kegger? Or was this about something worse?

CHAPTER EIGHT

HER HANDS COVERED with latex gloves, Wendy wiped her moist brow with the back of her arm. The fluorescent lighting in the clinic's emergency room cast a sickly glow over everything. She blinked to make her eyes focus. The wall clock read 3:36 A.M. Where was the sheriff? Had the kegger been scotched without a hitch?

"We're almost done here, Wendy." Dr. Doug, the grandson of Old Doc Erickson, snipped the last suture on the drunk's forehead. He turned to the young deputy standing in the doorway. "You can take this one now. I'll send over pain meds as soon as I'm done." He looked to Wendy. "How many left?"

"I'll see." She tore off her gloves and dropped them into a biohazard container. Victims from a brawl at Flanagan's had overwhelmed Dr. Doug and the two night nurses. Since Sage had come home safe and sound, Wendy had been able to come in. Now she hoped Rodd had taken care of the kegger and was home in bed after a day's work well done. He was due for some good news. Mind-dulling fatigue lay across her aching shoulders, threatening to bring her to her knees. Too many long days and short nights for too long. *I needed the sleep I didn't get all week and that nap I didn't get today.*

The radiologist, who also had been called in, met Wendy outside the ER near reception. "These are your Uncle Dutch's X rays. He's the last." He motioned toward a lone gurney against the wall.

At the mention of his name, Uncle Dutch glanced over. "Am I dead yet?" His voice was slurred with alcohol and fatigue.

Fighting a sinking feeling, Wendy sighed. "I'll take him to Dr. Doug."

"Fine," the nurse at the desk agreed. "I'll finish up all the paperwork so you can leave when he's done."

Wendy nodded but knew she'd barely have time for a catnap before she started her morning schedule for the day after Thanksgiving. Before she pushed her uncle's gurney toward the ER, she leaned over and kissed his forehead. "How are you feeling?"

"Rough."

Wendy believed him. His lip was split. One eye was swollen shut and his neck was bruised. It wasn't the first time she'd seen him like this, but it pained her more each time. Had the sheriff been at the brawl too? She shied away from that thought. "You're not twenty anymore," she murmured, wishing she could convince her uncle to give up drinking and brawling. Over ten years ago, her mom had finally gone to AA, but not until she'd been threatened with the loss of her children.

Dutch gave her his usual cocky smile, but his split lip made it more of a half smile. "Just need the love of a good woman to settle me down."

You need the Lord, she mentally corrected him. She'd shared the gospel with her uncle—or had tried to—so many times. As a child, Harlan had taken her to Sunday school each week. When she would come home, she'd always sing Uncle Dutch her Sunday school songs. And when she'd invite him to go to church with her, he'd laugh but would always swing her into his arms for a big hug. She swallowed deeply and blinked her eyes, warding off the tears. In spite of this, one tear trickled down her cheek.

"Don't cry, Wendy girl. I'll be fine. A patch of ice got me. That's all."

A patch of ice in the middle of a brawl outside Flanagan's. Sucking in air, she nodded and tried to give him an encouraging smile.

A deputy passed her, leading away the disheveled prisoner-patient Dr. Doug had just finished. Wendy pushed her uncle into the ER and handed Doug the X rays.

He clipped them up and studied them. "You won't be fighting again anytime soon, Mr. Rieker."

"Why?"

"You've broken your left wrist."

Uncle Dutch started to swear, then stopped. "Sorry, Wendy girl."

She patted his shoulder.

"Guess it's good I'm right-handed," Dutch muttered. The muted sound of a siren outside made everyone's head turn.

"Wendy, I can take care of putting your uncle's cast on. Go take care of the incoming emergency." The doctor motioned her away. Suppressing a yawn, Wendy hurried out into the hall.

Rodd burst through the automatic doors with Mrs. Zabriski in his arms. "She's having trouble breathing and she's hurt her ankle!"

Wendy grabbed the closest wheelchair and ran to him. The icy cold of the dark hours of early morning flew in her face from the open door, the sudden shock making her feel faint.

"What next?" the night nurse at the desk complained.

Wendy agreed wholeheartedly but merely nodded, too tired to waste breath talking. She pushed her wheezing gray-haired patient into an examining area and began to take her vitals.

"I'm . . . fine, Wendy, except for . . . my ankle . . . and my asthma. You know . . . being out in this cold is no . . . good for me. And I'm so tired. I'm too . . . old to be up . . . all night."

Wendy nodded reassuringly and proceeded to take her blood pressure. Rodd had followed and hovered nearby. His presence made Wendy more jittery, more shaky. Taking off the cuff, she suppressed the urge to question him about the kegger. Mrs. Z's health pushed everything else to the back of the line.

Then the light before Wendy's eyes began to flicker. She forced herself to continue the preexam. "How did you hurt your ankle? Why . . . how did the sheriff . . ." Wendy fell silent, her fatigue slamming her in waves.

"Wendy dear, sit . . . down. You look . . . faint." Mrs. Zabriski turned to Rodd. "Get her . . . a chair, Sheriff."

Wendy swayed slightly. The glue that held her together seemed to be dissolving.

The sheriff steadied her and settled her on a chair against the wall.

"I'm all right." Wendy tried to stand up, but Rodd nudged her back. "I . . . just . . . need a cup of coffee."

"And about eight hours of sleep," Dr. Doug said as he came in. "I called one morning nurse to come in early. She'll be here within the hour." The doctor turned to the sheriff. "Can you drive Wendy home?"

Rodd nodded.

Wendy swallowed a yawn. "I just need a quick nap—"

Doug bent down and looked at her closely. "Go home, Wendy. We're fine now."

Wendy stood up slowly. "If you don't need me."

Rodd helped her on with her parka, then took her arm and led her toward the exit. She fought the urge to follow her instincts and lean against him, letting his strength seep deep inside her. Standing close to her, he spoke, "Mrs. Zabriski, I'll be back after I run Wendy home."

"Sheriff," Doug called after him, "if I heard Mrs. Z say her asthma was acting up, I'll be keeping her for what's left of the night."

"What about Rieker?"

"He finally passed out. I'll keep him too. Go home and get some sleep yourself, Sheriff!"

With a wave, Rodd hustled Wendy outside. The brittle cold took her breath again but revived her enough to stumble to his Jeep.

Inside, she gazed at the dashboard's green-lit speedometer in a stupor. Rodd's Jeep—even with all its police equipment—had become a familiar place. She felt herself relaxing. Finally, she sighed. "I can't remember being this tired for a long time." Thoughts, words floated in her mind, but she couldn't focus on one of them.

❋ ❋ ❋

RODD WATCHED WENDY'S eyes close and her head loll against the seat, asleep. Through deserted streets, he drove to the trailer park on the edge of town and found Wendy's trailer, which Harlan had pointed out to him recently.

When he pulled up beside the dark trailer, he glanced at her. Though he didn't want to wake her, he'd have to eventually. But the Jeep was warm, so he paused for a moment, letting his gaze linger on her. The glow in the car highlighted both the gold in her hair and the creaminess of her complexion. Everything about her spoke of delicacy and fine detail. But her frail appearance was deceptive. Wendy Carey was up to any challenge.

Observing Wendy in repose worked on him, gave him a feeling of peace that flowed deep inside him, soothing his jagged nerves. She was a lovely young woman, but the most beautiful thing about her was the boundless giving of herself. Wendy Carey had exhausted herself serving her community today. That's what Uncle George had called "true beauty of the heart."

Rodd gazed at her softly rounded cheek, so inviting. If he touched it, he might waken her. He shook his head. Where had that come from? He finally admitted his attraction to this woman. Why, how had this happened now? His job hung in the balance. What if he wasn't able to lure the Weasel into another trap? Would he be forced to resign? This was no time for romance.

And what if he acted on his attraction to Wendy? He'd not thought about marriage in years. Why was this time different? The answer to that was easy. Wendy was different, special. . . . He tried to come up with a word to express how he felt about her and couldn't. He couldn't act on his feelings now, anyway. It was all too new, too uncertain. After he'd caught the Weasel . . . leaning his head back, he stared at the roof overhead.

With a jerk, he awoke. The dashboard clock said he'd been asleep about half an hour.

As though she sensed his waking, Wendy stirred in her sleep and opened her eyes. Blinking, she straightened up.

Thinking that she looked like a sleepy fawn waking from a nap, he grinned. "Hello."

She yawned and stretched. "The kegger?" Her arms lifted gracefully over her head, then drifted down again.

He took a deep breath. "I thought you'd ask about that." Disquiet churned inside him. "It was a decoy."

"A decoy?" Her eyes widened. "You mean . . ."

"I was set up." Remembering one unpleasant surprise after another in the past twenty-four hours gave his voice an edge. "Someone spread the rumor about a kegger to keep me and some of my deputies busy." He clenched his teeth. Why hadn't he become the least bit suspicious about the kegger before he got the breaking-and-entering page? He glanced at her sideways. "This is confidential—"

"I wouldn't—"

"I know you wouldn't." He drew back his lips, irritated with himself for even intimating he didn't trust her. "That's why I'm talking to you. I've gone over and over today's events in my mind, trying to figure out what should have tipped me off."

"I shouldn't have told you what my uncle told me—"

"No!" Her apology grated on him. "Anytime a citizen has information about a crime, possible or already committed, I want to hear about it." The dried oak leaves on a nearby tree rustled in the wind, sounding like faint laughter, laughter at him. "You weren't the only one who heard the rumor about the kegger."

"Who else knew?"

He let out a gust of air. "Carl at the Grill told me about the rumor when I stopped at his place, and Mrs. Beltziger called my office."

She drew up her legs under her. "Tell me what happened."

Her soft, sympathetic voice acted on him like someone running a finger around the back of his neck, sensitizing him to her. "I set up the stakeout to stop the kegger before it got very far." He forced himself to go on, spelling out what had gone wrong. "About eleven o'clock, kids showed up on snowmobiles—one even started a fire in a stove in the barn. We moved in—just as the kids realized they'd been tricked. There was no keg in the Dietz barn. As my deputies and I were arresting the kids for trespassing, I was paged about a possible break-in on the other side of the county."

"Whose house?" She angled herself toward him.

"Clyde Sparrow—"

"Clyde? He's gone to Chicago to spend the week with his granddaughter—"

Her words only added fuel to his sizzling frustration. "I should have asked who would be away for the holiday—"

"Sheriff," she interrupted, "I could have given you a long list. How could you cover every one of them all over the county? And people around here generally know who's going to be gone. People talk." She shrugged. "Is this a new MO?"

Somewhere in the darkness, something metal crashed over and rolled with the wind. Wendy glanced around. "Raccoons," she explained. "Someone left a garbage can open."

Shaking his head, Rodd answered her question. "No, this isn't a new MO. The first four burglaries fit an opportunist. Now it looks like that MO was planned as a smoke screen too. This kegger took obvious planning. It also shows that the perp must have known Clyde would be away—without watching your movements. As you just pointed out, people knew Clyde made a habit of visiting his granddaughter for holidays."

"The thief might have just taken a chance," she suggested. "If he'd seen Clyde was at home, he might not have gone through with the burglary. The kegger might just have been a coincidence. Or someone might have dreamed up the kegger to get Elroy into trouble."

"Very good." He grinned at her. "You have been learning."

⁂

WENDY GAVE HIM a muted grin. "I can't stop thinking about it. The victims have all been friends of mine." The sad, weighed-down sensation hit her midsection again. *Lord, help Rodd solve these burglaries. Don't let the thief go on hurting people!*

Then she wondered if Rodd was praying about this himself. Probably not. She sensed his resistance to accepting help—even from God.

"I've gone over and over it in my mind. It's all too well executed to be coincidence." He touched her shoulder.

She accepted his comfort, fighting the urge to rest her cheek on his warm hand. Should she ask him to pray with her about this? "Where did Mrs. Z come into this? Was she hurt by the burglar?"

"No, the burglar hit Sparrow's place before she went over to check on the house. She'd planned to go earlier, she said, before dark. If she had gone in daylight, I think she'd have missed everything, and I might not have known about the burglary until later today when she went back."

Wendy absorbed this information. How she wished she could help him more! Or get him to ask God to help him more! "Mrs. Z is Clyde's closest neighbor. She must have been there to feed Clyde's cats." Wendy glanced up at him. "Then how did Mrs. Z get hurt?"

Rodd stretched his long legs out in front of himself as best he could. "She called in the burglary and waited for me in her house. When I arrived, I drove her back to Sparrow's. I wanted her to get the cats out of the crime scene. After I took down her information, I looked things over while she coaxed the cats out of hiding and fed them. Then I was called away to Flanagan's—"

"The brawl?" She took her eyes away from his long, lean figure. Why did this man have the power to tempt her to forget that she didn't want to fall in love? She couldn't risk stirring up her mother's past and all the old gossip. And what if Mom came home without Jim? Would it start all over again? The drinking . . . everything?

"Yes, by then the brawl was a four-alarm fire!" He raked his fingers through his hair. "We finally had to use pepper spray."

Wendy shook her head over it. "I know. The two who got it are going to be in bad shape for a couple of days."

He let his hands drop to the steering wheel. "We used it because it took the fight out of everybody. The ambulances and my deputies wouldn't have been able to get the injured off to the clinic and the guilty off to the county jail without it."

Remembering the chaos the brawl had unleashed at the clinic, she folded her arms around herself. "That must be when Dr. Doug called me in."

He nodded. "It was just after midnight. When I finished closing Flanagan's down for the night, I went back to Sparrow's and tried to secure the crime scene. Then I got a call to go back to Mrs. Zabriski. She'd fallen in her home. Dispatch called me since she knew I was right down the road. The ambulance crews needed a break, so I picked Mrs. Zabriski up."

The fatigue had started working on Wendy again as though she were a balloon being deflated. "That's right. Her place isn't far from Flanagan's."

Rodd nodded, then glanced over at her. "I think the perp may have chosen Sparrow's house because of its nearness to Flanagan's."

"Why?" Wendy didn't like the direction of this conversation. Her uncle had been at Flanagan's.

The sheriff went on as though talking to himself, "The idea of the brawl itself shows intelligence."

"A brawl—intelligent? How?"

"Because the brawl at Flanagan's was timed to start almost as the kegger would be discovered to be a setup. After sparking the brawl—which wouldn't have been difficult, considering almost everyone there had been drinking for most of the day—the perp then could have slipped out of Flanagan's, committed the burglary, and come back and thrown himself into the brawl."

"I see what you mean." She looked down, not wanting to admit how much sense his words made.

"Or it might have just been intended to keep things confused, stirred up. But another fact that shows the brawl was a smart move was that it involved practically every possible suspect in the county."

"How was that smart?" She looked at him in spite of herself. So near her, his aura of restrained strength was powerful. Who had been foolish enough to choose this man as an adversary?

"The burglar guessed that I'd connect the closeness of Sparrow's place to Flanagan's. By involving all the suspects, the perp could spread suspicion around with a broad brush."

❋❋❋

TONIGHT, RODD HAD planned to do what he'd been elected to do—protect and defend his county. He'd laid his plans so well. . . .

She touched his shoulder. "You did your best. No one can ask for more."

Wendy's touch didn't soothe him. He let out a sound of disgust.

She leaned closer. "You are doing everything you can do. You expected to tie this up weeks ago, that night at Olie's place. But you aren't calling the shots; the burglar is. All you can do is try to anticipate him. I've been praying. The church is praying." She paused. "You should go on doing everything you can do. And start praying about it." She paused again. "Then you have to be patient. The day will come when you'll get the thief."

Awareness of Wendy filled his senses—her light strawberry scent, the sound of her even breathing, her sympathetic touch. She understood his frustration. He reached for her hand and held it in both of his. "Thanks, I . . . thanks." The desire to draw her hand to his lips nearly overwhelmed him. He fought it. He didn't want to mislead her. She was too fine a woman for that. And he had no time for romance now. He made himself release her hand. "I better let you go. It's late. . . ."

"Will you pray about this, Rodd?"

His conscience tugged at him as he considered her request. "I'll try."

She looked away; then she pointed forward. "Look." A gray winter-coated doe, followed by two fawns, strolled in front of the Jeep.

Rodd sat up. "Deer in town?"

"Edge of town. A few people here leave dried corn out for them. Besides, town is safe." She grinned in the half-light. "No hunting in town." They watched the graceful family until the three disappeared into the gloom.

"What are you going to do now?" she asked him.

Her question made Rodd realize he'd already unconsciously formed his next moves. "I'll have to run down where the kegger rumor started. That might give me something to go on."

"And then?"

"I'm going to have a private talk with Gus Feeney and get my trap in place. This thief is no opportunist and will not just stop when it becomes harder to steal." That much he'd learned tonight. But something just didn't gel. How did the careless burglaries themselves fit a thief clever enough to orchestrate a kegger ruse and brawl cover-up? He'd have to really be on his toes to entice this thief into a trap.

Wendy yawned. "Sorry." She grinned apologetically. "I'm going in to take a nap now. I just have time for one before I go on duty in the morning."

He shifted to unfasten his seat belt.

"Don't." She lifted her hand, motioning him to stop. "I'll just run in. No need for both of us to go out in the cold." She let herself out.

He watched her run the few feet to the small trailer and let herself in. Then he backed out and headed for home. Wendy was the first woman he'd really found it easy to talk to like this. And going over everything with her had helped him put facts into perspective. The Weasel wasn't a garden-variety thief. Rodd would need all his patience and skill to catch him. *But I'll get you, Weasel. Your luck is about to run out.*

Then he heard Wendy's voice again: *"Will you pray about this, Rodd?"*

* * *

FEELING LUCKY, THE smartest man in Steadfast leaned back in the one comfortable chair he owned. Last night's brawl had certainly been a free-for-all. And the sheriff getting tricked with the story about the kegger—ha! That was the real joke. Half asleep, he laughed to himself—even though it hurt to laugh. Who would have thought that the smart cop from Milwaukee would get skunked? It was rich all right. And the thief got clean away one more time! He laughed again, holding his chest. He'd have given a hundred dollars to have been at Dietzes' barn and seen the sheriff's face when all he'd found were a few dumb kids and no keg!

❋❋❋

"RIEKER," RODD SAID a few days later as he planted himself right in front of the man on Main Street, "how's your wrist?"

"Still broken." Dutch grinned.

Rodd wondered how someone could make a grin look so sly. "Wanted to ask you where you heard about the kegger."

Dutch eyed him, his grin broadening. "You mean the one over at Dietzes' that didn't pan out?"

Rodd ignored the man's taunting grin. "Where'd you hear about it?"

Dutch folded his arms and rested his chin on his good hand. "Think it was over at the truck stop on 27."

"Who had the info? What did they say exactly?"

Dutch's grin broadened. "I was hungover from the night before. Just tryin' to get enough coffee in me to qualify as alive again."

Rodd clenched his jaw. He couldn't do anything to "prompt" Dutch to be more exact in his recollection. But he hadn't expected much from Rieker. Carl Kainz from the Grill could only say he'd heard it from a beer-truck driver, but couldn't remember which one. Rodd believed Carl but not Dutch.

"Sheriff, maybe you should move along. Old Cram's heading right for you." Dutch chuckled. "That was quite an article he wrote about you being caught napping on Thanksgiving."

Rodd turned to face Cram.

"So you're reduced to talking to Dutch Rieker now?" the newspaper editor snapped. "Anyone could tell you that Dutch Rieker knows nothing and would lie about it if he did!"

Rieker bristled.

Rodd nodded to Cram and started to walk away.

"You better do something about this thief!" Cram called after him. "Decent people are starting to think twice about leaving their homes for a night. Some older citizen could die by refusing medical attention for fear of going into the clinic overnight!"

Rodd kept walking. He was on his way to meet Gus Feeney to give him the particulars about a possible trap after the Bingo Fund-raiser. The crusty veteran had yet to agree to let himself become a target. Trading words with Cram wouldn't catch the Weasel. *God, please keep everyone out of my way and let me do my job. A clear shot at the Weasel—that's all I need! I won't ask for more!*

❋❋❋

"HI, SHERIFF; THIS is Wendy."

"Wendy!"

The pleasure in his voice touched her. They'd seen little of each other in the week since Thanksgiving. That had been torture. She'd wanted to see him, but she avoided him—not knowing what to say. Her dreams had been filled with snowstorms, snowmobiles, and Rodd Durand.

Today the home-health call to visit Patsy, Carl Kainz's wife, had just come in a half hour ago. A check of Patsy's vitals had convinced Wendy to take Patsy in, and she'd known she needed to call Rodd. Her inner turmoil over the sheriff had made it difficult to get up the nerve to call him. But she'd had to. "Where are you?" she asked.

"Just outside the courthouse. Why?"

She imagined him standing outside the gothic courthouse in Steadfast. "I knew you'd want to know that I'm going to drive Patsy into the clinic."

"She'll be staying overnight?"

She heard the lift of interest in his voice. Yes, this would give him another chance at the thief. "That's right. She'll be staying overnight. Her heart is acting up. The thief might not hit their place since Carl will come home tonight. Leaving the house unattended concerned Patsy since Carl won't be home till well after midnight. The thief might know that—"

"And hit the place before Carl got there?" he finished for her.

"Right." Patsy, white haired and plump, waved to Wendy from her back door.

"Where's her place?" Rodd asked.

"Out on Gunlock Lake Road, just south of the lake itself. I've got to go. I called from my car so Patsy wouldn't hear me contact you."

"Good. I'll drive by Kainzes' place as soon as I've dropped one of my deputies off at your grandfather's to bring my snowmobile. I want both a Jeep and snowmobile there." He paused.

"I've got to go. Bye." She hung up just as Patsy opened the car door.

"It's all this hurrying for the holidays," Patsy said as she got in and hooked her seat belt. "I've got just about everything wrapped up and ready to send off."

"Calm down, Patsy. Old Doc just wants you to come in for the night. You don't want a second heart attack for Christmas." Wendy kept up a soothing flow of chatter as she drove Patsy to the clinic. All the while she thought about the sheriff. Would the thief hit the Kainzes'? Why couldn't life be less stressful? Boring might be pleasant for a change. She pulled into the clinic parking lot.

"Oh! I forgot my prescription eyedrops, and our mutt is still outside!" Patsy exclaimed in dismay.

"Do you need the drops?"

"Yes, they're the special ones from that doc in Duluth. And Carl won't be home from the Grill until real late! The dog will be frozen!"

Wendy reassured her. "Don't worry. I'll go back and bring the drops in with me. Give me your key and I'll get your dog inside, too."

"Wendy, you're a lifesaver." Patsy patted her arm.

Soon Patsy was safely deposited at the clinic. Wendy drove out of town, back toward Patsy's. When she turned the last curve, she spotted something unexpected by the Kainzes' back door—a snowmobile.

CHAPTER NINE

AFTER WENDY HUNG up, Rodd called one of his deputies to ride Rodd's snowmobile from Harlan's to the Kainzes'. Then Rodd headed for the Kainz place to look it over. It was farther out than he'd thought. When he drove around the curve toward the house, what he saw poleaxed him. Wendy's station wagon, still running, was parked cockeyed just outside . . . the damaged back door.

He barked his location and code three into his radio. Then he slammed on his brakes and shoved open the Jeep door.

He pulled his gun. "Police!" He ran toward the house, shouldered inside the demolished door. "Police! Wendy!" His heart pounded. He raced through the kitchen and burst into the living room. "Police! Wendy!"

She lay facedown at the foot of the staircase.

"Wendy!" he roared. He bent and found her carotid pulse—weak but steady. She was breathing normally. He turned her over slowly. No blood anywhere.

Rising, he made a quick search of the downstairs, checking closets and under the one bed. Then he started up the steps. "Police!" But upstairs, he also met no one.

When he trotted back down, he discovered a big dog sniffing Wendy. Holstering his gun, Rodd knelt beside her, pushing the mutt away.

She moaned.

"Wendy, it's Rodd. I'm here." His pulse pounding in his ears, he swiftly ran his hands over her limbs, looking for any wound or injury. He pulled his phone from his belt and punched the speed dial for the clinic.

Wendy's eyes fluttered open. "Rodd?"

"Where do you hurt?"

She blinked. "My head. Oh . . . ," she moaned again.

"Nowhere else?"

She shook her head and winced.

The clinic answered.

"Durand here. Wendy has been attacked at Kainzes'. I'm with her. She says her head hurts. I see no signs of serious injury—"

"Hit from behind," she muttered, running her hand gingerly over the back of her head.

"She says she was hit from behind. Yes, she's conscious. Right. I'll bring her in immediately."

Rodd hung the phone back on his belt and gently gathered Wendy into his arms. Her body was so light that it made the assault on her even more awful. What if he hadn't come right away? Had the thief seen or heard him coming and fled?

"Wait," she murmured.

He didn't pause. "Dr. Doug says he wants you in right now."

"Shelf over sink. Need to get . . . Patsy's eyedrops there. Needs them."

He pressed down his impatience and his rage at whoever had hurt Wendy as he entered the kitchen. "Fine. I'll pocket them on my way out."

"I'm not critical, just headachy. Keep dog . . . inside."

A dog at my crime scene is just what I need! He couldn't have anything tampering with possible evidence. "No, I want the dog out of here! I'll radio the nearest deputy and he should arrive anytime. After he secures the crime scene, we'll worry about the dog."

As he passed the sink, he grabbed the plastic eyedrop bottle. He pressed his cheek against Wendy's silky hair and silently cursed the Weasel. If the thief had appeared right then, Rodd was sure he could have choked him with his bare hands.

⁂

EARLY THE NEXT evening, Wendy lounged in her gray sweats at her kitchen table with the *Steadfast Times Extra* lying in front of her. She couldn't remember when Mr. Cram had last put out a special one-sheet *Extra* issue between regular weekly editions.

Sage opened the door to leave the trailer but turned back to Wendy. "I just wish we could do something to help the sheriff—"

The phone rang. Sage paused while Wendy picked up the receiver.

"Hello, Wendy, is that you?"

For a moment the voice on the phone disoriented Wendy, whose head still ached from the blow and from Cram's caustic prose under the headline: "Local Nurse Felled by Burglar!"

After spending twenty-four hours in the clinic for observation, she'd gotten home late this afternoon only to find the unwelcome *Extra* on her doorstep. "Hi, Mom, how are you?" she asked automatically.

"Who cares about me? How are you? I just got off the phone with Harlan and he told me you'd been attacked! Jim and I are so upset." Her mother sounded worried, edgy.

"I'm fine, Mom. I asked Grandfather not to worry—"

Sage closed the door. "Does Mom want to talk to me? I've got to get going."

"Mom, Sage is about to go baby-sit Zak. Did you want to talk to her quickly?"

"Well . . . if she's in a hurry, tell her I'll call her tomorrow."

Wendy recognized her mother's apologetic tone and tried not to betray any emotion. This was the tone she used when she was going to do something for Sage and not Wendy. "Sage, go on. She'll call you tomorrow."

"I'll call you later, Sis. Try to rest," Sage urged as she left.

"Wendy," her mom began, "I wish I were there. Why would anyone hit you like that?"

"I'm fine. Old Doc said he always knew I was hardheaded." For a few minutes, Wendy let her mother fuss over her about being assaulted.

"What's wrong with that new sheriff—"

"Mom, this isn't his fault!" Wendy snapped, her head throbbing. Cram's headline had continued, "New Sheriff at Fault." Now her mother's negative question . . . Wendy rubbed her temples.

Silence. Then her mother said, "Dutch told me you and the sheriff have become an item of gossip. Do you have feelings for him, Wendy?"

Her emotions tangled and twisted inside her. She couldn't speak the truth to her mother: *He makes me feel special and completely trusted. I think I'm in danger of falling in love with him. No, I can't say that.*

Wendy sighed. "I'll be fine. You know what gossip amounts to, and the sheriff will catch whoever hit me soon enough. He's a Durand—that should tell you what kind of man he is."

"I just never imagined . . . ," her mother went on, then finally came to the point she'd really called to discuss. "Wendy, I was able to get a ticket for Sage to fly to Florida for Christmas. Jim saw a classified ad in the paper. . . ."

Her mother's voice rushed on, but Wendy only half listened to the words. Mom was going to fly Sage to Florida for Christmas. Wendy felt tears come to her eyes, but she fought them off.

"Anyway," her mom finished, "we got it for only one hundred dollars. And I know Sage will have two full weeks off this Christmas. Wendy, I wanted both of you to come, but I know you can't get two weeks off so sudden, and you're always so busy around the holidays—"

"It's all right, Mom," Wendy said. "I couldn't leave Grandfather alone anyway." *And you might need Sage. Maybe she can help you and Jim have a good holiday and that will help . . . everyone.*

"I had thought of that too, dear. Next year Jim promised me we'll drive up and stay with Harlan for the holidays. But we've just moved here and Jim says if we go home before we're completely settled in, I'll only get more homesick."

The headache, a tight band around her forehead that had been with Wendy since yesterday, worsened. She fought the urge to bite her thumbnail. "I think he's right." This sounded hopeful. At least Mom and Jim were talking and trying to make their new marriage and move to Florida work.

"Do you think Sage will want to come down?"

Wendy sighed. "I don't see her turning down two weeks in the sun—"

"But she's . . . I know she's serious about Travis. She may not want to leave him for Christmas."

"Don't worry. I think Trav will insist on her flying down. He wouldn't want Sage to miss out on something good like this."

"You think so? This isn't upsetting you? I—"

Wincing from the pain in her head, Wendy interrupted, "Mom, it's fine. I'll have Sage call you back tomorrow so you two can take care of all the details."

"Wendy, how are she and Travis? They're not staying out late—"

"No, she's abided by your curfew and she's doing well in school—"

"I just feel so guilty sometimes for leaving you two—"

"Mom, just be happy." Wendy cut in, too tired and hurt to continue reassuring her mother. *If you're happy and settled, Mom, we can all breathe easier.*

"I'm trying, dear."

"Good. Bye, Mom."

"Bye, honey. I'll call tomorrow to see if your head is better."

Wendy hung up. She pictured in her mind the photo her mom had sent of her new Florida house, with its sparkly white-and-peach stucco exterior and the palm trees in the yard. It was a house her mom could be happy in. Her mother had thought she'd overcome being a Rieker when Daniel Carey had fallen in love with her. But being widowed at seventeen and rejected by Wendy's grandmother and Veda had caused her mom to rebel with years of drinking and brief unhealthy affairs. Then after Sage was born, Mom had struggled in AA, trying to pull her life back together again. After all the years of pain, her mother deserved a happy ending. *Let it be, Lord. I can't bear another crisis right now.*

Wendy sat down on the couch and closed her eyes. She prayed for the grace to let Sage go to Florida and not resent staying home alone.

A knock sounded at the door.

Wendy woke up. She'd fallen asleep on the couch. She rose to answer it.

"Hi." Looking very neat and professional, the sheriff stood on her steps in the still night. "How are you feeling?"

"I'm fine." His crisp appearance made her self-conscious. Her gray sweats were baggy, and her flyaway hair needed cutting. She folded her arms against the chill and hoped she didn't have some crease or something imprinted on her cheek from falling asleep with her face flat on the couch pillows. *I must look a sight.*

"Did I wake you up?"

"I fell asleep on the sofa." She ruffled a hand through her messy hair. "Come on in." A momentary thought of Miss Frantz watching from across the street flitted through her mind, but she opened the door wide to let the sheriff in. Then she remembered Cram's *Extra* lying on her table. Had Rodd seen that?

"I'm going to your grandfather's to take out the snowmobile again. I'm trying to learn the terrain and trails. But I wanted to see you first," he explained.

Intensely aware of him, she shut the door behind him and walked to the couch, steering him away from the table and Cram's scathing accusations and blame. She sat down and motioned him to sit next to her. Should she say something about the *Extra*? No. She couldn't talk about that. Rodd had suffered enough because of her foolish, impetuous act at the Kainzes'.

Bringing her mind back to snowmobiles, she said, "If you leave the groomed trails, you know there are danger spots, hidden boulders, thin ice over lake springs—"

"I'm going to stick to marked trails again tonight," he reassured her.

"Good. Be sure you heed the speed limit," she scolded him with a mock scowl, glad to have some way to show concern for him. "No more than fifty miles an hour after dark."

"Don't worry." He raised his hand as though taking an oath. "I never overdrive my headlights."

She gazed at him in the low light. Having him here beside her eased the odd feeling of being unprotected and exposed that she'd suffered since being struck from behind. The impulse to slip her arms around his chest and ask him to hold her swept through her like a whirlwind. She fought it, but inside her strength had shriveled up. Tears hovered just beneath her control and she couldn't keep silent. "Rodd, I'm so sorry I went into Patsy's—" With her words, something like a sob slipped out.

Fierce anger at the Weasel—anger that Rodd had banked down for the past twenty-four hours—flared hot. "You shouldn't have run inside like that!" He stopped the flow of words, which had come out accusatory when he didn't mean that. He took her hand. How he wished he could hold her, comfort her. For her sake, he tried to keep his voice even. "I know you probably didn't mean—" But his own passion broke through. "Anything could have happened to you!" He pulled her nearer him.

With her free hand, she wiped away tears. "I know, but . . . I've heard of people seeing red. I just thought that happened in books. But I think it really happened to me. I was just so angry and wasn't thinking—"

"Never do that again!" He tugged her closer to him. Still fighting the urge to wrap her in his arms, he cradled her hand, then pressed it to his heart. "I'd never forgive myself if something happened to you."

"I just ran in shouting—I don't know what. I was just shouting! Anyway, I sensed someone behind me—and that's the last thing I remember." She tucked her stocking feet up under her, then rested the side of her head on the sofa back.

Rodd moved even nearer. An invisible thread seemed to be drawing him to her. His attraction to her and his desire to protect her became entwined. He leaned forward. "Whenever I think of him striking you . . ."

Her angelic face looked up into his. "I never would have gone in if I'd had the slightest idea that the thief would break in during daylight. Patsy needed her eyedrops, and I didn't even consider that the snowmobile could belong to the thief." She searched Rodd's eyes. "That changes the MO, doesn't it?"

Rodd let out a ragged breath. At this point, what did he know? "I don't think we can even guess what this burglar's MO is. It's whatever he wants it to be, day by day. The opportunist I thought I was dealing with at the start was just a cover, too. But he must still be keeping track of you. Did you notice anyone, tell anyone you were going back to the Kainzes'?"

"Just Old Doc." She started to shake her head, but stopped herself as though it pained her.

This cut him to the quick. *I should have been there to protect her!*

"There were snowmobiles out riding—plenty of them," she continued. "But I didn't take notice of them. I guess since it was daylight, I didn't think any of them would be the thief's."

"Understandable." He was also guilty of not considering that the thief would work in the daytime. But how does one catch a quick-minded thief who leaves no physical evidence, no traceable loot, and no witnesses?

"Did you find anything at the crime scene?" Wendy asked.

He let out a sound of disgust. "Nothing. The thief never leaves so much as a hair behind."

"It's the snowmobile suit. He's covered from top to bottom. And you said before, he takes off his boots just outside the door."

Rodd nodded, his mind engrossed in awful possibilities. Now his fear that someone might get in the burglar's way had come true.

What if the Weasel started hitting houses with senior citizens at home? Wendy was young, in good health, and Rodd had found her immediately. What if an older person with health problems were injured and no one discovered him or her for hours, even days? What if being assaulted brought on a stroke or heart attack? The possibility of a tragedy hung over Rodd like a sword. He knew the only way he'd be able to end this case was to catch the Weasel red-handed. And what were the chances of that!

God, what do you want from me? Did I ask for the wrong thing? What do you want me to ask for? Is this some kind of test? Why did you let Wendy get hurt? Just let me do my job. Give me some clues! I can't make bricks without straw!

"Well, one thing this proves: it couldn't be my uncle. He's got a broken wrist and he would never strike me. He never even spanked me when I was little!"

Rodd didn't contradict her, but he still considered Rieker a suspect. Though Rieker's left wrist was in a rigid cast, he was right-handed. He could still steer a snowmobile and batter in a door. And though it wouldn't occur to Wendy, Rodd believed Dutch would rather knock his niece unconscious than let her find out that he was the Weasel.

CHAPTER TEN

A WEEK LATER, at just before ten in the morning, Rodd walked into the brightly lit, hollow-feeling Steadfast VFW hall to redeem his promise to Zak that he'd help set up the Senior Bazaar.

"Sheriff!" Zak, dressed in blue corduroy overalls, barreled straight for Rodd.

Rodd bent and scooped up the little guy, swung him in a circle, then set him down. "You, mister, have too much energy. We need to work that off."

"I'm helping," Zak declared. "I—"

"Zachary," Miss Frantz, the woman who'd just greeted Rodd, said in a sugary voice, "your mother needs you."

"Yes, Zak, please come back!" Penny called from the kitchen doorway.

"Okay, Mom!" Zak turned, and with his arms outstretched like Superman, he "flew" back to his mother.

Rodd got the strong impression that Penny wanted Zak with her to keep him out of Miss Frantz's way. He didn't think he liked that. It was certainly unusual. Zak always evoked smiles from the people he was around. What kind of woman was Miss Frantz?

"Now, Sheriff, we need you to help Harlan put out the tables." Miss Frantz gestured toward the kitchen just as Harlan sauntered out of it with Lady at his side.

Rodd and Harlan began stretching open and locking the folded legs under the tables, then righting and arranging them around the walls of the long rectangular room. A knot of three older women hovered near the coffeepot, chattering. Occasionally, they would consult a stack of papers on a clipboard.

Wendy walked in and headed straight for Harlan. "Hi, Grandpa. I'm here to pick up Lady." She knelt down to greet the frisky sheltie. "I hear you need a bath and your nails trimmed, Lady."

A loud, sharp voice sounded from the main doorway—Veda McCracken. "Is that all you people have done this late in the morning?"

Rodd stiffened. Harlan took in a quick breath, but Wendy didn't flinch. Harlan said in a low voice, "Rodd, we only have three more long tables to put up."

"Talking behind my back, Harlan?" Veda barked.

"Good morning, Veda," Harlan said without glancing at the woman and without his usual warmth.

Hoping to avoid a scene for Wendy's sake, Rodd kept his peace.

"I see you, Sheriff." She humphed, advancing on them. "Why aren't you out doing your job?"

Rodd faced her, but before he could speak, Veda shook her finger in his face. "If you weren't so busy keeping late hours with Doreen Rieker's worthless daughter, maybe you'd have time to do your job! Sitting in your Jeep at four in the morning the day after Thanksgiving—"

Shocked and outraged for Wendy, Rodd took a step forward.

"Veda, doesn't it ever occur to you that no one is especially interested in your opinions?" Harlan said without turning to face her. The older man's words seemed to make the old witch angrier.

Veda scowled. "I'm not the only one who's noticed that it's Wendy's patients who are getting robbed. She's probably telling her uncle who's away, so he can do the dirty work for her."

At first, Rodd was too stunned to react. How could anyone accuse Wendy, a warmhearted, good woman—

Harlan thrust past Rodd. Wendy grabbed his arm and Lady began barking.

Rodd stepped between Wendy and Veda. He lifted his voice over Lady's agitated barking. "Miss McCracken, you have just opened yourself to the charge of slander. Harlan and I can both testify that you have publicly defamed Wendy Carey's reputation by accusing her of crimes she didn't commit."

Veda's lumpy, round face turned red. "How do you know she didn't commit them? Have you arrested someone?"

"When I arrest the perpetrator, I will advise Ms. Carey to bring legal action against you." Rodd stood his ground.

"And I'll pay the lawyer," Harlan said, his anger giving force to each word.

Veda glowered, then swung away from them, barking orders to the other ladies. They scurried into the kitchen for white plastic to cover the tables. Veda, dressed in purple polyester slacks and a matching overlarge sweatshirt, marched behind them as if she were their commandant.

Silent and ashen, Wendy stood, still holding on to Lady's leash. Lady barked on.

Rodd didn't know what to say to Wendy. How could he counter the abuse that he'd just witnessed unleashed on her?

"Wendy—" Harlan began.

"I'm fine," she answered. She forced a weak smile. "Come on, Lady." She hurried outside.

Rodd watched her go, trying to think what else he could have done. But Veda's attack had come so quickly, it had taken him by surprise. And he couldn't have clapped a hand over an older woman's mouth. Veda's nastiness was so outside the realm of normal politeness that it left one without a response. Veda was beyond anything he'd experienced before, and this time she'd crossed the line. Slander was against the law. And he'd be happy to proceed with a civil suit against her.

Penny and Zak hurried toward Harlan. "I guess we'll be going now," Penny said.

Rodd didn't blame them for clearing out.

"We're done here too," Harlan muttered.

Asking without words, Zak reached up and Rodd swung him up high. Zak muttered in Rodd's ear, "I don't like that mean purple lady. Her voice hurts my ears."

Rodd gave the boy a big hug and set him down. "Be good and help your mother."

"I always help her," Zak said in a wounded tone.

"I couldn't do without him." Penny smiled, but Rodd thought she looked a bit pale today. Maybe the cold weather was keeping them all inside too much. Bundled up warmly, Penny and Zak departed for the short walk to their house.

"Rodd, can you give me a lift to Harry's Shop?" Harlan asked, straightening himself as though his back were stiff.

"No problem."

Outside, Rodd brushed the fine layer of snow off the front and back windows. The sharp, fresh air cleaned away the last of Veda's nastiness.

Sitting beside Rodd in the Jeep, Harlan let out a long breath. "Over the years, I've just ignored Veda, but it's getting harder and harder."

Rodd drove out of the parking lot. He'd wanted to ask Harlan about Veda many times but had always shied away from prying. This time he couldn't help but comment, "I don't know how you and Wendy have put up with her." He waited to see if Harlan would respond.

Harlan lifted his hands in a gesture of hopelessness. "Veda has delighted in causing trouble since she was a child. My late wife, Nelda, left home early to marry me partly to get away from her younger sister."

Rodd turned right at the snow-piled corner of North Center and Main.

"And I soon learned that my wife and I were happier when we had as little to do with her sister as possible." An edge crept into the older man's voice.

"Veda never married?"

"No, she was all-right-looking when she was younger, but she couldn't tame that tongue of hers. James, brother of Jesus, called the tongue 'a flame of fire.' I think he had Veda in mind. Veda just seemed to have been born bitter, always looking to make trouble."

Rodd frowned. "Can I ask you why Veda hates the Riekers so much?"

"It's not the Riekers. They've been a troubled family for generations. But I told you, Nelda and I were happy if we limited Veda in our life." Harlan turned his head to face Rodd. The old man appeared to age before his eyes. "Then when our son, Daniel, got Doreen Rieker pregnant and married her, Veda saw her chance to drive a wedge between my wife and me. I think she'd waited for this opportunity for ages. Anyway, she made things as bad as she could between us.

"She kept stirring Nelda up until she had Nelda believing she couldn't accept Daniel until he got rid of Doreen." Harlan's voice picked up speed and volume. "Daniel wouldn't do that, of course. He'd done wrong, but he loved Doreen. He married her and gave Wendy his name just as he ought. But even when he left for Vietnam, Nelda wouldn't say good-bye."

Rodd held his peace but wondered if Harlan's love for his late wife blinded him to a certain degree to his wife's culpability. Veda may have made everything worse, but Nelda could have made peace with her son.

Glancing away, Harlan went on as though talking to himself. "Then Daniel died in Vietnam. I think Nelda turned all her guilt onto Doreen and Wendy. She couldn't live with what she'd done, with how she'd turned her back on her son when he needed her most. So she used Doreen and Wendy as her scapegoats. And even after Nelda died, Veda has kept it going. Telling everyone Doreen had put Nelda in an early grave." Harlan fell silent.

As Rodd pulled up in front of Harry's Auto Repair, a fifties-vintage gas station and garage, he remembered Uncle George telling him years earlier about Harlan losing his son in the war. He'd never realized all the pain Harlan had suffered. How could a man handle his wife's rejecting their only son and then losing both of them?

"Hatred and bitterness bring only unhappiness, strife," the older man muttered. Then he looked over at Rodd. "When Daniel didn't come back from Vietnam, I helped Doreen get the trailer and I tried to look out for her. But I didn't help her as much as I should have. When she got to drinking too much to take care of the girls after Sage was born, I took them home and wouldn't let her have them back until she started going to AA. I just hope I've made everything up to her and Wendy."

"It's obvious to everyone that Wendy and Sage love you very much," Rodd said with deep sincerity.

"They have been a blessing to me." Harlan looked into Rodd's eyes. "Sage is going to be a blessing in Trav Dietz's life, and Wendy will be a blessing to any man who has the sense to marry her."

Evidently, Wendy's grandfather believed some of the romantic gossip that had started about Wendy and him. Why shouldn't people believe that Wendy was a woman a man could find it easy to love? But at times, Rodd questioned whether he'd be good enough for Wendy. Today, she'd certainly not returned evil for evil.

Feeling Harlan's intense scrutiny, Rodd belatedly nodded.

Harlan opened the door and got out. "Thanks, son." He waved and walked toward the repair shop to pick up his car.

Rodd felt a tide of sadness for the man who'd lost his wife as well as his son and carried deep regret. He knew how regret could gnaw at one's soul. Especially after the fatal mistake he'd made in Milwaukee. Letting out a long breath, he drove to the courthouse on the square to take care of a few mundane details.

TWO DAYS LATER Rodd sat at Harlan's kitchen table, wondering what he'd do next to try to tempt the Weasel into a trap if Gus refused to cooperate. Gus Feeney, a wiry man in his eighties, sat with them. Rodd had enlisted Harlan to help him convince Gus to be part of the next—and Rodd hoped the last—trap. If anyone could persuade Gus, Harlan could.

"I still don't know how you're going to get that burglar to move his dirty work from Steadfast to LaFollette." Gus folded his arms over his thin chest.

"That isn't your problem, Gus. Something else is," Harlan pointed out. "The thing is, we just can't wait around. The sheriff here has got to get the thief before he hurts someone seriously. I was over at Carl's Grill the other day visiting with him. He says he won't go to the clinic overnight or leave his house unattended during the day. He won't leave his home unprotected again."

"So?" Gus asked, a glint in his eye.

"So if people here around Steadfast stop leaving their homes to go to the clinic or going away for the holidays to see their kin, where's the thief going to look for money? He could head right over to your neck of the woods. This is a preventative strike, Gus. Just think how our lives would have been different if the U.S. had moved against Hitler while he was still gathering his strength. But we let him march through Poland and then the Netherlands and into France, and we just sat on our hands and watched like he'd never look our way."

Gus eyed Harlan. "I get your drift. We need to nail this guy before he really hurts someone badly."

As the point hit home, Rodd nearly jumped to his feet and pounded the veteran on the back.

Gus scraped his chair back from the table. "Okay, Sheriff, I'll do it. Just call me and let me know what you want me to do and when. I'm not too old—" he paused to grin—"to take on another bully."

THE RINGING OF the phone woke Wendy late in the night. Rubbing her eyes, she got up and staggered, sleep-drugged, to the phone in the kitchen. "Hello."

"Wendy!"

"Sage, is that you?" Wendy slumped down at the table. "What's the matter?" She yawned. "You sound upset."

"I'm sorry to wake you, but I was afraid you might wake up and wonder where I was."

Wendy looked at the clock: 1:36 A.M. "Aren't you at the Weavers' baby-sitting?"

"Yes, but I'm going to stay the night with Zak. Bruce called me from the restaurant in Woodson where they were having dinner. He had to rush Penny back to the clinic."

"Why?"

"She's having some trouble." Sage's voice showed her worry. "She might lose the baby."

"Baby?" Wendy sat up straight. "I knew they were trying, but I didn't know she was expecting—"

"She didn't tell anyone since she'd miscarried again last spring. She's only about two months along."

Sympathetic anguish for Penny cut through Wendy. "Oh, dear."

"I feel like crying." Sage's voice thickened. "Penny's so sweet. Why can't she have another baby?"

The pain of watching friends and loved ones suffering never became easier. Wendy faced it every day. "I know what you mean, Sis."

Sage sniffled into the phone. "Well, I didn't want you to worry about me like you did on Thanksgiving night."

"Thanks, kid."

"Good night, Wendy."

"I'll be praying for Penny. If they haven't come home by morning, call me and I'll bring over a change of clothes for you for school. If Bruce needs someone to watch Zak, I can take him on rounds with me."

"You're great, Wendy."

"And you're tired. Try to get some sleep."

"Night."

Wendy hung up the phone and pressed her face into her hands. *Oh, Lord, may it be your will that Penny and the baby are fine. She's a great mother. And Bruce is such a good father. Bless them with more children. Be with them and comfort them tonight. Please.*

CHAPTER ELEVEN

ON SUNDAY MORNING, Rodd stifled an unusual restlessness as he sat in church. Two things distracted him: a mysterious phone call from Mrs. Benser, which he'd received very early this morning, and the fact that Wendy was absent. The sanctuary felt hollow, empty without her. He was well aware that his feelings for her were intensifying. In time, would they deepen into lasting love? He hoped so, but he didn't know if she cared for him in the same way. Always cheerful and kind, she kept her heart under wraps.

"I want to thank all of you," Pastor Bruce spoke from the pulpit, which was adorned with fresh evergreen branches and shiny gold ribbon, "for all the meals you've brought in. For those of you who have helped care for Zak during this very . . . stressful . . . week." The pastor paused, plainly getting his emotions back under control.

Rodd felt for the man. Penny's problems had lasted for days now. Usually Zak sat beside Rodd in church. But his mama's staying overnight at the clinic had moved Zak onto Rodd's lap, where he now sat. As usual, the little boy brought Rodd memories of his childhood visits with Uncle George.

Living single into his thirties had left Rodd feeling separate from others. Being "the law" only reinforced this separation. But with Zak on his lap, he was no longer isolated. Zak liked him and trusted him. He wished the rest of the county agreed. The newspaper editor had just fired off another article demanding reasons why the Snowmobile Burglar hadn't been arrested yet. Didn't Cram realize that no one felt this continued failure more keenly than Rodd himself? He was counting down the last few days till the Bingo Fund-raiser.

Hope stirred. Perhaps Mrs. Benser's call meant that she had some lead about the burglaries. What other reason could Mrs. Benser, who sat in the pew ahead of him, have for calling him? He didn't think he'd exchanged more than a polite nod with her before. He tried to keep a lid on his anticipation. She had said nothing about the burglaries during the call.

Harlan, sitting beside Rodd, leaned over and ruffled Zak's hair. "Don't worry. Your mom is going to be okay." Sucking his lower lip, Zak nodded.

Rodd tightened his hold on Zak, telling him without words that he was there and would stand by him. Zak snuggled deeper into Rodd's arms. Was this how Uncle George had felt when he'd held Rodd in his arms? Rodd placed a kiss on the top of Zak's head—just as he vaguely remembered Uncle George doing to him so many times, so many years ago.

"On to other news." Pastor Bruce picked up where he'd left off. "The Senior Craft Bazaar and Bake Sale yesterday was a rousing success. A total of $293.96 was raised to be added to the new doctor's tuition fund. We thank the seniors who worked so hard in this cause. And finally, don't forget our Christmas caroling party is coming up next week. Remember this is our holiday outreach to our community. We want to make Steadfast ring with the joy of Christmas." He raised both his hands. "Let's rise for the next hymn." He smiled at his son. "I've chosen Zak's favorite carol to get us into the Christmas mood."

Setting Zak to stand on the pew beside him, Rodd rose. They sang, "'Away in a manger, no crib for a bed, the little Lord Jesus laid down his sweet head.'" Zak's high, childish voice found the notes. Uninhibited, he swayed to the music. "'The stars in the sky looked down where he lay, the little Lord Jesus, asleep on the hay.'"

When all the verses had been sung, the congregation settled down. Back on Rodd's lap, Zak squirmed until he found just the right position. Rodd stretched his legs out under the pew in front of him and relaxed. Fresh pine greenery had been added to every window sash and scented the chill air in the sanctuary. Cold wind always seeped into the old, white frame church.

The pastor began his sermon by reading Scripture. "Matthew 7:7-8: 'Keep on asking, and you will be given what you ask for. Keep on looking, and you will find. Keep on knocking, and the door will be opened. For everyone who asks, receives. Everyone who seeks, finds. And the door is opened to everyone who knocks.'" The pastor looked up from his Bible. "These familiar verses seem to be a rather simple list of statements. And they are. But how often we humans ignore the simple fact that God is able to meet all our needs."

Rodd shifted in the pew. He'd been seeking all right, but when would the finding start?

Pastor Bruce paused, his eyes scanning the faces turned toward him. "Why do we resist this? I've spent this week trying to come up with an answer. Could it sometimes be our pride? That we don't want to humble ourselves and admit we need help?" Again he gazed out, gathering everyone's attention. "God is able to meet all our needs," he repeated. "The old 'God helps those who help themselves' mind-set shuts God out. We are not to depend on ourselves alone."

Rodd bristled at these last words. He didn't shut God out. But catching the Weasel was his job, not God's—wasn't it? Rodd shifted his attention to the back of Mrs. Benser's silver head. He recalled seeing her at the VFW hall when he'd set up tables. Was she a crony of Veda McCracken's? Why had she called him? And why today at 6 A.M.? What did she want to discuss with him privately? She'd asked him to meet her at the truck stop north on Highway 27 after church.

The request struck him as more than peculiar. But after the past few months, he had no doubt about her motive for secrecy. A desire to avoid gossip must have prompted her. But if she didn't want to discuss the burglaries—what else? Nothing else occurred to him. Had she heard something, noticed something suspicious? Bringing his mind to the present, Rodd tuned back into the sermon.

The pastor was pleading. "Why do we think God doesn't care about what concerns us, what troubles us? This is an improper form of humility. It doubts God's love for us. We matter to him! Maybe it doesn't seem logical that the Creator of the whole universe and whatever may lie beyond our universe should be concerned with us—small, frail, imperfect humans. But praise God! We *do* matter to him!"

Rodd had never doubted that God cared about humans. He didn't usually disagree with the pastor. Maybe it was sitting so still; it made Rodd really feel his fatigue. His inner thigh muscles ached from hours on the snowmobile. Every night after ten o'clock, he spent at least two hours patrolling the county on his snowmobile. It made for a long day—sheriff duties, cattle care, and night patrol. But long days weren't anything new to him. Rodd swallowed a yawn.

Pastor Bruce's voice called him back to attention. "God has given each of us different talents and he expects us to use them. 'Those who wait on the Lord will fly high on wings like eagles.' How much more can we achieve if God is with us giving all our efforts extra energy, more power! His wisdom and his Spirit guide us with his unbelievable clarity."

Rodd's mind echoed the pastor's words: *"How much more can we achieve if God is with us."* Why had those words jumped out at him? Would it have made any difference if he had asked God for help in solving the crimes, not just in keeping others out of his way? His mind struggled with this thought, images from his recent nights intruding.

The nightly snowmobiling had been exhilarating to Rodd at first, but Wendy had impressed on him that he needed not only to know the dynamics of riding a snowmobile but also to learn the topography of the county. Most snowmobilers stuck to marked snowmobile trails, but other, more experienced "beelers" didn't. They used these hardy winter vehicles to get around in the snowbound countryside.

The pastor's words replayed in his mind: *"If God is with us giving all our efforts more power!"* The whole church had already been praying for more than a month for the thief to be caught and brought to justice. If prayer were going to help, wouldn't he have already brought the Weasel to justice?

Rodd rubbed his aching thigh. With Christmas still a couple of weeks way, the county had already received nearly ninety inches of snow. The weathermen were having a field day with dire predictions of a record-breaking winter of icy temperatures and snowfall totals. The important fact, however, was that so far his midnight patrolling had brought him no insight or clues to the identity of the thief—who evidently had decided to hibernate or go on a winter vacation.

He hoped not—he'd pinned his hopes on the Bingo Fund-raiser. Gus Feeney had been to Steadfast inviting other vets and their families to attend and support the fund-raiser. Harlan had paid for an ad promoting the Bingo Night in the *Steadfast Times* and Ms. Keely Turner, the LaFollette village board chairwoman, had donated additional money, raising the big jackpot to five hundred dollars. The Black Bear Café had buzzed with that news yesterday morning. How could the Weasel resist a prize like that? Rodd tried to keep a rein on his optimism.

A change in the pastor's voice signaled the end of the sermon: "So whatever your motivation—pride, misguided humility, or lack of faith—stop doubting. Start believing and take everything to God. He can and does want to help you with whatever problems you face. Let's rise now and sing our closing hymn, "'I Must Tell Jesus.'"

Rodd wondered if the pastor had chosen this message with him in mind or because of the pastor's own week of tension and worry over Penny and their unborn child. Being forced to watch someone beloved suffer could make even the strongest man feel helpless.

The memory of Wendy lying unconscious flashed in his mind. He owed the Weasel something for attacking someone as sweet as Wendy Carey, a woman who was dear to many people, not just to him. Rodd longed to see the thief in a jail cell.

As the organ played the introduction to the hymn, Rodd gently roused a dozing Zak and set him in the pew. Sharing a hymnal with the small boy who hummed along added to Rodd's enjoyment in singing the familiar melody: "'I must tell Jesus all of my trials; I cannot bear these burdens alone. . . . If I but ask him, he will deliver, make of my troubles quickly an end. . . . I must tell Jesus! I must tell Jesus! I cannot bear my burdens alone . . . Jesus can help me, Jesus alone.'"

As he sang, Rodd prayed silently, *Dear Lord, bless Penny and heal her. Zak and Bruce need her.* He missed Wendy, but he was glad she was at Penny's side at the care center today. Rodd sensed Veda McCracken's forbidding presence as he glanced a few pews ahead of him and saw her large form. How did Wendy face that woman's frowns every Sunday?

When the last note of the hymn had been sung, Rodd observed Mrs. Benser walk past him up the aisle. The way she pointedly ignored him gave him a frisson of wariness. What she needed to talk to him about must be serious or she wouldn't avoid even looking in his direction. What does she know?

❖❖❖

AFTER WENDY FINISHED checking on her other two patients during her Sunday morning shift in the tranquil care-center wing of the clinic, she walked to Penny's room. She hesitated at the door. Penny lay with her eyes closed, though Wendy doubted she was asleep.

"Wendy?" Penny's flat voice called.

"I'm here." Wendy went to her side and noted Penny's eyes were puffy and red. "How are you feeling?"

"I can't . . . stop crying."

Snagging the nearby chair, Wendy sat down at her side and took Penny's hand. "You have something to cry about." After days of medication and bed rest, Penny had miscarried earlier this morning.

Penny covered her face with one hand, appearing to try to suppress the sobs that forced their way out of her throat. "I haven't called Bruce. I can't bear to tell him. I didn't want to upset him before he had to preach. He'll be sad for the baby, sad for me. I hate to think of his pain."

The sound of absolute desolation cut Wendy's heart in two. She added her other hand to her grip on Penny and bowed her head. "God, comfort, comfort your people," she whispered, aching to smooth away all of this dear woman's sorrow.

As Penny sobbed and held her abdomen to suppress the painful vibrations, Wendy repeated this prayer. The anguish of the moment allowed no embellishment. Wendy recognized the sound of despair. It awakened a turbulent welter of sensations from her own past. She'd heard despair like this before. Her mother had wept this way many lonely nights in their small trailer, after she'd come home from another "fun" night at Flanagan's.

Wendy tightened her hold on Penny. *Lord, she doesn't deserve to suffer like this. She's a good mother who wants another child to love. There are so many neglectful mothers who hurt their children. I don't understand. Why is this happening to Penny? What's your plan?*

Finally, Penny gained control of the heaving in her breast. Tears still ran nonstop from her eyes, but she tried to smile. "Sorry—"

"Don't apologize. You have a right to cry. Holding back your grief won't help you." Wendy had recited these phrases so many times during her years of nursing, but the simple words still rang true. So much suffering in this sad world.

Penny bit her lower lip and eased her sobbing. "Three miscarriages in two years. It's almost more than I can bear."

Wendy nodded in sympathy and concern for her friend.

"But I must. Zak and Bruce depend on me."

Wendy handed her several tissues from a box on the bedside table. Penny used them to wipe her eyes and pink nose. But still the tears leaked out as though a spring inside her had been uncapped.

"What did Old Doc say?" Wendy asked.

"He says I should stop trying to conceive for six months at least. He said my uterus needs time to recover if I'm ever to carry another child to term."

Hearing defeat in Penny's tone, Wendy only nodded again, saddened by it. She didn't think this was the time for "Nurse Cheerful."

"I'm going to follow his advice, of course."

Wendy encouraged her with a slight smile.

"Bruce and I have just been approved as foster parents by the county."

Wendy had a mixed reaction to this. Being a foster parent was like running your heart through an old-fashioned wringer washer. Wendy didn't think she could ever let herself stand in such a vulnerable situation. Yet she tried to sound hopeful. "That's so good of you. I know Social Services always needs more families than they have."

A smile glimmered on Penny's flushed face. "They warned me not to do it, thinking I'd be able to find a child to adopt instead." She paused. "That is a temptation, but I'm trying to focus on being a blessing to a child in need."

"That's the best attitude." *But a difficult one. Caring for children, then letting them go. Tough duty. Too tough for me.*

Making the hospital bed's motor hum, Penny adjusted the bed to a semireclining position. "I know I have so much to be thankful for—" Tears overcame her again.

Wendy claimed one of her hands again. "Don't try to make light of the pain you're suffering. God doesn't expect us to. Let yourself mourn. You've lost a child. God knows what that feels like."

"I hadn't thought of that." More tears flooded Penny's eyes, cascading down her flushed cheeks.

Wendy clung to her hand, giving the grieving mother an anchor. The only sounds in the quiet wing were the TVs in the other rooms and Penny's weeping. A quiet Sunday morning in the care center.

As Wendy held Penny's hand, she wondered what it felt like to live Penny's life. She compared and contrasted their lives. Penny was a little older than Wendy—thirty-one. Wendy was single. Penny had a loving husband and a sweet son—two blessings. On the surface, they might appear to have different lives. But Wendy knew something of Penny's feeling of loss, what it felt like to want children and face a future without them.

After watching her mother's years of suffering—the shame of

out-of-wedlock pregnancy, the difficulties of young widowhood and single motherhood—Wendy had decided not to marry. But by deciding to stay single, she'd given up having children too. A part of her still grieved for the home and children she'd never have. But she didn't doubt the wisdom of her decision. Rieker women had little luck in love. It wasn't just her mother, either. Her grandmother Rieker, Doreen's mother. And her sister Sage . . . the odds were against her.

Now her mother's rocky adjustment to a second marriage and a move to Florida only reiterated Wendy's need to stay uninvolved. If her mother came home with her second chance at love shattered, she'd need Wendy to help her keep from repeating old mistakes, old patterns. Love could sometimes be a burden.

Rodd's concerned but determined face came unbidden to her mind, as it had too often in the past month. She forced herself to face reality. Yes, she'd been spending too much time with the sheriff. Their duties brought them into contact with each other too often. Working with him on the case had brought them even closer. She'd have to guard her heart better. Rodd attracted her like no other man had. Whenever he came near, he kindled feelings she'd forsaken.

When she'd decided to come home to Steadfast after college, she'd come back for Sage, for Ma, for Old Doc who'd helped her get her education. All good reasons, but her family's track record and Veda's nastiness had only confirmed her decision to stay single. She could only hope that time would solve this problem, this unwanted attraction she felt toward Rodd. Wendy Rieker Carey wasn't wife material for a sheriff—not in this county.

Still, she worried about him. She hoped he wasn't expending too many late hours alone on the snowmobile. That was a prescription for disaster. She'd tried to warn him about the hazards—drift-hidden fences, spring-fed lakes, sudden ravines. Had he taken her warnings seriously? And the Bingo Night trap—would it bring an end to Rodd's struggle to catch the thief? *Oh, Lord, let it be so!*

❋❋❋

THAT SUNDAY EVENING, steeped in a deep gloom to match the icy night, Rodd and his deputy got out of his Jeep. The wind had died down for the night, and the cold, clear air magnified every sound with its clarity—the grinding sound of their boot soles on the dry snow and the whir of truck tires on the highway a half mile away. They breathed out white puffs as they approached the worn-down farmhouse.

His interview with Mrs. Benser had been an eye-opener. Her information had nothing to do with the burglaries, but opened a completely different can of worms. After an afternoon of checking her facts, he'd been forced to come here, the last place in Wisconsin he wanted to be. And to do what he didn't relish. He hated this kind of nasty little crime. And it took time he'd wanted to devote to preparing for the Saturday bingo stakeout and trap.

The youngest of his deputies caught up with him at the bottom of the porch. They walked side by side up the creaky, rickety steps, making Rodd recall delivering Thanksgiving dinner here. As he knocked on the door, he muttered, "Remember, don't say anything. Just keep your ears open and remember everything that's said."

"Yes, sir."

Veda opened the door. "What do you want?"

"Good evening, Miss McCracken." Rodd took off his hat. "There is something we need to discuss."

She grimaced at them as if they were naughty children. "I don't need or want to discuss anything with you." She started to shut the door.

Rodd had anticipated her action and had his boot wedged in her doorway. Without a change in his even tone, he continued, "Then I'll have to take you down to the police station for questioning—"

"Questioning! What are you up to?" She glared at him, ignoring the deputy.

"There is a matter I need to question you about. I can do it here or down at the station." He met her angry gaze without flinching. "It's your choice."

She fumed at them in silence.

He waited for her to open the door wide and let them in. Most people would have at this point. No reasonable person wanted to be taken into the police station.

"And if I refuse?"

He'd anticipated her obstinacy too, but couldn't quite credit it. "Then I'll have to take you by force."

Her breathing began to wheeze, and her face had turned an unpleasant scarlet. "Come in then!" She threw wide the door and stalked away. A stream of foul language spewed from her. The young deputy's eyes widened as he and Rodd entered the room. Veda snapped off the TV and thumped down into a worn recliner. "What's this all about?"

While Rodd eased down into an ancient rocker facing her, he motioned the deputy to sit on the sagging sofa along the wall. Veda exuded a malevolence unexpected from an older woman. He didn't blame Mrs. Benser for taking great pains to keep Veda McCracken from knowing she was the one who'd given the sheriff information; this was one grizzly bear of a woman.

Rodd took his time, arranging himself in the chair, taking off his hat, and opening a small dark notebook. Then he looked across at Veda. "Miss McCracken, since this is a small community I decided to try to settle this privately—"

"Then why's he here?" She jabbed her thumb toward the deputy.

"Police procedure specifies that an officer must always have a witness when questioning anyone. Now this is a matter concerning yesterday's Senior Bazaar—"

"What about it?" she snapped.

"You were the sole treasurer at the bazaar?" He watched for her reaction.

"So?" She gripped the patched arms of her avocado green recliner.

Rodd leveled his gaze at her, aiming at the spot right between her eyes. He could gently ease up to the point for this visit, but why? Why not just fire the charge at her? "You stole $103.50 from the Senior Bazaar profits—"

"What!" Veda reared up in her chair. "Who says so? Which of those mealymouthed—"

He continued his attack. "My source isn't important. I've—"

"Liar! Whoever told you this is a liar—"

"I checked my facts before I came," he went on in a calm but insistent voice. "Each participant—"

"Those women can't be trusted to get anything right."

As though she hadn't interrupted, Rodd continued. "Each participant kept track of her sales and her total money taken in. The final sales figure of crafts and bake-sale items came to a total of $103.50 more than you reported."

"That's a lie."

"Those are the facts."

Veda glared at him, her face beet red. "This is just a plot to take the attention away from your botched investigation of the snowmobile burglaries! Think arresting an old woman will make you a big man?" she sneered.

Her venom still had the power to surprise him. And she'd attended church this morning as usual! He kept his tone colorless. "I think stealing is stealing."

She crossed her arms over her breast. "It's their word against mine."

"No, it isn't." Still amazed and somewhat amused at the craftiness of the elderly bazaar women, he looked her straight in the eye. "The women who collected the money marked the bills."

Veda's eyes narrowed. "I didn't see no marks on any bills."

"They were very subtle. But every woman who collected money at the table marked each greenback that she put into the till for the event."

A cunning look came into the woman's eyes. "What kind of marks?"

I'm not telling you, lady! "Each woman had her own mark and will be able to identify it."

"Those—" Another stream of foul invectives about the character and appearance of the women who had worked so hard on the Senior Bazaar followed.

Rodd felt uncomfortable sitting there with his young deputy, listening to such language coming from an old woman. He had heard enough of it in Milwaukee to last him a lifetime. But in the vulgar and profane department, Veda McCracken could top any suspect in the city.

"Evil words come from an evil heart." Rodd recalled the verse from Matthew. He had no problem believing the portrait of Veda that Harlan had painted for him. *Lord, what went so bad in this woman's heart?* His mind answered, *"The human heart is most deceitful and desperately wicked."*

He dragged in a ragged breath. "Miss McCracken, this is useless. Now, give me the money and the ladies won't press charges against you."

Caught up short, she seethed at him, rapidly breathing in and out in wheezing puffs. "What if I don't?"

Her bullheadedness shouldn't have surprised him, but it did. He pressed on. "If you don't give it to me now, I'll have to serve you with a search warrant—it's in my pocket. Then this deputy will keep you in that chair while I tear your house apart looking for the marked bills. And if you make me do that, you will be arrested and everyone will know what you've done."

"Everyone will know anyway!" she growled. "You don't think those old biddies will keep quiet!"

"Some of them may talk, but that's much different than this appearing in the newspaper." He raised his eyebrows at her. "It's much different than going to jail." He stood. "Now let's get this over with. Just give me the money and we'll leave."

She glared at them, and then with a vicious curse she rose. She stomped out of the room and returned with a wad of cash in hand. She threw it at Rodd. "Here! Take it and get out of my house!" Another stream of obscenity.

Noting the tiny incriminating marks, Rodd counted the money, then pinned her with his gaze. "You owe the bazaar another fifty cents."

She dug into her pocket and threw a handful of change at him.

He didn't bother to pick it up but stared at her. "A word to the wise: Don't volunteer to be the treasurer of any other cause in the future. Good night, Miss McCracken." He and his deputy walked out. She slammed the door behind them.

"Whew!" the young deputy observed. "She turned out to be an ugly customer."

Rodd nodded. The expression on Veda's face had been murderous. Mrs. Benser said that the women had grown suspicious over the past three years, but had been unable to oust Veda as self-appointed director and treasurer of the bazaar. Whenever they had put someone else in the position, Veda had simply barreled in and taken over anyway. In desperation, they'd finally come up with the plan of the separate tallies and marked bills. It had worked. Veda's skimming had been unmasked.

His past experience with people like Veda caused Rodd to be seriously concerned now. Would she take her anger out on the women who had worked together to catch her stealing? Her kind of hatred would seek vengeance. He'd keep his eye on the honest women and protect them as best he could. Evidently, they'd hoped in the safety of numbers; he hoped it worked. He'd have to watch his own back and—a gut feeling alerted him—Wendy's too.

Veda might be the Weasel. The idea stunned him. But Veda had the strength to batter down a door. He'd seen her snowmobile beside her garage. She'd do anything that might cast suspicion on the Rieker family. And now he knew she wasn't above larceny. Could it be possible? Maybe he'd find out this Saturday night after bingo. The waiting was killing him!

Then for no reason, the sound of Zak's voice singing this morning's hymn came to him: *"I must have Jesus. I must have Jesus. I cannot bear these burdens alone."*

CHAPTER TWELVE

OUT OF THE frosty mid-December night Rodd walked into the brightly lit VFW hall in LaFollette. A haze of cigarette smoke hung above the crowded hall. Small children ran around the tables playing tag while the adults with multiple bingo cards in front of them sat shoulder to shoulder along long institutional-looking tables.

The size of the crowd affirmed what Wendy had predicted. This Bingo Night would bring in a large sum of money—one that should tempt the Weasel. *God, just give me a clear shot at him. That's all I need.*

As Rodd stood in the back of the long room, he saw heads turn toward him, then away. He was used to that. People always noticed a police officer in their midst—kind of like a Martian dropping in. His khaki-and-brown uniform with its badge, and the belt with handcuffs and gun, pointed him out as different.

"B-3!" The caller at the front of the room barked into the microphone.

". . . letter from that old bat in Steadfast. She really laid into him. . . ."

Rodd caught a snippet of conversation and felt himself stiffen. Of course, by now everyone in the county had read Veda's letter to the editor in Friday's *Steadfast Times.* She'd vented on him all her anger at being caught red-handed stealing from the Senior Bazaar, vowing to start a petition to have him removed from office for malfeasance for not stopping the burglaries.

"N-34!"

"If she thinks anyone would sign a petition, she'd start—" someone to his left said, then cast a glance over his shoulder at Rodd.

He hadn't thought of that, but Veda's own unpopularity would work for him. *But if I don't catch the Weasel I'll resign anyway.* The thought pained him more than he'd thought possible three months ago when he'd taken his oath as sheriff. Even though he knew she wouldn't be here, his eyes sought out Wendy's golden head. Would he be forced to leave her, never knowing if they could have had a future together? But what right did he have to let her know of his feelings when he might have to go back to Milwaukee—beaten by a small-town thief?

"O-65!"

Suddenly the large number of the people congregated in the room bothered Rodd. After doing a rough head count, he walked back to the entrance and read the sign specifying the allowed occupancy of the building. The number in attendance exceeded the limit. What could he do? If he emptied the room, he'd spoil his plan. Why was it always something?

"G-52!"

He walked toward the front of the hall. Only a half hour left till midnight, but he had to do something to mitigate the possibility of injury. He put his hand over the mike. "I'm sorry to interrupt," he said to the veteran calling the numbers, "but everyone needs to make sure that all personal items on the floor are under the tables. I need unobstructed aisles in case of emergency—"

The players started shouting, "Go on with the game!" "What's the problem?" "Don't stop now!"

The vet, a tall white-haired man, held up his hand for quiet. "Sheriff, why—"

Rodd interrupted him. "I should clear the room. You have exceeded the occupancy of this hall, but since the game's nearly over, I just want clear egress in case of emergency."

The vet nodded. "Okay."

Rodd took his hand away, then walked to the nearest exit to check that it was clear and unlocked.

The vet explained the concern, and the crowd, though grumbling, shifted everything under the tables.

"I-29!"

As the game proceeded, Rodd checked all exits, making certain everyone would be able to get out safely. Gus Feeney sat at the front table, his gaze never meeting Rodd's. The big clock behind the bingo caller ticked away the minutes till midnight.

"Bingo!" a woman in the third row shouted and stood up. "That's my fifteenth one!"

Some applauded and some groaned.

After her card had been checked for accuracy, Gus rose and walked to the scoreboard. "That makes you the big winner so far! Come on, folks, just seven more minutes!"

The caller stepped up his pace. The anxious players eyed their cards intensely. "B-5! N-39! O-70!"

The caller's rapid announcements kept rhythm with Rodd's heartbeat. He had all his deputies stationed to anticipate any contingency on the road to Gus's house and at Gus's house. Two of them were on snowmobiles—one along the way to the house and one at the house. He'd follow Gus home at a discreet distance. By now, he realized that he had to be prepared for anything.

The clock struck midnight. The plump woman who had won fifteen times went forward and received her five-hundred-dollar prize. Other people accepted lesser awards. Then Gus announced that the Bingo Fund-raiser had brought in nearly nine hundred dollars. The crowd whistled and applauded.

As everyone gathered up their belongings, children, and grandchildren, Rodd's insides were jumping. People streamed out through the exits, laughing and talking. Rodd hung back by the main entrance to the parking lot, nodding to people who greeted him.

BOOM!

The sound of an explosion brought screams and shouts from everyone.

Rodd pushed his way through the crowd out into the parking lot in front of the VFW. Flames lit up the sky farther down the street. Rodd raced toward them, barking into his cell phone, "Fire on Turner Street—LaFollette!"

He jogged toward the fire—the crowd at his heels. "It looks like Garvey's Garage!" someone shouted. "Yes!" and "That's right!" others agreed.

He reached the fire, which engulfed a garage behind an aged storefront. "Stand back!" he ordered. "We don't know what kind of fire it is! Get back! There could be another explosion!" Surging in front of the crowd, he had to shove a few men back for their own safety.

BOOM!!!

A second explosion behind the fire detonated. People covered their ears and screamed. A few dropped to the ground, shielding their heads with their hands and arms. Burning debris showered all around. Rodd prodded everyone back farther, helping up an old woman who'd fallen.

"Everyone back to the VFW!" He began herding them back down the street. He bent down and picked up a stray child. "Stay in the middle of the street! Something else might explode!"

Fear now ran with the crowd. The people huddled together as they hurried, helping the older ones keep pace, picking up children and running, running. Infected with the alarm of the adults, children screamed and babies cried out, sobbing, "Mommy! Mommy!"

The child trembled against Rodd, clutching his jacket. Protecting the rear of the crowd, Rodd kept urging everyone on with calm, even shouts. "Just head to the VFW! The firefighters are on their way—"

The siren of the LaFollette Volunteer Fire Department drowned out his voice. The sound bolstered the crowd. They ran, but the hysteria waned. They funneled back into the VFW hall, suddenly a haven in the chaos. Inside, a mother came and lifted her son from Rodd's arms. She thanked him and wept over the child's head.

In the front, Gus held the proceeds from the fund-raiser in a bank bag and on each side of him, two vets with guns drawn hovered protectively. "No one got the—" Gus's voice was interrupted by an urgent shout.

"Help!" Came a yell from the back door. "Help! I've been robbed!"

* * *

ON THE FOLLOWING wintry Monday morning Wendy met Rodd at the Foodliner on Main Street. Rodd had volunteered to pay for the ingredients for the hot cocoa and fresh gingerbread that would be served at the church caroling party, and Wendy had volunteered to do the actual shopping with him.

Wendy led him down the baking goods aisle. Rodd pushed the cart with one rattling wheel while Wendy chose flour, sugar, baking cocoa, and spices. Performing this domestic chore together gave her a peculiar sensation. What would it be like to be married to Rodd and . . . she halted this fairy tale. This was definitely not the moment for flights of fancy.

She watched him from the corner of her eye. By now, everyone knew what had happened Saturday night. The snowmobile thief had set explosions in LaFollette to distract everyone. The ensuing commotion from the second blast had made the slick theft possible.

Evidently, the thief had been lingering by an exit at the end of Bingo Night, saw who won the money, then targeted that person when everyone ran outside after the first explosion. A man in snowmobile gear had been overlooked in the mad rush. He'd come up behind the woman and knocked her unconscious at the rear of the VFW, then made off with the money on his snowmobile. The woman who'd been robbed hadn't seen her attacker. The only blessing had been that she hadn't been seriously injured.

The whole debacle in LaFollette had left Rodd looking grim. Unreachable.

"That's about it," Wendy said with a bright smile, wishing with all her heart she had some idea to offer him.

Rodd nodded.

In light of his gloom, she reined in her smile. *Lord, help me give him hope that he will succeed in arresting this awful burglar. He's such a good man and he's tried so hard. How could he possibly have known that the burglar would blow up part of LaFollette?*

Rodd pushed the noisy, irritating cart to the checkout line. Wendy was very aware of the glances directed at the sheriff. Bruno Havlecek and Leo Schultz had greeted them both. From the other few shoppers, Wendy didn't detect any hostility, only curiosity.

"There you are!" Fletcher Cram's distinctive scratchy baritone boomed through the thin crowd. "I saw your Jeep outside! What is going on with you? You let the thief blow up Garvey's Garage on Turner Street! Good heavens! What's next?"

Instinctively, Wendy took a step backward, closer to Rodd.

Rodd stared at Cram. "I didn't let the thief do anything—he doesn't ask my permission—"

"You know what I mean! For the first time in over fifty years I agree with Veda McCracken! You should resign if you can't do the job!"

Bruno, who was in line in front of Wendy, scowled at Cram and demanded, "What makes you think you can speak for us?"

"That's right!" Leo Schultz chimed in. "Just because you run the newspaper don't mean you're in charge of the county!"

Wendy sensed Rodd's discomfort. What could he say in his own defense? What could she say?

"I have the right to demand that a public servant do his job!" Cram retorted.

"I am doing my job." Rodd surprised Wendy by speaking. "I've secured the crime scene around the explosion site. One of my men is standing guard around the clock until the explosives expert from the state crime lab gets here later today to go over the scene for evidence."

"That's all well and good," Cram blustered, "but what are you going to do if that expert doesn't find anything you can use?"

Rodd and Cram faced each other. The rest of the customers

watched. Wendy searched her mind for some words to say, something that would support the sheriff without embarrassing him.

"Cram, I would resign right now if I could." Rodd's voice sounded as though it had been ripped from deep inside him.

"What does that mean?" Cram growled. "No one's preventing you!"

"Who would take my place as sheriff?"

Everyone became very quiet. The checker stopped running items over the scanner.

"Who would take my place?" Rodd repeated.

"One of your deputies. Until a special election," Cram complained.

"My deputies are all green. None of them has even a year's experience. I have nearly fifteen years in law enforcement, and I . . . haven't . . . been . . . able . . . to catch him. How would one of them? If I resigned now, it would amount to dereliction of duty. I can't resign now, even if I wanted to."

Cram fell silent. His prominent Adam's apple bobbled, but he said nothing.

"This thief," Rodd continued, "isn't a garden-variety one. He's got brains. He's fearless. And he's very good. I don't have one shred of hard evidence to connect anyone to any of the burglaries, and that isn't because I haven't looked. I don't think, Mr. Cram, that you have a clue as to what law enforcement is all about. So why don't you go write yourself another article about what a bad sheriff I am—but that won't make anything better either. It will just give you another chance to vent your sour spleen!"

Applause broke out spontaneously.

"That's tellin' him!" Schultz chortled.

Cram turned on his heel and stomped out of the store.

"Good riddance!" Bruno pronounced.

Wendy stood, shocked. She was speechless.

The checkout line resumed and moved along; the checker tallied the charge for their groceries; they drove to the church.

In the church kitchen, Wendy unloaded the bags, which Rodd had carried in for her. In the stillness of the empty basement, she could hardly breathe she was so aware of Rodd. She heard each breath he took, and her hands ached to cup his face and bring his lips down to hers. But beyond this grew a sense that she needed to confront Rodd. Over and over when she'd mentioned prayer or asking God for help, he'd pulled back. *Lord, am I to say something to him? How can I when everyone's already sniping at him?*

Finally, she knew what she had to say. "Rodd, I know you never miss a Sunday here, but have you really learned to turn things over to God?"

He glanced at her, a wariness in his eyes. "What do you mean?"

"Have you asked God to lead you to the thief?"

He made an impatient sound. "I asked God to keep everyone out of my way so I could get a shot at him."

"That's not the same as asking him to help you. . . ."

"God has better things to do than my job. And I can do my job if I just get a chance, just one little piece of evidence."

Wendy shook her head. "God isn't too busy to handle anything that is important to us."

"If God does everything, what am I supposed to be doing here? I'm the sheriff."

She cocked her head to the side, appealing to him to listen to her. "A good sheriff takes all the help he can get, doesn't he?"

Rodd studied her.

Then her own conscience hit her. She'd been fretting about her mother and Jim—wasn't that God's business, too?

❖❖❖

HOLDING THE WARM mug, the smartest man in Wisconsin stood looking out the cracked, taped window. Outside, snow fell dizzily, as if it had a hangover—a lot like he felt. His head ached and the coffee tasted bitter on his tongue, but that didn't dim his amusement. The explosions had been seen for miles!

He sucked in another swallow of the hot murky brew. Picking up his tattered copy of Cram's latest *Steadfast Times*, he glanced over the letter to the editor again. The old biddy had unloaded both barrels at the sheriff again and she'd been loaded for bear! He tossed the paper back down.

Did the sheriff suspect old Veda of being the Snowmobile Burglar? No doubt Elroy Dietz had made the sheriff's list and even good old Dutch Rieker. What did Durand plan to do next?

His empty stomach burned. No one in the county knew what was behind the burglaries except him. And he wouldn't end it until he'd gotten exactly what he wanted—and that wasn't just a few lousy bucks.

CHAPTER THIRTEEN

FEELING A STRANGE mix of emotions, Wendy walked between Sage and Grandfather through the small utilitarian airport, a county away from Steadfast. They'd come to see Sage off on the first leg of her journey to Florida. Grandfather had bought Sage a ticket out of the small airport to Minneapolis, where she'd catch her flight south. Wendy felt tears just waiting to fall. Hurt over being left behind wouldn't leave her in peace and the sadness of being parted from her sister was worse yet

The sound of many different footsteps on the polished linoleum reminded Wendy that the three of them were not alone. Trav sauntered beside Sage, holding her hand. Behind them came the startling threesome of Elroy Dietz, Sheriff Durand, and Uncle Dutch. The reason for the strange trio accompanying them was purely circumstantial.

Uncle Dutch had been expected to come to see his niece off. Elroy wanted to borrow Trav's truck, so right after Sage took off, he was going to drop Trav at his job on the way back to town. Finally, Rodd had called and insisted on driving Wendy and Harlan because the roads were slick again. Wendy had wanted to refuse, but she had seen that her grandfather had wanted her to accept. She'd wanted it too—though she would never have asked him. The roads had been snowpacked. They'd be safer in Rodd's Jeep than in Wendy's wagon. And Wendy admitted to herself that she drew unexpected strength from Rodd's presence.

The intimate glances that passed between Sage and Trav in some mysterious way heightened Wendy's consciousness of Rodd just a foot behind her. An invisible force seemed to be urging her to turn around and throw herself into Rodd's arms, where she would feel safe and strengthened. She tried to block the feeling, but it persisted.

"I can't believe I'll be in Florida tonight." Sage, wearing a new dark gold slacks-and-jacket outfit, grinned and squeezed Trav's hand.

Trav smiled back. "Just don't get sunburned."

Sage chuckled. "I never burn."

"But you'll be out so much," Wendy interrupted. "I just don't want you—"

"You just want me to have the perfect vacation!" Sage beamed at her.

Sage's excitement proved contagious. In spite of being a mismatched group, Wendy noticed that they were all smiling when they reached the exit where the turboprop commuter plane was preparing to take off. Wendy welcomed the lift of mood. But her unsought attraction to Rodd continued. Her gaze wandered to him despite her wish to appear unaffected by his nearness. *Lord,* she prayed silently, *bless Sage and Mom this Christmas. Don't let us miss each other too much, and help us rejoice in the celebration of your birth!*

"Well, Sage," Grandfather said as he opened his arms, "give your mother our love."

"I will, Gramps." Sage hugged him. "Remember to put the presents I left under your tree. I'll miss you so."

"We'll miss you too." Harlan stepped back.

Wendy blinked away tears. When Rodd rested a comforting hand on her shoulder, her emotions scattered like dry snow before wind.

Uncle Dutch stepped forward. He pulled a smudged envelope from his pocket and handed it to Sage. "You remind that Jim that he'd better be takin' good care of my sister. Here's some cash. Buy your mom something from me and put it under the tree and get yourself something. You know I'm no good at gift wrappin'."

Wendy choked back a sob, a sudden flash of memory recalling a scene from a long-ago Christmas. Still too little for kindergarten, she'd awakened in the middle of Christmas night. From the doorway of her bedroom in the trailer, she'd watched Uncle Dutch arranging a miniature tea set for her under a scraggly Christmas tree. That night she'd discovered that her uncle was her Santa Claus.

"Thanks, Uncle Dutch." Sage stuffed the envelope in her pocket and gave him a big hug. In spite of the cast on his wrist, he lifted her off the floor and swung her as he always used to do with both Wendy and Sage when they were little. Sage giggled with delight.

Wiping tears from her gloved hand, Wendy smiled too. Why didn't their uncle ever let his good side show away from family?

He set Sage down and stepped back. "Merry Christmas!"

Clearing his throat, Rodd stepped forward and offered his hand. "Hope you have a safe trip, Sage."

Craving more of Rodd's comforting touch herself, Wendy balled her hands into tight fists at her side.

Sage shook his hand. "Thanks, Sheriff. You watch out for Wendy while I'm away."

Rodd nodded. "You can count on it."

Her sister's request made Wendy turn a fiery red. Though Rodd made no sign of it, she hoped he didn't take Sage's request as a slur on his ability to protect her. She knew that the attack on her had filled him with helpless anger at the thief—but most of all, at himself. *He's such a good man, Lord. Help him solve this case.*

Sage gave a little wave to the scruffy man hanging back, just behind the sheriff. "Bye, Elroy. Merry Christmas."

Elroy nodded, appearing subdued by the presence of the law, his longtime enemy, and Harlan, an elder of the church. Wendy never felt comfortable around Elroy. She had a feeling he was a quieter, sneakier version of Veda.

Sage touched Wendy's arm. "Walk me outside."

Wendy had expected Sage to ask Trav to walk with her to the plane. She glanced up into her sister's eyes and read the silent plea there. "Okay."

Sage kissed Trav and whispered something into his ear. He hugged her and kissed her again. Then with one final wave, Sage walked outside. Wendy went with her. When they reached the plane, Sage paused. "I know your feelings are hurt. . . ."

"No, I—"

"Don't." Sage's determined tone stopped her. "I'm sorry Mom could only afford one ticket—"

Again, Wendy tried to interrupt.

Taking both Wendy's gloved hands, Sage stopped her. "If there had been any possibility you could have gotten away, I would have paid your fare."

"Sage, your savings are for college." Wendy felt guilty for feeling left out.

Sage put her arms around Wendy's shoulders and with a sigh drew her close. "You're more important to me than college." Sage hugged her. "I'll miss you, Sis. We've never been apart for Christmas, and I wouldn't go if Mom didn't need me."

"I know." Wendy's throat threatened to close up on her.

"I love you, Wendy."

"I love you too." Wendy tightened their embrace. "You were the best gift Mom ever gave me."

Sage straightened up. "You've always been there for me, and now that I'm nearly an adult I'm going to be there for you."

Sage's pledge touched Wendy's heart. She brushed away more tears. "Give my love to Mom."

"I will. Here, I won't be needing this." Grinning, Sage shrugged out of her winter jacket, gave it to Wendy, and turned to go. "Be kind to the sheriff. He's having a rough time and something in his life should be going right!"

Feeling healed and refreshed, Wendy called a last farewell, and then she walked back inside. What did her sister's cryptic comment about the sheriff mean? Had Sage guessed Wendy's attraction to Rodd? Was it that obvious?

Back inside, Wendy and the small group watched the plane taxi away and take off. Suddenly she was glad Sage was the one flying away. She felt relieved she was staying home for Christmas. The early winter had been disturbed by the burglaries and made her want to cling to the familiar. Wendy imagined all the cheerful cleaning, shopping, wrapping, and baking her mother had no doubt been doing the last two weeks. She grinned to herself. It was wonderful Mom would have Sage with her. *Good-bye, Sage!* And though she knew she shouldn't, she drew strength from the sheriff's formidable presence.

THE EXCITEMENT PAST, Rodd noticed everyone's mood had sobered. The six of them turned and paraded back through the tiny airport. They walked more slowly and didn't speak.

Rodd was glad he'd insisted on driving Harlan and Wendy. She had looked crushed about saying good-bye to Sage. But being Wendy, she was trying to smile for her grandfather's sake. She possessed such a sweet spirit. The memory of seeing her lying facedown at the Kainzes' would haunt him forever.

Rodd had again been contemplating the possibility of either Elroy or Dutch being the Weasel. Since the VFW debacle, Rodd had gone over the burglary file repeatedly. And again, no incriminating physical evidence had been found at Garvey's Garage. The simple incendiary devices used to ignite an auto garage amply supplied with oily rags and other flammable substances had been the simplest possible—made with items that could be purchased at any discount or hardware store. He now had a collection of evidence from the explosions, but nothing that pointed a clear finger at anyone. Though he did doubt Veda would know enough to plan and craft the explosives, Veda, Dutch, and Elroy still remained his most likely suspects.

Today at the airport, the tension between Dutch and Elroy had been palpable. But the feud between the two men was widely known and long-standing. And it didn't seem to have anything to do with the burglaries. People tended to think that, of the two enemies, Rieker had the brains. But Elroy had what Rodd, as a cop, recognized as that natural furtive cunning that some criminals had. It was almost like a natural talent for anything twisted or illegal.

When was the Weasel going to make a mistake or go too far? Rodd was disgusted that events had reduced him to that thin hope. After the showdown with Cram, he'd contemplated helping the county find a replacement; then he'd resign and go back to Milwaukee. But he couldn't leave this crime unsolved, and what officer in his right mind would take up a mare's nest like this?

Outside, the farewell party headed to their parked vehicles. With a wave, Elroy and Trav set off in Trav's truck. Rodd wondered what Elroy needed the truck for. Did he have a Christmas kegger in mind? How had Trav, by all accounts a good kid, popped up in a family like the Dietzes'?

Dutch turned to go toward his car.

With Wendy beside him, Harlan lifted his hand. "Wait, Dutch. I wanted to invite you to join Wendy and me for Christmas dinner."

"Hey, that's great, Harlan. But I've got plans." Dutch grinned.

Harlan nodded as though this response hadn't surprised him. "The invitation will stay open. If your plans change, just show up when you can."

Wendy leaned against her grandfather affectionately. "Yes, Uncle Dutch, please try to come."

"I'll keep that in mind. Thanks." Dutch shook Harlan's hand, then turned away.

Rodd admired Harlan. Harlan and Uncle George had been two of a kind. Harlan never let anything get in his way of reaching out to others. He always practiced the Golden Rule. Today he looked broken up over Sage's leaving. Rodd wished he could do something for him.

Rodd walked beside Wendy as they headed for his Jeep. He hadn't detected any friction between the sisters. Perhaps Wendy knew that she was needed here—Harlan needed her. But Rodd resented anything that made matters hard for her. It was obvious to him she was holding back her emotions. Touching her shoulder inside the airport had been the least he thought he could show as merely friendly regard. But he longed to put his arms around her, to let her know of his concern.

"Hey! Wait a minute, Sheriff!" Dutch called. "This battery of mine has been giving me trouble. Wait and see if I can get it started, okay? I might need a jump."

"Sure." Rodd, along with Wendy and Harlan, waited while Dutch climbed into his beat-up Camaro. The battery cranked but didn't catch.

After a few minutes of grinding, Dutch got out. "I've got jumper cables in my trunk."

"I'll drive over next to you," Rodd called over his shoulder. Helping Wendy into the Jeep while Harlan climbed in back, Rodd gave her a reassuring smile and was rewarded with one in return. He got in and drove over to Dutch.

Rodd got out to help Dutch hook up his battery cables to the Jeep. Slipping outside, Wendy hovered nearby. She looked tired. Had she been working too much? He wished he could stop her from shouldering too much responsibility. So many people depended on her. "Wendy, why don't you get back in the Jeep?" Rodd invited gently. "We weren't inside very long, so it's still warm. This won't take long."

She looked at both of them. He tried to read her expression. What was she concerned about now?

"I guess you don't need another pair of hands." After touching Dutch's shoulder affectionately, she walked to the passenger side and got in.

Dutch grinned at him. "Think she was afraid I'd try to give you a hard time?"

Rodd shrugged. Leaning under the hood, he looked at the date on the oil-smeared and corroded battery. "You should start shopping for a new battery."

"Oh, this one's got a few more miles on it! Back in the county, I just leave the motor running for short stops. But here someone might have driven off with it."

Rodd doubted any car thief would be interested in a twenty-five-year-old rusted-out Camaro, but he didn't say anything.

"So, Sheriff, are you seeing my niece?"

The unexpected question threw Rodd. "We aren't dating."

"Well, seems to me that whenever I see Wendy you're somewhere in the picture."

Rodd gave him a noncommittal reply. "Our jobs bring us together—"

Dutch cut in, "I just want you to know, no one hits on my nieces. I took Trav aside and let him know what would happen to him if he hurt Sage. You treat Wendy with respect or else. I don't care if you are the law."

Rodd gazed at Dutch, reading his intent stare. "Wendy is a fine woman. She has nothing to fear from me."

"Okay, I'll take your word." Dutch shook his head slowly. "You notice that skunk Dietz giving me the eye?"

Rodd shrugged, wondering where this was leading.

"He thinks he's gotten something over on me since he started seeing Carlene, my fiancée."

Rodd nodded.

"Carlene and me been informally engaged for nearly three years, and as soon as this wrist is back in condition, I'm going to teach little Elroy a lesson."

Rodd couldn't figure out why Rieker was telling him this. Just male ego?

"Okay, Sheriff, get in and start her up!" Dutch wiped his hands on a grimy rag from his pocket.

Rodd slid behind the wheel of his Jeep and turned on the ignition, starting his vehicle. Dutch did the same. His motor fired and chugged to a start.

Dutch hopped out of his car, disconnected the cables, and waved Rodd away. "Thanks, Sheriff! See you, Harlan, and see you, Wendy girl!"

As Rodd adjusted the defroster vents, the thought occurred to him that Dutch could have used the money he'd just given to Sage for Christmas presents for a car battery instead. Veda McCracken attended church every week but was capable of stealing money from a local fund-raiser. Dutch Rieker drank too much, brawled, and had trouble holding down a job, but he gave generously to his family.

Everyone was a sinner, and experience had taught him that human nature never fit into neat little slots of good people/bad people. But Rodd didn't deem Dutch as irredeemable—though some church members might quibble with him, especially Veda McCracken. Why did Veda bother taking up a pew each Sunday morning when she seemed intent on hating everyone in the congregation? in the county? Was it just her way of keeping tabs on what was going on so she could use it for her own bent purposes?

"Thanks for driving us here, Rodd." Harlan hesitated. "Did you hear about Elroy's good luck?"

Rodd picked up the reluctance in the older man's voice. "Good luck?"

"Yes, seems his truck was in Garvey's Garage when it exploded."

"That's good news?"

"It is since he'd just upped his auto insurance policy to include replacement value."

❋ ❋ ❋

AT TWILIGHT THE wind died down, but Wendy still shivered in the church parking lot. It was the day before Christmas Eve, and the congregation had gathered for caroling. She tried to give Rodd her usual smile. Nothing new about the case had turned up in the week since the explosions. But their showdown with Cram at the Foodliner had only been a prelude to more hate from Veda. She'd begun accosting people on Main Street, trying to get them to sign a petition to remove Rodd from office. Plus she had written another letter to the editor—a damaging one because it had recounted . . . Wendy shook her head, trying to get rid of the empathetic pain she'd felt for Rodd when she'd read Veda's hate-filled exposé of something from Rodd's past that he certainly didn't want reopened.

"Okay!" Pastor Bruce gathered everyone's attention. "We're lucky. A new snowstorm is predicted for tomorrow, but tonight the sky is clear. So I hope you all dressed warm and wore your most comfortable boots. In spite of the snow and cold, we're going to take our usual route all through town. Many in Steadfast still don't know what the baby born in Bethlehem means in their lives. This is another chance to share the Nativity with them and show we care for them."

"I suppose you're going to make us sing at Patsy and Carl's," Miss Frantz grumbled.

The pastor looked at the frail woman sternly. "Over the past five years, I've been called to the care center by older men we've sung to at Christmas at Carl and Patsy's. I've been privileged to lead a few of them to Christ just before they went to meet him. If we hadn't reached out to them, I doubt they'd have called me to comfort them in their final hours."

Harlan quoted, "'Therefore go and make disciples of all nations, baptizing them in the name of the Father and of the Son and of the Holy Spirit, and teaching them to obey everything I have commanded you.' That includes going to Carl and Patsy's."

"Thank you, Harlan." Pastor Bruce nodded.

Wendy smiled at Grandfather while she stomped her feet to keep warm.

Pastor called out, "Let's stop talking and get going. We have to get back here for hot cocoa and warm gingerbread right out of the oven!" Muted applause from mittened hands greeted this agenda. Little Zak jumped up and down next to Rodd and Wendy.

Pastor Bruce beamed at them. "We'll start with 'God Rest Ye Merry, Gentlemen.'" He blew the first note on his pitch pipe.

Along with everyone else, Wendy began singing the familiar melody. When she voiced, "'Let nothing you dismay,'" she couldn't help herself; she glanced over at Rodd's face.

In the days since the explosives expert had found nothing incriminating, Rodd had begun not speaking unless spoken to, and tonight, even though he was part of the group, his gaze was fixed forward. Wendy was certain he also still felt irrational guilt over her being assaulted and for not somehow divining that the thief would turn to explosives. None of what had happened was Rodd's fault. She was beginning to think only God could catch this thief.

Wendy looked around, wondering if they'd meet up with Veda. She'd spent most of the last two days parading up and down Main Street, bad-mouthing Rodd, usually to people hurrying to get away from her. No one would sign Veda's petition, but that didn't bother her. It just gave Veda more to harp about—loudly. Righteous indignation surged through Wendy. How did that woman know exactly what to do to make others miserable? It was like some sick talent.

But Rodd's low spirits hadn't kept him away tonight or affected his singing. His deep voice gave a firm foundation to her soprano. Pride in his faithfulness made her smile. And the sound of his bass voice ignited a warmth that flowed through her. As he walked, Zak clung to Rodd's hand, jumping and hopping to keep up. The picture of the serious man and the carefree child tugged at her heart. What a wonderful dad Rodd would make!

Getting her rampant emotions under control, she faced forward again and caught several carolers looking over at them. Then she realized that though she hadn't intended to, she and Rodd had ended up side by side. She blushed.

How had that happened? She hadn't tried to get close to him. She knew she certainly hadn't noticed Rodd making his way toward her. The other carolers must have arranged themselves around Rodd and her, making them a twosome. Her face warmed even more. Just because her grandfather and the sheriff were friends. And just because the sheriff's duties and hers had brought them into contact often . . .

Who are you kidding, Wendy Carey? her conscience goaded her to honesty. *You've allowed yourself to let people see you and Rodd together—not just in connection with work. The trip to Duluth and letting Rodd drive you to see Sage off at the airport weren't business. You want to be with the sheriff. Being with him gives you more pleasure than anything else this world has to offer. You want to be beside him tonight and forever. And you know it!*

What had happened to her ability to resist becoming involved with a man? Had she abandoned it just because her and Rodd's lives had become so entwined as they worked together to uncover the thief? No.

Wendy admitted more than this had sparked her attraction to Rodd. Everything about him and his character drew her to him irresistibly. The question was, where did they go from here?

During "I Heard the Bells on Christmas Day," Wendy tried to drift away from Rodd's side. She had to put distance between them. She had to resist his lure. But the singers around her thwarted her. As they walked down the snowy streets, they hemmed Wendy in beside Rodd. Did they realize what they were doing, keeping Rodd and her together? Had the sheriff noticed? She glanced up at him again. His brooding expression acted like a magnet on her—how she wanted to wrap her arms around him and comfort him! This thought sent shivers through her.

The grim set to his jaw and the bleak look in his eyes brought her back to reality with a dull thud. How could she be so concerned about what people thought about her—about them—when he was bearing so much? Not being able to catch the thief must be torture for a man so concerned about meeting his responsibilities. And then Veda's petition and her damning letter had to make matters worse. That was Veda's specialty.

Wendy sang: "'And in despair I bowed my head. "There is no peace on earth" I said.'"

Over the years of Wendy's life, Veda had never failed to make things for Wendy and her sister and mother as difficult as she could. A particularly nasty memory of Veda when Wendy had been about thirteen surfaced. She'd been walking four-year-old Sage to the café to eat supper with their mother, and Veda had begun shouting at them on Main Street, yelling that she'd killed her grandmother with worry and shame! Wendy had picked up Sage and run the rest of the way to the café. The memory brought back the public humiliation and outrage of that moment in full force. *Lord, I've never understood why she decided to hate us so. But why had the Pharisees decided to hate Christ? Pride, greed, lust for power? Did hatred have to have a reason?*

The voices around Wendy lifted: "'For hate is strong, and mocks the song of peace on earth, goodwill to men.'"

But more importantly now, why had Veda decided to make the sheriff her fresh target? Something more than his friendship with Wendy must have triggered the three cruel attacks on him. When Wendy had read Veda's latest letter to the editor, she'd felt as though each of Veda's words leaked some form of corrosive airborne acid.

"'God is not dead, nor doth he sleep,'" Wendy sang along with the voices lifting in the chill night.

What had the sheriff done to make Veda so vengeful? Wendy had overheard snippets about Veda and the Senior Bazaar. But in her own past, gossip had made her life so miserable that Wendy refused to deal in gossip for any reason. Was it just that Veda was doubly against Rodd because she thought he might be interested in Wendy? Or was the woman becoming so hateful with age that she no longer needed a logical reason to unleash her vindictiveness? Was her twisted mind disintegrating?

"'A voice, a chime, a chant sublime, of peace on earth, goodwill to men.'" Wendy hung on to the last note and thought of peace as the carolers reached Carl and Patsy's Grill. The pastor opened the door and led them into the darkened interior, except for Miss Frantz, who remained outside. The carolers filed in around the bar. Carl greeted them with an enthusiastic "Merry Christmas!" The old men with beaming faces turned around on their barstools. The pastor blew his pipe and started: "'The first Noel, the angel did say, was to certain poor shepherds in fields as they lay.'"

Wendy wondered if a few of the shepherds who had witnessed the songs of angels that night near Bethlehem had been like these men. She knew each man here who was enjoying their singing. When she noted a few of them wiping their eyes, she felt her own eyes moisten. *Lord, let them feel your love in this moment. Let it draw them to you. You love them so!*

"Noel, Noel! Born is the King of Israel!" At the end of the carol, the men applauded, beating their gnarled, work-worn hands together to show their gratitude for being remembered, included in the celebration of the babe in Bethlehem.

When the applause died down, the pastor said, "Remember, even if you don't attend our church, if you ever need help, please don't hesitate to call on us. We are Steadfast Community Church. It's your church too."

Old Leo Schultz at the end of the bar spoke up. "You'll have to get rid of that old McCracken woman before I'd ever step foot in your church—"

Olie Olson turned and glared at him. "It's not the reverend's fault! What can he do about that old battle-ax?"

Wendy agreed silently. What could anyone do about a woman who knew no shame?

"Gentlemen," the pastor called them back to him, "it's not up to me to decide who gets to come to church."

"That's right, Pastor! Hypocrites in church ain't anything new!" Patsy had joined her husband behind the bar. "Hey, Pastor, how's your wife?"

"Thank you for asking." The pastor's voice softened. "She's getting back to normal."

Wendy heard the catch in Bruce's voice.

"Tell her she's in our thoughts and prayers!" Patsy said with a warm smile.

The pastor shook Patsy's hand. "She told me to thank you for the supper you sent us last week. It was delicious."

Giving his hand a hearty shake, Patsy turned pink with pleasure. "I was pleased to do it. You take care of her."

Olie stood up, catching everyone's attention. "We just want you to know, Sheriff, that we're behind you one hundred percent. Your Uncle George raised you right. We know that! It's just like Veda to bring up something you'd just as soon forget. Old biddy."

Like a flame bursting inside, Wendy felt Rodd's embarrassment as her own.

The men around him rumbled their agreement.

Olie went on. "So you made a mistake when you was just starting out—well, who didn't?"

More growls of approval and nods.

Wendy knew that to the sheriff this show of approval was like pouring iodine on a fresh cut. But he didn't disappoint her.

With Zak in his arms, he stepped forward and nodded. "Thanks for your support."

"Like the movie—we support our local sheriff!" Carl joked and was greeted by more merriment.

"Thank you! Merry Christmas!" The pastor led them outside to the tune of "O Little Town of Bethlehem." As they filed out, Carl pressed a silver half-dollar into Zak's hand. Wendy drew as close as she could to Rodd, giving him her silent encouragement. She longed to pull him aside and in the chill shadows of this night heal his wound with tender kisses. Her breath caught in her throat, sensations of tenderness cascading within.

"'Yet in thy dark streets shineth the everlasting light; the hopes and fears of all the years . . .'" A few snowflakes swirled onto her face, melting instantly, bringing her back to the December night. More snow! The weathermen were forecasting a snowstorm for Christmas. Had it started already?

Crossing Main Street, Wendy recalled in years past that a fresh snowfall while they caroled would have caused a lift in their spirits and plenty of *oohs* and *ahs*. This treacherous winter, however, had changed their appreciation of a white Christmas. A few shook their heads. A few moaned as they sang: "'O come to us, abide with us, Our Lord Emmanuel.'"

Singing carol after carol, they gathered in front of the Black Bear Café, next Harry's Auto Repair, then the hardware store, the Foodliner, and one by one, covered all the streets in town.

Wendy stopped trying to drift away from Rodd. Walking beside him, noticing how he measured his stride to hers, how he carried Zak in his arms, how he sang in his deep voice—all enfolded her in a cloud of sweet sensation. Never before had any man sparked such awareness, enticing her when she wanted to resist. Letting go, she accepted this moment of unexpected joy, reveling in their lush closeness, their unseen but powerful connection.

She walked beside him up the church steps. Rodd held the door open for her to pass in front of him. Tossing caution into the winter night, she gave him a smile, one full of the joy being with him had brought her. Then she stood on tiptoe. Her cheek brushed his as she whispered into his ear, "Merry Christmas!" Other words threatened to bubble up and spill out, but she couldn't say them! Not here. Not now. His return smile, though reluctant at first, broadened and deepened and warmed her to her cold toes.

❋❋❋

IN THE CROWDED entryway where the carolers peeled off their layers of cold, dampened outerwear, Rodd helped Zak out of his bright blue snowsuit and boots. He let Zak's excited chatter cover his awareness of Wendy. Her smile had, at last, freed him from the dark cloud he'd walked in since Veda's latest "nasty-gram" to the editor. Wendy's regard counted for so much more than that unhappy woman's.

Penny and Mrs. Benser had stayed behind to mix the cocoa and bake the gingerbread. From the cloakroom, the spicy aromas beckoned everyone to hurry to the basement. Hand in hand, Rodd and Zak walked down the steps, Wendy beside them.

Sniffing the air like a hound on the scent, Zak let go of Rodd's hand and raced toward the kitchen. "Mama! Mama!"

Rodd sensed someone at his elbow and glanced down.

Mrs. Benser handed him a steaming mug of cocoa. "Here, Sheriff, you look chilled."

"Thanks." He lifted the warm mug.

"Be careful," the older woman warned him. "It's hot."

He nodded.

She took a step closer. "I'm so sorry about Veda," she whispered.

"Nothing Veda does is your fault." This well-intentioned but painful reminder dimmed his rising mood.

Mrs. Benser pursed her lips in a straight line, then muttered, "Don't worry. Everyone realizes that letter is just Veda's way of paying you back for showing her for what she is, and what happened to you years ago in Milwaukee doesn't mean anything here and now."

Rodd felt himself stiffening. He knew the words were meant kindly, but that didn't make them any easier to swallow. Then he remembered Wendy standing just inches away. The pained expression on her face told him that she'd overheard his exchange with Mrs. Benser.

What did Wendy think of Veda's poison-pen letter to the editor? The answer was easy. It had hurt her. No doubt it had made Wendy remember Veda's years of nastiness against her.

If even half of what he'd been told were true, Veda's treatment of Wendy had been criminal. He wished meanness were a punishable offense. Arresting Veda for all the times she'd wounded Wendy would be very satisfying. *"All have sinned and fall short of the glory of God"* Rodd recalled Uncle George's voice and took a deep breath. If Veda succeeded in angering Rodd, it would only make her happy.

He had better things to think on. He would be spending Christmas with Wendy and Harlan—a pleasant thought. Though with the unsolved burglaries hanging over him, Rodd had hardly felt in the holiday mood. But he'd do everything he could to make Wendy's and Harlan's Christmas without Sage as cheerful as possible. Wendy deserved his poor best and she would get it!

"Merry Christmas!" Bruno, with Ma at his side, appeared at the bottom of the stairs. "Sorry we missed the caroling."

"No gingerbread for you then!" Pastor Bruce shook his finger at the older couple.

"You'll forgive us." Bruno beamed at everyone. "We had to drive to Rice Lake before this next snowstorm moved in for Christmas."

"What did you have to do in Rice Lake?" Harlan asked, a smile splitting his face.

Bruno held up Ma's left hand. "We had to buy a ring. Lou has consented to be my wife!"

CHAPTER FOURTEEN

ON CHRISTMAS EVE the wind howled around Harlan's eighty-year-old farmhouse as Wendy hung another gold glittered but faded red glass ball on the Christmas tree. Fresh pine scented the air. At her elbow, Bruno was hanging silver tinsel, strand by strand. "This is so much fun! I haven't helped decorate a proper Christmas tree for years," Bruno said.

In spite of her inner turmoil, Wendy smiled at him. "We never have room for a big one in the trailer." Once more against her will, she glanced toward the back door with longing. *Stop that!* She dragged her mind back to Bruno. "Grandfather's tree is the one Sage and I always look forward to. Don't you want to help, Ma?"

Ma sat on the sofa, crocheting an afghan. "No, it's just fun watching you two fussing around. Besides I can't put one strand on at a time like Bruno can. Too impatient, but I do like how it looks when he does that."

Noticing how Ma's gruff voice had softened, Wendy hung another ball, this one a pale blue satin. The ball trembled on the short-needled branch. Ma marrying Bruno! Who would have thought it?

An image of the sheriff popped into her mind. *Where are you, Rodd? You should be here by now.* Her effort to appear unconcerned about the sheriff's delay tightened Wendy's neck. She shrugged her shoulders, trying to release the tension.

"Are you tired, Wendy?" her grandfather asked.

Startled, she shook her head. She'd hoped she'd masked her worry better.

Grandfather turned on the small radio by his recliner. Lady was asleep at his feet. "Let's hear the weather report."

Wendy had noticed that he'd been repeatedly glancing toward the back door too. Grandfather wouldn't relax completely until all his "chicks" were in for the night.

Ma humphed. "Why? You know it's going to be bad news. Blizzard warning has been on since last night."

Bruno spoke up. "It's kind of pleasant to enjoy the contrast." He paused with a string of tinsel between his thumb and forefinger. "I mean, here we all are—friends and family—snug by the fire, plenty of food, a Christmas tree. But outside the snow is blowing and it's icy. It just makes me feel all the more cozy—especially since you're here with me, Lou."

Ma blushed a fiery red. "That sweet talk of yours." She shook her crochet hook at him. "It's all right for you, but here is Wendy. She's on call. What if someone gets sick? I don't want her to have to go out in this. And the sheriff should have been here an hour ago!"

"Oh! I didn't think about that!" Bruno's face lost its glow.

"Don't—," Wendy started to speak.

Out of the crackling static, the radio announcer's voice came in clear. "You won't want to hear this, but more snow tonight. Aren't we lucky? We're going to have the whitest white Christmas in America. And watch out for those powerful gusts—the windchill is subzero! Santa had better wear his long johns!" Then the radio played a rollicking "Here Comes Santa Claus."

A motor sounded outside. Everyone turned toward the back windows; even Lady lifted her head. But night revealed only headlights. *Oh, Lord, let it be Rodd!* The back door opened. The sound of the thrashing wind outside zoomed in volume. "It's me, Harlan!" Rodd slammed the door and stamped the snow off his boots in the back hall.

Wendy recognized the voice and her heart thumped with relief.

Rodd had made it safe and sound. She tried to moderate her reaction to Rodd's arrival, but in vain. *Now it can be Christmas! Thank you, Father!*

"Glad you didn't bother knocking, son!" Harlan called out with a big smile on his face. "We saved you some of my chili and Ma's home-made ice cream and chocolate chip cookies."

"Sounds wonderful! You did say *your* chili, right, Harlan?" Rodd's teasing voice carried through to the living room.

Wendy's joy exploded. How good of Rodd to come in so cheerful. "Hey! It's Christmas Eve," she joked back. "Watch the comments about my cooking or you'll get coal in your stocking!"

"Okay! Okay! I haven't eaten since breakfast. I'm so hungry I'll eat anyone's chili!"

Trying not to show her eagerness to see him, Wendy strolled into the kitchen. "I'll fix a tray for you, and you can join us in the living room. Bruno and I are decorating the tree."

Rodd walked to the sink to wash his hands. "Thanks. I'd appreciate that."

The cold air that had blown in with him couldn't compete with the warmth she now felt having him near. She watched him from the corner of her eye as she dished up a generous serving of the chili still simmering on the stove. Now that he'd safely arrived, she could try to help him put Veda and the investigation behind him for tonight. After the caroling party last evening, she'd fretted and finally decided she would speak to Rodd about Veda's letter. But would she have a chance for a private word with him tonight? Not very likely, with a houseful of people looking on.

Rodd finished drying his hands on a towel. His gaze captured hers and her hands stilled. His eyes told her she was beautiful. Rolling his weight to one side, he leaned his hip against the counter. The pose somehow sharpened her awareness of him. She blushed and turned back to the task at hand. She poured him coffee, added crackers beside the heaping bowl of chili already on the tray.

"Let me carry that for you." Rodd stepped close to her as she turned from the stove.

His nearness shivered through her, sharpening her connection to him. Was it only her concern about him or was it his powerful presence that worked on her emotions? Still, she managed to give a cool reply. "Glad you were able to come." She handed him the rectangular tray.

"Me too. Looks like we're going to have a house party."

"Yes, I'm glad Grandfather decided we should all come prepared to stay the night." How could her voice still sound nonchalant? She glanced up and focused on his eyes. In the dim light, they glowed silver blue.

Rodd nodded for her to precede him. "I took care of my stock earlier in the afternoon. I didn't want to wait until the weather got so bad that I couldn't get to them. They're all safe and snug in the barn. I won't have to check on them again till tomorrow late. I'll probably use my snowmobile to get home."

Just before they entered the living room, he leaned forward and whispered to her, "Thanks for pointing out that Harlan would worry about me if I didn't come to stay over." He raised his voice. "I hope other people think ahead. It would take a load off my mind."

She agreed. That's what she wanted to do, take the load off the sheriff's mind . . . and heart. Now she realized how hard it had been for him to accept this invitation. In light of the dangerous weather, she'd expect that Rodd would want to be out making sure everyone in his county was safely accounted for. Thinking he might refuse Grandfather's invitation, she'd called him earlier that day and put the invitation to him as a favor to her grandfather. It had worked and it was true. Grandfather would have fretted over Rodd's spending the holiday without friends or family.

"I wish this snow would let up," Grandfather said from his place near the fire.

Side by side, Wendy and Rodd walked into the living room, extra warm from the glowing fireplace. Rodd settled on the couch beside Ma, ready to enjoy his supper. As Wendy returned to the tree, she felt the sheriff's gaze follow her, warming her all the way through.

"How are the roads?" Bruno asked.

"Treacherous." Rodd picked up his mug of coffee. "The county has shut everything down. The road crews can't keep up with the drifting. Except for one, I sent all my deputies home. That way they're spread out around the county. If an emergency comes up, the dispatcher will call the nearest deputy."

"Sounds like good thinking." Ma moved the shiny pink crochet hook in and out of the off-white yarn. "But with all the warnings and predictions, most everyone should be smart enough to stay home or inside."

Wendy hoped that included the snowmobile burglar. She didn't worry about her trailer in town being burglarized, but Bruno, Ma, and even Rodd had left their homes unattended. She also didn't want to point out that in her experience, some people didn't have much common sense. This was a night ripe for emergency calls—for both of them. *Please, Lord, no burglaries!*

But now with Rodd sitting on her grandfather's sofa, Wendy was able to let the soothing setting sink in. She began humming along with the carols on the radio. The wind flapped the shutters outside, while Rodd ate two helpings of chili and Ma finished several more rows on the afghan. Harlan dozed in his recliner. Wendy and Bruno continued decorating the tree. She sighed and said a silent prayer of thanks. Tonight, even thinking about Veda's nastiness didn't have its usual power to depress her. What a lovely, peaceful Christmas Eve.

At last the tree was decorated. When the room lamps were switched off, the tree glowed with green, red, and white twinkle lights along with the firelight. Wendy sat down in the rocking chair in the shadows, gazing at her handiwork and Rodd. She'd sensed Rodd's reassuring aura filling the room. How did Rodd have this effect, this way of taking charge in any setting? Did he make everyone feel safe and protected just by being near? Or was it just her fancy?

Outside, the roar of a motor interrupted their peace. Everyone looked toward the windows—though the night and falling snow made it impossible to see out. Lady barked. Rodd rose from the sofa. Leaning forward at the window, he cupped his hands around his eyes, trying to see. "It's a truck."

Wendy got up, folding her arms around herself, feeling a sympathetic chill for the person outside.

Rodd reported, "Someone's getting out."

She started toward the back door.

Rodd reached out and stopped her. "I'll get it. Whoever it is doesn't look too steady on his feet."

She looked into his eyes with an unspoken concern. It might be Uncle Dutch after hours of drinking at Flanagan's. She worried her lower lip.

The sheriff gave her a subtle but reassuring nod, then went to the back door and stood looking out through its high window.

"Who is it?" she asked, keyed up.

"I don't recognize him. That's a good sign." He glanced back at her.

She locked gazes with him, then looked away. His attention only attuned her responsiveness to him more. Who was the intruder? Would the sheriff have to go out? Would she?

At the first knock, Rodd opened the door. "Yes?"

"Wendy, got to talk to Wendy." The man lurched inside. Bitter wind poured through the open door.

Slamming it shut, Rodd reached out and steadied him. "Are you ill? Is someone injured?"

The tall man buried in a fleece-lined jean jacket stared at Rodd and then jerked away. "I need to get . . .Wendy. Juanita . . . will listen to her."

Wendy recognized the man. "Kane," she said as she approached him, "what's happened?"

Kane looked at her as though trying to identify her. "Wendy! You gotta . . . talk to Juanita. She won't let me in. But . . . it's Christmas. Gotta be with my kids."

Rodd questioned Wendy with a lift of his eyebrows. He hovered behind Kane, ready to restrain him.

She responded with a slight movement of her hand, forestalling

Rodd. "Kane." She sighed aloud. "You know she won't let you in if you've been drinking."

"I didn't drink too much—just a few beers."

Why did he even bother with explanations? "Kane, you know you can't handle liquor."

"Wendy—"

She held up both hands to stop him from more useless pleas. "I'll call Juanita if you sit down here and stay calm." Wendy's stern voice worked on the man. She pushed a kitchen chair forward and Kane slumped into it. "Now I'll call, but it will be Juanita's choice if you see them tonight or tomorrow."

Kane stared at her. "Gotta see my kids," he pleaded.

Wendy studied him, then walked to the wall phone and dialed. "Hello, this is Wendy Carey. Kane's here at my grandfather's."

"Keep him there," Juanita snapped. "I told him if he wanted to be—"

Wendy agreed, but why hadn't Juanita told him to spend the night with friends or his family? "I already told him it was your decision whether or not he could see the kids."

"Tell him he can see the kids tomorrow when he's sober." The woman's voice softened. "He shouldn't be out tonight, Wendy." She paused. "Please keep him there. Tell him if he stays there overnight and sobers up, he can come and see the kids as soon as the roads open."

Wendy frowned at Juanita's passing the responsibility to her. But who was she to judge? "Okay, I'll tell him. Are you okay? Do you need anything?" Kane's family lived in a double-wide trailer about a mile away.

"We're fine, and we're staying put till this storm is over. Sorry we had to bother you. I thought he'd go to his mom's. Merry Christmas, Wendy."

"Merry Christmas to you." Wendy hung up. "Kane, Juanita says you can go home in the morning if you stay here tonight and sleep it off."

Kane reared up. "No, Christmas Eve—"

Rodd stepped up to the man, ready to push him back down. "No argument. If you try to go out to drive in your condition, I'll arrest you before you get out of the yard. Now give me your keys."

Kane eyed Rodd as though trying to size him up as an opponent. Kane had come from a rough family and could be unpredictable when he drank.

Wendy inched backward. She'd witnessed slugfests before and knew the best thing she could do was get out of the way so Rodd could handle it. Still, her nerves began to jump. She hated scenes like this. She'd seen too many.

Kane continued to stare at the sheriff, then slowly put his hand in his pocket.

Wendy held her breath, hoping Kane wasn't pulling out a weapon. *Lord, don't let our peace be broken.*

Kane glanced at Wendy. "Don't worry, Wendy. Don't want to hurt anyone." He handed Rodd a ring of keys. Then he put his head in his hands. "I've made a mess of everything." Kane's tone turned maudlin. Now remorse for his drinking would kick in. It was a cycle Wendy had endured with her mother's drinking for most of her childhood. Wendy felt a little sick.

Harlan had come up behind Wendy. "Kane, I have the cot set up downstairs as usual. You know where it is. Turn on the electric blanket. You'll need the extra warmth down there tonight."

Kane began to cry. "Thanks, Harlan." Kane stumbled toward the basement steps, his weeping growing louder.

"Rodd will walk you down, Kane," Harlan ordered in a no-nonsense tone. "You don't look too steady on your feet."

With a quizzical expression, Rodd trailed Kane down the steps. Within a few moments, Rodd returned to the kitchen.

Harlan motioned for Wendy and him to come back to the living room. "Kane rents and farms most of my land and has a trailer on it for his wife and kids. She won't let him in if he comes home after he's been drinking."

"He's not a bad guy. He just can't drink," Wendy explained further.

"Juanita, Kane, and I went to school together. He's really trying to overcome a lot of stuff from his childhood."

Harlan shook his head. "Yes, Kane's come a long way, but he's going to have to give up drinking and go to AA or he may lose everything."

"I take it this has happened before?" Rodd asked.

"Yeah," Ma answered from the sofa. "Harlan takes in a lot of the strays around here. Juanita is expecting again."

Wendy looked up, surprised. "So soon? Their youngest is only six months old."

Ma shrugged. "They're both young and babies happen."

Rodd moved the fire screen and added two logs to the fire. Bruno tossed in a few branches they'd chopped off the base of the tree. As the fire consumed them, it crackled and flared with golden sparks.

Breathing in the fresh pine fragrance, Wendy wondered how Juanita's fourth pregnancy in seven years had slipped by her. She usually knew the medical condition of most of Steadfast. "I'll go over this week and talk to her about getting some help with all those children."

She knew from experience that preventing abuse and neglect usually proved more effective than picking up the broken pieces. Kane and Juanita both had a backlog of childhood abuse, and now faced money problems from farming and Kane's drinking binges—heavy loads to carry.

"I'll be glad to watch her two oldest ones for one afternoon a week, let her take a nap with the baby," Ma offered as she counted stitches in her crochet pattern.

"You have such a generous heart, Lou." Bruno beamed at her.

Ma blushed for the second time that evening.

They all took their places again. The cozy minutes passed with gentle laughter and nutmeg-sprinkled creamy eggnog. Wendy felt the ache of being separated from her mom and sister ebb in the warm setting. She'd called them earlier, afraid the storm might take the phone lines down. Mom had called Sage in from sunbathing!

Now as Wendy studied Rodd, she tried to come up with a way to speak to him privately. But the urgency had lessened. If she didn't get to talk to him tonight, there was tomorrow. Christmas Day—snow-bound with Rodd.

After the ten o'clock TV news with its dire predictions of a blizzard with record-breaking snow and drifting, Ma and Bruno retired upstairs to get ready for bed. Ma and Wendy would share a room while Bruno and Harlan bunked in together. Rodd would sleep on the couch downstairs.

"What a blessing. I have a full house tonight," Harlan joked. "Basement to the rafters."

Wendy kissed his lined cheek, and then pausing on the bottom step, she turned to Rodd. For a long moment, their gazes held. The Christmas tree glow filled the room—the crackling fire, the scent of pine. Wendy gripped the smooth wooden banister to stop herself from going back to him. She longed to rest her head on his hard chest . . . instead, she cleared her throat. "Did I give you enough bedding?"

"Plenty, and I think this couch is going to feel really good when I stretch out." Rodd sounded happier than he had for several days. The evening must have mellowed his spirits too. She was glad.

"Well, good night then." She started up.

"Good night."

His watching her as she climbed the steps made her feel alive, attractive. Her heart fluttered. Before Rodd, she'd been able to block any man out of her mind. But not this man, not Rodd Durand.

Upstairs, while Ma finished in the bathroom, Wendy waited on the bedside rocker in her bedroom. After Ma eased into the high double bed, Wendy lingered in the rocking chair by the window, staring out at the swirling snow under the yard light. The power lines whipped around like jump ropes. She dreaded possible power outages tonight. The sound of the wild wind sharpened all her senses.

Despite her fatigue, the knowledge that Rodd slept downstairs kept her from easy sleep. She tried to analyze what was different about him from the other men she knew. How did he manage to linger in her mind and refuse to be rooted out?

Her goal tonight had been to help him put Veda's nasty letter into perspective. The letter had hit him hard—hard enough to shake his confidence seriously. Cram had irritated Rodd with his jibing editorials, but he hadn't upset Rodd as much as Veda had. Veda had revealed that damaging story from Rodd's past at just the wrong time. His confidence had already taken a beating because of the unsolved burglaries. His joining in the holiday spirit tonight only demonstrated his good heart.

Oh, Lord, help him catch the thief. I've been hoping that the burglaries would just stop. But even if they do, Rodd will always feel like he's been put to the test and failed. That's an awful feeling for a man like him. Help him ride out this storm, and please keep Veda's barbed darts from digging deeper into his flesh. Don't let her have any power to hurt him.

WENDY WOKE WITH a start. She'd fallen asleep in the rocker. What woke her? She glanced out the window and saw Kane getting into his truck. Oh no! Jumping up, she raced silently down the steps to the living room.

Rodd was already at the window. "Blast it," he breathed in a low voice. "He's crazy!"

"He must have had an extra key. He probably woke up and thought he'd slept it off and decided to head home." Wendy hurried to Rodd and peered out the window. "He won't get far. By now the roads will be drifted shut."

"Where's his place?"

"Just east of here. He'll stay on this road until his mailbox; then there's a short access lane to his trailer."

"It's good I didn't undress." Rodd sat down on the couch and started pulling on his boots. "I have to go after him."

She wanted to object but held her peace. Of course Rodd had to go after him. Long before he reached home, Kane would be mired in a snowdrift and stranded; he could die of exposure before morning. The thought sent a shiver through her. "You'll take your snowmobile?"

Rodd nodded, then headed for the back hall. "I've got my stuff here."

Fretting, Wendy followed him and watched him pull on his shiny black-and-white snowmobile gear, including a face mask and helmet. "I should come with you."

"If I need you, I'll call. Stay by the phone."

"Promise?" She caught his eye.

"Promise. And say a prayer for God to protect that fool from himself." As Rodd let himself out, a frigid blast of air burst in.

Her arms folded, Wendy stepped to the back-door window and, on tiptoe, watched Rodd enter the metal machine shed and lift the overhead door. He barreled out on his snowmobile. The snow surged in white veils around him. *Lord, keep Kane and Rodd safe.*

While she waited, she stoked the low fire in the hearth to warm up the chilled living room. Then she stood by the front windows, looking down the lane to the country road in front of her grandfather's house. The snow swirled into higher and higher drifts like ocean waves, as the frenzied storm rampaged over the sleeping landscape. Quivering inside, she paced in front of the window.

The phone rang. She ran to it, lifting it on the second ring, not wanting to wake anyone else.

"Wendy!" Rodd's voice came through heavy static. "Kane wrapped his truck around a telephone pole."

Shock tingled through her. "How bad is he?"

"He's breathing. His nose is pouring out blood. Must be broken. I need you to come and see if I can move him back to Harlan's. I called the ambulance, but they can't get out. The roads are closed till morning."

Her heart pounded. "Where are you?" *Oh, God, please don't let it be anything serious!*

"About a mile down the road east."

"I'll be right there."

"Be careful. I'd come back for you, but I'm afraid he might do something stupid like try to get out of the truck and wander off."

"I'm on my way." Wendy hung up and ran to pull on her navy blue snowmobile suit. She hurried outside. The frigid night tried to suck the warmth from her. Icy snow flung itself at her. The wind buffeted her, trying to sweep her off her feet. She fought her way to her grandfather's large machine shed, rattling metallically in the gale. Inside, she swept off the tarp over her grandfather's machine. She straddled the snowmobile and slid in the key. The motor vroomed to life. She eased it around the pickup and out into the snowy night. Her first time out on the snowmobile this year, she took it easy as she skirted the pasture fence.

She kept her mind focused on the snow under her machine. She didn't want to hit a low spot and kill her engine. Rodd and Kane needed her. Quickly. It took all her concentration to keep the snowmobile on track, following the fence line in the driving storm. Finally, up ahead, she glimpsed Kane's red truck smashed into a pole. She pulled up and cut her engine next to Rodd's snowmobile.

Rodd turned to meet her as she plunged through the knee-deep snow. He motioned her to the open door of the pickup. "He'd have killed himself if the snowdrift hadn't slowed him down!" Rodd shouted above the frenzy of the wind.

Wendy peeled off her insulated gloves and pushed in between Rodd and Kane within the shelter of the open truck door. With Rodd shielding her back with his body, she quickly examined Kane's nose, opened his drowsy eyes, checked his pulse, slipped her hand into his fleece-lined jacket to check his chest for broken ribs, then slid her hands down his frame checking for broken legs and ankles. "Kane!" she shouted. "Can you feel your feet?"

"Yeeaaah."

"Do you think you can walk?" she demanded.

He flapped his head in a sluggish nod. "Need help."

She turned to Rodd and shouted close to his face, "We've got to get him back to my grandfather's! I don't think he has any broken ribs or has injured his spine. He may have internal injuries, but we can't get him to the clinic in this!" She stepped out of the way. "Get him out and onto your machine."

She slogged over to her grandfather's 'bile and uncoiled the length of nylon rope he always kept wound around the seat. She returned to Rodd, who was helping Kane straddle the snowmobile. She motioned Rodd to get on behind Kane; then she looped the rope in a large slipknot under both their arms and cinched it in front, giving Rodd the knotted end. "That should help! Kane, hold on tight! Sheriff, I'll follow you."

"Get on your machine. I won't leave till you're on your way!" Rodd shouted.

"Don't worry!" She climbed through the shifting snow to her seat and piloted the snowmobile around toward home. Her winter gear was holding in her body heat, but the oppressive cold enveloped her, a life-threatening force. Keeping an eye on her patient, she raced off after the sheriff, the snow sliding under and whooshing up behind her like a tail.

She sped through the gray black night. The frigid wind beat against her, nearly stealing her breath away. She huddled behind the shelter of the windshield and breathed in through her nose, warming her air. She clung to the snowmobile as if her life depended on it. Because it did.

CHAPTER FIFTEEN

BACK IN GRANDFATHER'S snug basement, still in their snowmobile suits, Rodd and Wendy laid Kane on the foldaway bed after Rodd had half carried him down the stairs. In spite of her heavy fatigue, Wendy did another, more thorough examination of the half-conscious man, feeling for tender spots, asking him if her touch hurt. She straightened up. "I think he's managed to come through this with only a banged-up face and a couple of cracked ribs."

Rodd dusted off his hands. He'd just added more wood to the basement stove. "The snow slowed him before the impact and he was still drunk—as limp as a rag doll—so he didn't break anything." Rodd shook his head. "The luck of the crazy."

Wendy sighed, gratitude flooding her, making her feel weak. "We can go upstairs. He doesn't show any signs of internal bleeding or even a concussion. Normally we'd take him in anyway. But tonight, going out would be life threatening for all of us. I'll still come down and check him hourly till morning, though."

"How about some coffee then?" Rodd offered. "I'll make it."

She smiled as she led him upstairs. "Did someone tell you about my coffee-making abilities?"

"Only everyone."

"So . . . I'm not made for kitchen work." She felt the heady release from the tension after dealing with an emergency. They both peeled off their snowmobile suits and hung them on the highest hooks in the small rear hall. Rodd filled up the confining space around her, making it difficult for her to take a breath.

In stocking feet, they prowled around the kitchen, Rodd making coffee and Wendy getting out more of Ma's chocolate chip cookies, both of them trying not to wake anyone. And, Wendy noted, both careful not to come too close to each other. Was Rodd fighting attraction just as she was?

Kane's gravelly snores were already wafting up from the basement when Wendy led Rodd into the living room lit only by firelight. He put Grandfather's red Christmas coffee mugs on the table and went to stir up the low fire. He added two more logs, and the orange flames circled them eagerly. Pinesap snapped and crackled in the fire.

Wendy felt a little funny sitting down among the sheets and blankets that Rodd had been sleeping in earlier. It seemed too intimate somehow. But she couldn't say that—it would only expose her sharpened perception of him.

Rodd settled himself beside her and murmured, "I should call in and see if I'm needed."

The solid weight of him dipped the sofa cushions and threatened to send her closer to him. She squirmed, trying to lever herself away. "Wouldn't they call you?" she whispered back.

"Yes, but—"

"But you think you should be there making certain everything is all right?" Gravity won. She let herself slip the few inches to the spot next to him.

He looked at her. "I know it sounds silly. Like I could do anything in a storm like this."

"We just saved Kane Thorpe from dying of exposure. In this blizzard, you couldn't help anyone very far away. We had to follow Grandfather's fence line or we could have gotten lost out there ourselves."

"You're right." Rodd nodded, but reluctantly.

Shadows cast by the flickering fire leaped and danced on the ceiling. The moaning of the blizzard only made the nest of blankets on the couch cozier. Wendy gave in to the delicious moment. She leaned her head back against the soft sofa and propped her feet on the coffee table. Sipping her coffee, she concentrated on its flavor, trying to block her sensitivity to Rodd.

Beside her, Rodd took a long swallow and lifted his stocking feet onto the coffee table too. A sideways glance at him in the firelight revealed that the relaxing moment was having its effect on him. His shoulder rested beside hers. He settled his mug on one thigh.

She decided it was now or never. They were alone, at ease, and could talk without interruption. Putting down her mug, she chose her words with care. "I'm sorry Veda McCracken decided to open up your past. She's the kind of person who collects nasty facts about people and saves them for when she can use them to inflict the most pain. I guess that years ago she read about you and that case in the *Milwaukee Journal*. There're always a few copies at the café every day."

Wendy held her breath, waiting to see if he would open up and talk to her or not. Would he?

* * *

"YES, IT WAS in the paper at the time." Rodd's voice sounded rough even to his own ears. He took another swallow of coffee and looked at Wendy. In the low light, she glowed like some classical portrait of a heavenly being, the golden highlights in her hair like a halo, her fair complexion, the pale ivory of her blouse tucked into snug jeans. So lovely. So innocent. Yet she knew firsthand how Veda McCracken's venom could sting and burn.

He struggled with his reluctance. But he'd kept this inside so long. The regret had become a knot within him that he couldn't untangle. Maybe voicing it could help him loosen it. "I thought I'd put that . . . experience . . . disaster far in the past." He set his mug on the coffee table. "I learned from it."

"What really happened? I can't rely on Veda's account."

He gazed at her, drinking in her sweetness, her natural charm, her honest concern. He leaned back again, letting himself settle close beside her deceptive softness again. A man could trust Wendy with the burden of his soul. "I was just a rookie cop. My partner and I were the first ones on the scene of a home invasion and murder." He fell silent, seeing the scene come up before his eyes. He'd never found a corpse before. It had shaken him, made him uncertain.

He drew in a deep breath. "I had studied the procedure for crime-scene preservation backwards and forwards. If no one's life was in danger and no suspect was present, we were to call for a crime-scene investigator and stand watch to preserve the crime scene as is. I tried to call for backup, but my partner said no, he wanted to look around first." Rodd stared into the flickering orange flames. "I knew that wasn't correct procedure—not in a big-city police department. MPD had specialists trained to examine murder scenes."

Wendy rejoiced at every word he spoke, knowing that his speaking of it could help him release the guilt. "Why did he do that?" she prompted.

He glanced at her, then at the steady fire. "He had been at this house before. It had been a meth lab previously. He thought he knew who the perp was. He went over everything, walking where he shouldn't have, lifting things. He nearly drove me nuts. Finally he let me call for backup and left me to watch the scene while he followed up on the guy he suspected."

"Yes?" She let herself lean even closer to him on the sofa, giving him her silent encouragement.

"When the detective came, I told him what my partner had done. What else could I do?" Rodd's voice hardened. "He asked me and I told the truth. He was really hot, said my partner never learned."

"Your partner got into trouble?"

He nodded. "Yeah, and since the crime scene had been compromised by the delay and by his prowling around, a lawyer who knew his stuff got the case thrown out of court. The perp walked. My partner and I were reprimanded."

She grieved for him and searched for a way to ease his self-reproach. "Maybe they didn't arrest the right man—"

His voice, hard and quick, interrupted her. "The detectives arrested the right guy and the worst part of all . . ." He paused. "Even Veda doesn't know the worst. . . ."

Wendy touched his sleeve, such a soft feminine wisp of a touch. He longed for understanding, for absolution. "The worst was that the suspect my mistake let off, murdered again—a woman and her three children. A SWAT team finally took him out."

The stark words seared Wendy like hot razors. He'd suffered so. *Oh, Rodd, no.* She turned to him and leaned her forehead against his. "Rodd," she whispered, "how awful for you."

"I'm not the one who was killed—"

"But you've carried the guilt . . . for years. Needlessly. You made a mistake. You were just a rookie."

"I still knew my duty and I didn't do it."

She pulled back a few inches and looked into his troubled eyes. "Rodd, we've all have fallen short of the glory of God. You aren't perfect. No one expects you to be. And you shouldn't expect it of yourself."

He shook his head slowly. "Wendy, I can't forget the faces of the people he murdered. Because of my mistake, four lives were lost. A man lost his wife and kids."

She touched his shoulder. "It wasn't your fault alone—"

"Yes it was." He pulled away and stood up. "I can't duck responsibility just because my partner was more experienced. I knew what I was supposed to do. And I should have done it regardless of what my partner said."

Bereft of him, Wendy rose and followed him. How could she help him put this into perspective? She stared into the blue flames deep in the hearth. "Don't you think I know how you feel?" She motioned toward the back hall. "I checked Kane over as well as I could, but I don't know if he has injuries that I couldn't detect. If the roads weren't closed and there wasn't a blizzard outside, I'd take him in for X rays. I'm a nurse, not a doctor.

"I had to weigh the danger of possible undetected injury against more damage or even death to my patient and us—if we tried to get him to town on the snowmobile!"

"That's not the same as my failing to do my job. Maybe God's just bided his time and is punishing me now—"

"No, Rodd! God doesn't work that way! You and I have jobs where we make life-and-death calls. But we're not God, so sometimes we have to live with a wrong choice made in the urgency of the moment. That level of responsibility sometimes threatens to overwhelm me."

Their gazes locked. "But I go on because God called me to this life. I've always felt I was born to be a nurse. That's just part of what I am, who I am. Someone like Veda doesn't understand that. She's too tied up in her petty, nasty little world—"

Rodd suddenly pulled Wendy to him and wrapped himself around her. She twined her arms behind his back, reveling in his warmth, his touch. "I understand, Rodd. I—"

He bent his head and kissed her.

She realized she'd been craving his kiss for a long time. Joy surging with each beat of her heart, she kissed him back, not wanting his touch to end, willing him to go on. His lips moved over hers, strong but not insistent—almost tentative as though she might evaporate. She tugged him closer, wanting to comfort him with her warmth. He responded and his tenderness brought tears to her eyes.

He pulled back and cupped her face in his hands so he could see deep into her eyes. "I didn't have the right—"

"I wanted you to kiss me." She said the truth, plain and simple.

He grinned. "That's my Wendy—straight to the point. I've fought wanting to kiss you for weeks now. I don't know why I waited." He gazed into her eyes as though searching her soul. "I've never known anyone like you."

Her face grew warm. She tried to look away.

But he held her gently and lifted her chin. "You're so good. It sounds funny to say that, but you are good to people, good to be with, good to look at."

Uncomfortable with his praise, she tried to pull away again. "I'm not—"

"You are." He tightened his embrace. "Why can't you see it? Everything about you—your honesty, your caring for others. You're just beautiful." A fierce protectiveness surged inside him; his expression darkened. "I just wish you didn't know how it felt to have Veda McCracken hate you. Why has everyone allowed her to abuse you?"

Wendy released a ragged sigh. "Veda McCracken is a law unto herself."

"She's hurt you—"

She looked away. "Every chance she gets. Some Sundays it has been difficult to pull together enough courage to face her in church."

He rested his cheek on top of her silky hair. "Why didn't you give up?"

"You didn't give up." She pulled him closer, resting her face against his cotton flannel shirt, hearing his heartbeat, rapid like hers. "I decided that I wanted to be near Grandfather and God, and I wasn't going to let that ugly old woman stop me."

He moved his cheek in a nodding motion against her hair. "I guess I better adopt the same attitude."

She pressed her face tighter against his chest. "Don't let her get to you. That's what she wants. Nothing would make her happier than to run you out of your job, out of the county."

"I've never had a case like this before," he began.

She stilled in his arms, then nodded against him.

"I keep thinking that maybe I showed pride when I took this job, this being sheriff—maybe I'm in over my head."

"That's not what your Uncle George believed! I was his home-health nurse for nearly three years, and I heard about your cases every time I visited him. I know you've risked your life over and over and saved countless others—"

He tried to interrupt.

She swept on. "And you should feel pride. Forget Cram. Forget Veda. Focus on your job and God—"

He kissed her again.

She leaned against him as he supported her. She sighed, drawing back. "You make my knees mush."

He chuckled and led her back to the sofa. They snuggled close together.

"I don't want you to violate a confidence, but from what I've heard, Veda did something at the Senior Bazaar, didn't she?"

"I'm not at liberty to say." His hold loosened as though giving her permission to draw away.

"That's okay. I'll hear about it eventually. Steadfast can't keep a secret. As my mom always said, 'Everything comes out in the wash.'" Fatigue hit her. Wendy yawned and tried to smother it. "Your fine-tasting coffee isn't working." She gave him a sheepish grin. "I think it's time I tiptoe down to see how Kane is doing." She got up, even though she longed to linger beside him.

"He's still breathing." Rodd commented on Kane's loud snoring with a wry smile. But his gaze tarried on her.

Rosy from his regard, Wendy smiled back and then slipped out of the room and down the steps. Kane lay just as they had left him. She stood over him, looking for any signs of anything she should be concerned about. But he slept, his chest rising and falling in a normal pattern. *Sweet dreams, Kane.*

With her arms folded against the chill, she walked back upstairs and into the living room. She sat in front of the fire with Rodd's arms around her for long moments, too content to need to speak. When Rodd fell asleep, she smoothly extricated herself, picked up the coffee cups, and took them into the kitchen. Then she gently pushed Rodd's head down onto the pillow and pulled a blanket over him. Across from him, she curled up under an afghan on the recliner. She'd sleep down here. She might not be able to hear Kane from upstairs.

She studied Rodd. He must have been exhausted to fall asleep so quickly. Yawning, she pushed back the chair, bringing up the footrest. *He said I'm beautiful, Lord.* She smiled, remembering the experience of being held so close and with such tenderness. *Thank you. I've always wanted someone special to tell me that. Just once, to hear those words. But you knew that, didn't you?*

❋❋❋

ON CHRISTMAS MORNING, the bright cold sun on the pure white snow dazzled Wendy. She slid on her sunglasses over her face mask and then pulled the helmet over her head. She'd wakened this morning with a joyful spirit, glad to celebrate Christ's birth and to deliver Kane safely home.

"Okay?" Rodd called to her from where he sat on his snowmobile in front of her grandfather's machine shed.

Grinning, she waved her hand, and he started off with Kane behind him on his snowmobile. Wendy followed on her grandfather's machine, swishing over the snow. The wind whistled inside her helmet, filling her ears with a constant hum. They headed to the fence line that would lead them to Kane's trailer.

They swerved in and out around the drifts piled over and under the wooden fence posts. Despite the frigid cold, speeding over the snow exhilarated her. In some places, the county road opened up, but huge drifts several feet high and long blocked other parts of the road. They passed Kane's truck; the antenna and part of the windshield were visible. The rest had been buried by snow. Seeing the aftermath of the storm awed her. Such power unleashed, but God had kept them safe through the night!

Wendy had checked on Kane hourly all night. No sign of concussion or more serious injury had developed. His banged-up face was purple, and his bruised ribs were very sore. He could have been killed driving drunk like that. He'd been very lucky, blessed, even though Rodd fully intended to cite him for drunk driving. Wendy agreed. Kane had to be held accountable if he was ever going to turn his life around.

Farther up the road, they swerved into the lane to Kane's trailer. Ahead, the tan double-wide appeared to be wearing a white shawl of snow. They parked as near as they could to the door. The black metal landing outside the front door had been cleared of snow, and a red snow shovel had been stuck into the drift at one side.

Rodd got off and plowed his way through the knee-high snow and retrieved the shovel. He attacked the snow heaped over the steps to the trailer. Wendy watched, reveling in Rodd's strength and his willingness to serve.

Inside, a dog began barking, and Kane's family appeared at the storm door. The two small children pressed their faces against the glass, while their mother stood behind them, holding an infant. Kane slowly dismounted from the snowmobile and lumbered toward his family. "Merry Christmas, kids!" he called out with a smile.

As the children jumped up and down, Wendy burst into a smile too. Inside, she shouted, *Merry Christmas! Joy to the world! Jesus Christ is born!*

Just as Rodd finished clearing a path to the door for Kane, Wendy's cell phone rang. She lifted her helmet and brought the phone from her belt to her ear.

"Wendy," Old Doc's strident voice asked, "where are you?"

"Merry Christmas to you too, Doc! We just took Kane Thorpe home. What do you need?"

"Old Schultz on Grass Road took a fall trying to shovel a path to his barn. Can you get to him by snowmobile? After his recent heart flare-up, I want him looked at to see if shoveling snow has done more to him than just sprain his ankle."

"Are his nephew and family there for the holiday?" she asked.

"Yes, so if it's nothing serious, you can leave him in their care."

"Great. How are the roads around town?"

"We're still buried. No electricity. No phone. Our emergency generator is keeping us going at the clinic. But it will probably be a few days before the power's on and the county's dug out. They're working on the highway now. We broke all records for snowfall and wind gusts."

"And I'm so delighted to hear that," she teased.

"Okay, smarty, get to Schultz's. Call me and tell me what you find. Merry Christmas. Ho, ho, ho!" Old Doc hung up.

From the trailer doorway, Kane shouted his thanks to Wendy. She waved at the Thorpes and wished them "Merry Christmas!" The beaming family waved back, then shut the door.

Rodd slogged toward her. "Who called?"

She filled him in on her next call.

"I'll come with you!"

She didn't demur. Though the snow had stopped falling and the wind had stilled, bitter cold held them in its icy grip. Today wasn't a day for going out alone. She hoped her patients all remembered that.

Schultz's place lay a few miles to the south past the Kainzes'. She turned her vehicle and headed down the fence line to the county road, with Rodd following. Since Kane was safely home, her mood lightened even more. Snow swished up behind her as the 'bile ate up the miles.

When she crested a rolling hill, she idled her motor and got off. The view of the gentle valley with Hunter's Lake was magnificent—tall evergreens wearing fleecy white coats of snow, the illusion of glinting diamonds scattered over the snowy expanse, the wind-sculptured drifts, the serene blue horizon that yesterday had been shrouded with snow clouds. Her heart sang wordless praise to the Creator.

Rodd halted and dismounted too. "It's something, isn't it?"

Delighted to have him beside her to share this special moment, she turned to him with an eager heart. "I never get over how God can take any circumstance and make it beautiful."

Rodd lifted her chin with his hand. "The landscape is lovely, but you are more—"

Wendy tried to interrupt.

"No, let me say this." He paused, gathering his words. "My past failings and Veda's spite aren't going to bother me anymore. I allowed her to have power over me for something that happened nearly thirteen years ago. You've faced her nastiness your whole life and she hasn't stopped you. I won't let her stop me either. I will face her just like you do and give God the victory."

Thankful he'd found peace, Wendy pressed her gloved hand over his. "I'm glad. Just accept the fact that she will do anything she can to derail your investigation. She wants the Weasel to win because she yearns to see you fail. With God's help, I know you can solve this case."

He leaned close to her face. "I wish you weren't wearing that mask."

She glanced up into his eyes but saw only his helmet, face mask, and sunglasses. "Why?"

"Because I want to kiss you."

Her pulse sped up and a warm glow blossomed inside her. No one had ever said that to her before—not like this. She leaned toward him.

He lifted off his sunglasses, helmet, and face mask, then stopped her from doing the same. With a featherlight touch, he lifted off hers. Then he pressed his cheek to hers and drew her into an embrace.

The chill of the tranquil winter air made the warmth of their meeting sharp and so exquisite that Wendy feared to take a deep breath, afraid she might shatter their connection.

He turned his face; his body-warmed, white breath puffed against her lips. She felt herself blush in spite of the frosty temperature.

"I better make this quick or we'll freeze into an ice sculpture, Frozen Couple by Lake." His mouth swooped down and captured hers.

It was an easy conquest. She forgot everything but the tender touch of his persuasive lips, the experience of being connected to the man she loved. As the thought registered in her mind, shock zinged through her. *I'm in love.*

She pulled away.

He chuckled. "You're right. We've stayed here long enough. And lucky us, we get to go wish Leo Schultz, one of Steadfast's most charming residents, Merry Christmas. What are we waiting for?"

Though she reached to take her gear from his hand, he silently insisted on replacing her mask, glasses, and helmet, and he did so with surpassing care. His tenderness heightened her sensitivity to him. *This is dangerous. I thought I knew what my future was going to be. How does Rodd fit in? Is my life about to change forever?*

Then he returned to his snowmobile and started off slowly, letting her catch up to him. The glittering white landscape broadened out into pastures, so Wendy came abreast of him. The snow sprayed up behind them in a white wake as they sped toward Schultz's property. Hearing their two motors surging and buzzing together gave her a new feeling of freedom, of joy. The moment was too precious to be analyzed. She gave herself up to the experience.

Soon they pulled up in front of Schultz's farmhouse, back to reality, to their duty. Wendy and Rodd dismounted and headed for the door. A path had been dug through a drift that had previously blocked the rear entrance. Rodd called out his name and Wendy's and opened the unlocked door. Today wasn't a day for formalities.

Inside, Schultz sat at the kitchen table, looking grumpier than usual. His nephew and wife stood nearby, obviously concerned. "Good morning," Wendy greeted everyone after pulling off her helmet, sunglasses, face mask, and gloves. "Doc called and said I should check you out—"

"I just took a fall. Why is everyone making a federal case out of a sprained ankle?" the old man blustered.

Wendy only smiled. She pulled off her backpack of medical supplies and set it on the table. Quickly she checked the older man's pulse and blood pressure, listened to his heart, and took his temperature.

"It's my ankle that's paining me!" he complained.

Wendy chuckled. "I'm ready to look at that now." When she knelt down, Rodd's phone rang. He was standing in the doorway of the kitchen.

"Durand here," he answered.

As Wendy gently examined her patient's ankle, she hoped Rodd's call wasn't anything serious. Though she didn't want to, she kept glancing over her shoulder, keeping an eye on his reaction to the call. Rodd put the phone back on his belt and she stood up. "Do you have to be somewhere?" she asked him.

"No, just dispatch calling. Two of my deputies borrowed snowmobiles and are checking the main county roads for stranded vehicles. So far everything looks good except that the road crews are making such slow progress."

"Good."

After Wendy finished her examination, she stepped into the adjacent dining-room doorway and called Doc to report Schultz's vitals. While she talked quietly on the cell phone, she watched and tried to listen to the exchange in the kitchen.

"So old Veda got you between her crosshairs?" Schultz growled at Rodd.

Wendy held her breath. Would Schultz undo all her work?

Rodd eyed the man. "You mean that letter?"

"Yeah, you gonna let that old battle-ax get under your skin?" The man glared at Rodd while his nephew and wife looked ill at ease.

Rodd cocked his head to one side. "I've dealt with the mob. One sour old woman's not going to bother me."

Schultz let out a bark of laughter. "Good for you."

Wendy rejoiced in silence.

"Is Uncle going to be all right?" the nephew asked her.

Stepping back in the kitchen, Wendy nodded. "Doc said your uncle should be fine. Just apply cold to the ankle for these first twenty-four hours, then the next twenty-four alternate between cold and moist heat."

"Thanks for coming out." Schultz's nephew shook her hand. "I didn't want to take any chances. He snuck out while I was in the shower. Then he looked so red in the face from shoveling. We were worried."

Wendy pointed her finger at Schultz and shook it. "No more shoveling."

Schultz rumbled at her, "How could I shovel? I can't even walk!"

"Good. Take your medicine as usual and you should be fine." She bid the family a "Merry Christmas," and she and Rodd left.

Outside in the crisp brilliant sunshine again, Wendy straddled her snowmobile, started it, and followed Rodd down the lane. The miles back to her grandfather's house flew by. In spite of sparse sleep the night before, she was refreshed by the beauty of the sparkling morning.

Over and over, the sensation of Rodd's lips on hers warmed her from head to toe. She'd let him kiss her twice now. And she had kissed him back. Had she really fallen in love with him? Her decision to remain single must have changed, but . . . she felt strange, new, not like herself at all. She wanted to dance, to sing, to roll in the snow and shout with laughter! She couldn't regret the kisses. *Lord, what's happening to me, to us?*

RODD AND WENDY arrived back at Harlan's house in time to wash up with water from the kettle on the stove and sit down to Christmas dinner. Sometime early in the morning Harlan's electricity had gone out. With Wendy beside him, Rodd sat down to an improvised feast of steaks pulled out of the freezer and broiled on the propane grill on the back porch, salad, cloverleaf rolls and pumpkin pie, which Wendy had baked yesterday. During the meal, Rodd thought over what he and Wendy had shared last night and this morning.

Snapshots of Wendy kept popping into his mind—her singing carols beside him, her concern for Ma the very first day they'd met, her walking bravely into Flanagan's to deliver Thanksgiving dinner. He'd been very attracted to other women he'd dated, but those women had been so very different from Wendy. None had ranked as high as she in his regard. He'd given up thinking about marriage years ago. He'd told himself he just wasn't the marrying kind.

After last night, he realized that his guilt over the botched crime scene years ago and the subsequent deaths of that woman and her children had stopped him from feeling free to love anyone. What right did he have to a wife or a family when he had caused another man to lose his? But Wendy's perception and genuine understanding last night had finally closed that old wound. And Wendy was too special to become involved with unless this was serious. But if he were to fall in love with Wendy . . .

Later that afternoon, Rodd rose from the sofa and stretched. "I hate to leave, but I have to go home and check on my cattle."

"I thought you'd want to see to them," Harlan said from his

recliner by the fire. "We'll expect you to come back, though. We haven't opened our gifts yet."

Rodd knew better than to try to excuse himself from the holiday. He could tell that Harlan wouldn't take no for an answer. And until the electricity came back on, they'd need him to carry in wood for the fireplace and woodstove downstairs and to carry up water from the hand pump. Besides, Wendy was here—and he wanted to be anywhere she was. "Okay." His phone rang. He pulled it from his belt, expecting it to be one of his deputies. "Durand here."

"Hi! It's Zak! I like my gift! It's cool!"

Rodd grinned. "You like it, huh?"

"Yeah, it's great! My dad helped me drive the car around the living room!"

Pastor Bruce's voice came on the line. "Hi, Rodd. Thanks for the remote-control car. Zak's been busy ramming furniture with it all day!"

Rodd chuckled. "Sorry."

"No problem. These cell phones are great, aren't they?"

"Right."

"Won't keep you. Here, Zak, wish the sheriff a Merry Christmas."

Zak's exuberant voice shrilled, "Merry Christmas, Sheriff! Jesus loves you and I do too!"

Rodd couldn't stop the grin that spread over his face. "The same to you, Zak!" He glanced at Wendy as he replaced his phone in his belt. His heart swelled at the sight of her. He'd never experienced such a pull toward a woman. The thought—though brand-new—wasn't unwelcome. *What is this, Lord? Is this how love that leads to marriage begins?*

About a half hour later, Rodd, followed by Wendy, snowmobiled up the fence line to his house. The sun sat low on the horizon. He'd check his cattle's water supply and feed; then they'd head back to Harlan's. Spending the holiday with friends and, more importantly, with Wendy, exerted an irresistible attraction on him. He admitted to himself that spending the rest of Christmas alone at home was unthinkable—especially after last night. Would he and Wendy have time alone tonight? He needed to talk to her, to investigate this new relationship they'd begun.

His lane was drifted over in spots. With Wendy close behind him, he navigated around the drifts until he stopped in a windswept area right in front of his barn. He slid off his machine and started toward the barn entrance.

Wendy's agitated shout stopped him.

He turned toward her. She was pointing toward his house. Looking over, he froze.

His back door had been smashed in.

CHAPTER SIXTEEN

AFTER DOING A cursory survey of the damage done to his door, Rodd went in search of Wendy. The blinding outrage that had burned through him hadn't lasted but a few moments. Rodd's unspoken hope had been that the thief would become overconfident and do something foolish. Cockiness like this always led to exposure. Pride goeth before a fall. The Weasel had made a fatal mistake. He'd catch the thief now—and soon. The Weasel had made it personal.

Rodd found Wendy in the barn at the hand pump, filling the water trough for his breeding cows. The barn, snug and lit by the fading sun, welcomed him. As he walked in, his attraction to Wendy drew him straight to her. The desire to coax her close and kiss her flowed through him like a vibrant current. Even in this rough setting, her natural beauty shone bright.

He wasn't surprised to see her busy. Her talent for recognizing practical needs and meeting them only revealed more of her caring personality. *Lord, she's so special. All I can think is, am I worthy of her?*

"You didn't need to do this, Wendy." *I need to take you home to your grandfather's and come back here alone. Please don't misunderstand.*

"Your cattle needed water. In the past when I came out to check on your uncle, I often helped him with this." She wouldn't meet his eyes as she went on pumping.

The squeakiness of the old pump grated on his nerves. Wendy shouldn't be doing his chores. And he needed to begin his investigation, and he couldn't involve Wendy now. This was his break. The Weasel may have left him something this time. Of course, she'd want to help. It was her nature. But he had to focus on the case.

And the only way he could do that was alone. After last night and this morning, Wendy had the power to distract him and he couldn't allow that.

"I need to take you back to your grandfather's." He drew off his insulated gloves. Would she understand? "I have to stay here and go over the crime scene."

⁂

WHEN WENDY HAD seen the broken-in door, she'd half expected Rodd to shut down again. She'd just gotten him to open up, to put Veda's attack and his past mistake into perspective, and now this! *Lord, I don't know why this is happening. How could this be? Why did the Weasel do something this brazen?*

With one glance at Rodd's shuttered expression, she repeated her thought aloud. "Why would the Weasel hit your house? It doesn't make any sense."

He frowned at her, then rested his ungloved hand on hers.

She had stopped pumping, but stood with her hand on the curved handle. His touch reassured her. What had passed between them in the past twenty-four hours had been real to him too. "Did you have much money around the house?"

"No. But this wasn't about money."

"What is it about then?" She combed her flattened hair with the fingers of her free hand, trying not to look so bedraggled for him.

He hesitated and then touched her cheek. She came into his arms as naturally as if they'd embraced every day of their lives. "What does this move mean? Why would the burglar take such a chance?"

Rodd held her tight against him, resting his chin on the top of her head.

She drew strength from his wanting her close to him. But would he let her be his sounding board?

Rodd inhaled deeply. "Unless he's totally stupid, it's a slap in my face. He's laughing at me because I haven't been able to catch him yet." His voice had dropped to a lower pitch.

"Then he's a fool." She lifted her face and stared into his eyes, letting her affection for him show in her expression, her voice. "He's a fool if he thinks you won't catch him."

His reply came in a swift kiss, one that left her nearly breathless. She remained in his arms, standing quietly, listening to the lulling sound of the cows' soft lowing.

"What will you do?" she asked, resting her cheek against his slick snowmobile suit, hearing his heart beating under her ear—wishing she were bold enough to initiate another kiss.

"I'm going to secure the crime scene; then I'll take you home. I'm going to get one of my deputies to come on his snowmobile to help me go over the crime scene. I don't want to miss anything. Then I'll be back at Harlan's for the night."

She nodded. "There's something else you need to do."

"What?"

"Ask God for his help."

"I—"

"Rodd, why do you keep resisting God? You remind me of Paul on his way to Damascus—Christ asked him, 'Why are you persecuting me?' and told him, 'It's hard for you to fight against my will.' I think God's trying to get your attention. Why don't you let him help you?"

Rodd gazed at her, thinking. "Maybe you're right."

She heard a softening in his tone and prayed that God would open Rodd's eyes—if she were right. *Lord, is that what you wanted me to say? Please let me help Rodd.*

They worked side by side feeding and watering the stock, then went out to their snowmobiles.

As Wendy pulled on her helmet, the impression that this break-in "felt" like something Uncle Dutch might do troubled her for a moment.

But she discounted it. The sheriff had done nothing that had irritated her uncle.

Next Veda came to mind, but Wendy dismissed her too. Veda was a physically strong and very vindictive person whose spirit was quite capable of this, but Wendy couldn't see her tackling such a long snowmobile ride in a blizzard. But then the break-in could have taken place early on Christmas Eve before the weather had deteriorated. Which left the field of suspects, including Elroy Dietz, still wide open.

THE NEXT MORNING, Rodd unlocked his front door and stepped inside. Fortunately, the downed power line hadn't serviced his house, so it was chilly but not icy, and he wouldn't have to deal with broken water pipes. But the fact that his home had been invaded gave him the sensation that he was stepping into alien territory. Home didn't feel like home. To alleviate the silence that threatened to deafen him, with his gloved hand he snapped on the radio in his kitchen.

The voice of the weatherman broke the stillness: "The morning after Christmas Day has dawned bright and—you won't believe it—warmer! The cold blast that had barreled down from Canada for Christmas Eve and Day has retreated north. Let's hope the Canucks will be able to handle it!

"Northern Wisconsin, as well as Minnesota and Upper Peninsula Michigan, is going to receive a break in this year's record-breaking winter. In the next few days, the weather should moderate—highs in the twenties. But don't get used to it. This is just a short vacation from frigid temperatures. Spring *isn't* just around the corner."

The weather report ended and was followed by an advertisement by the county funeral home. Rodd blocked out the words but kept the station on for company. He carefully took off his gloves and winter gear and put them in the hall closet, which hadn't been touched during the break-in. He and his deputy had been all over his house last night, but he wanted to go over it once more.

He'd read so much about the emotions that victims of home invasion experience. Now he was having to deal with those emotions himself *and* proceed with his investigation. His one hope was that the Weasel had had one moment of carelessness.

Motivated by this, he began again by examining the scene as a whole. The Weasel had touched and disturbed very little. He'd been in a hurry. Rodd's hope that the perp had made a mistake dimmed.

Two hours later, Rodd had discovered nothing new in the way of evidence. And the thief hadn't gotten much either—just a few bills and change that Rodd had left on his bedroom dresser. But he'd sent Rodd a message loud and clear—he thought the sheriff couldn't catch him.

Anger roiled inside Rodd. Anger at the Weasel. Anger at himself. If only the stakeout at Olson's hadn't turned into a slapstick comedy. . . . If only he'd seen that the kegger was a smoke screen. . . . If only he'd stayed at the VFW instead of running to the explosion. . . . If only . . . he stopped. That line of thinking never took anyone anywhere useful, according to Uncle George.

Wendy came to mind. He'd call her soon. He wanted to hear her soft voice.

The phone rang. He walked back into the kitchen and picked up the receiver. "Durand here."

"Hey, Sheriff, back home, I see." The voice had some quality of familiarity to it, but it was slurred and muffled.

"Who is this?"

"Well, that's the question, isn't it? Who am I?"

The hair on the sheriff's neck prickled. "What do you want?"

"I want to help you, since you don't seem to be able to figure out who the Snowmobile Burglar is."

"Who is this?"

A chuckle. "Check out the snowmobiles. You might find something interesting."

"Whose snowmobiles?"

"You know whose." The line clicked and the dial tone buzzed in Rodd's ear.

CHAPTER SEVENTEEN

UNDER THE LONG fluorescent lights, the Steadfast Community Church basement was crowded and noisy with village residents of all ages for its third annual New Year's Eve Carnival and Auction. Wendy glanced at the door from her job at the "fishing hole," where children flung fishing lines over a primitive painting of a bright turquoise, very "fishy" ocean to "catch" prizes. Bruno sat behind the ocean and tied the prizes onto the lines.

Wendy tried to keep herself on an even keel, but something didn't feel right tonight. An hour ago, Veda had swaggered into the carnival and, with her back to a wall, sat watching the activities.

Wendy knew it was fanciful, but the old woman looked like an outlaw from an old Western movie—she looked as if she were waiting for the sheriff to come for the showdown. Why had Veda come? Even though she never missed a Sunday morning service, she never attended any social function at the church. But how could one guess her twisted motive and prepare to meet it?

Was Veda here to confront the sheriff? Had someone told Veda of Wendy's deepening relationship with Rodd? But who would know, apart from Grandfather, Bruno, and Ma? And what was her relationship with Rodd, anyway?

Though he'd called her every day since Christmas, he had been busy with his investigation, and she'd been working overtime at the clinic in addition to her home visits. Flu season had descended.

"Look what I caught!" Zak waved a coloring book in her face, catching her attention.

Wendy smiled, peering down at him. "Oh, dinosaurs to color."

"Why isn't the sheriff here?" the little boy asked. "Why didn't you bring him?"

She wondered at Zak's assumption that she could make Rodd Durand do anything. The innocence of children! "He's going to come when he can, Zak. He's working. Being sheriff takes a lot of time."

She glanced at the clock above the kitchen's open Dutch door again. A few more hours until the new year came—and Rodd would be off duty. Would he be able to stop here before midnight? Would he kiss her like they did in the movies on New Year's Eve? The thought made Wendy's stomach turn to jelly.

She couldn't decide whether that was because thinking about another kiss from Rodd took her breath away—or because then everyone would know that they had become more than friends. How much more than friends were they? A tremor shivered through her. What made her think she—a Rieker—could become involved with a man like Rodd?

No doubt Veda would use it as a perfect opportunity to rake up every sin a Rieker had committed over the past two generations. Worse, Veda could use Wendy's family's reputation to castigate Rodd. Veda could make Rodd feel that he was letting his family down by having anything to do with a Rieker, or worse yet, make it sound like Dutch was the thief and Rodd was shielding him because of Rodd's feelings for Wendy. Wendy wouldn't put anything past that sour old woman!

Penny called out, "Time for children's games to end. Let's go, kids, to the Sunday school classrooms for the slumber party!"

Zak sped off. Other preschoolers and the school-aged children waved good-bye to their parents as they trooped to their separate rooms to watch videos and eat their snacks. Each had brought a sleeping bag and would spend the night under the watchful eyes of a few stalwart grandmothers and some young teens. Now the adult portion of the evening would begin.

Penny had just received her first two foster children, a Native American brother and sister whose Chippewa parents were having marital problems that had led to an abusive custody battle. The kids held on to Penny as if she were their lifeline. Penny, who looked happier than she had in weeks, waved at Wendy as she led them into the school-aged room where she would stay with them.

"Let's close up, partner!" Bruno stood up from his hiding place with a grin. Wendy and Bruno gathered fishing poles, folded up their "ocean," and propped it against the wall. Around the room, the other games, including the cakewalk and pin-the-tail-on-the donkey, were disassembled. Then several men moved the tables and chairs so that everyone could sit comfortably during the auction. Wendy ended up sitting at a table with Grandfather, Bruno, Ma, and Patsy Kainz.

This was the first time Patsy had come to the church. Since Wendy had invited Patsy for the past three years, she was delighted to see her here tonight. Now the plump, white-haired woman leaned over to Wendy's ear and asked, "Did you call to see if Sage's flight would be getting in on time?"

"Yes." Wendy smiled. Everyone in town knew that Sage was flying in tonight. Since the roads had finally been cleared and Harlan and Wendy had volunteered to work at the carnival, Trav had gone by himself to pick her up. "It arrived in Minneapolis on time."

Patsy nodded.

Ma leaned over and whispered into Wendy's other ear, "What gives with Veda showing up?"

Even though concerned herself, Wendy could only shrug and hope Ma didn't feel a need to confront Veda tonight. That would be a battle of the titans! *Lord, you are here with us, I know that. And you know what Veda's got up her sleeve. Please confound her intentions if they are wicked, but also open our eyes if this is a change for the better.*

"We're so happy that so many of you have turned out to this evening's fund-raiser," Pastor Bruce, standing at the front of the room, began. "As you all know, Old Doc Erickson is well past the age of retirement. His founding a clinic here and continuing to work in Steadfast is an invaluable service to our county. But in order to bring in another doctor to take up practice here, we've gone the route of other rural areas in supporting a medical student who will in turn practice here for the first ten years of his or her career. All the proceeds of tonight's auction will go to the tuition fund—just as the funds raised at the Senior Bazaar did."

A nervous rustle went through the audience—some people looking at Veda and some pointedly looking away. Wendy's uneasiness grew. She still hadn't been told what Veda had done at the bazaar. She tried never to participate in gossip, but this time, she'd had to restrain her curiosity.

Whatever Veda had done must have been bad because none of the women who had been involved in the Senior Bazaar would speak to her—not even Miss Frantz! Miss Frantz, who had lived across from Wendy all her life and had spied on her and helped Veda wound Wendy's mom many times by broadcasting gossip about Doreen. Their estrangement had begun a thread of gossip all its own. A few people had even called Wendy to find out what had caused Miss Frantz's turnaround. Wendy hadn't known what to think. What could Veda have done to cause such a seismic change?

Pastor Bruce picked up a wooden gavel. "Now some counties have people rich in wealth. But here in Steadfast we are rich in willingness to help each other and to use this to benefit the community. Over the past two months, residents all around the county—many who are here tonight and some who weren't able to attend—have offered various skills and services to be auctioned off tonight to the highest bidders. Doc is over at the Conlon VFW hall at another auction like this one, and Dr. Doug is on duty at the clinic. Otherwise, they'd be here."

The basement door burst open and Wendy looked back—would it be Rodd or Sage and Trav? It was none of them. To her surprise, most of the men whom they had caroled to at Patsy and Carl's trooped inside. "Hey, Reverend!" Olie Olson called out. "Did we miss anything?"

"Not a thing!" Pastor Bruce beamed at them. "Make yourselves comfortable—and I hope your wallets are full!"

The men hooted at this and found places around the tables where they were welcomed. Wendy's heart warmed and she felt the tug to cry. *Oh, Lord, soften their hearts so that they may see your love in action here and begin to respond to you. Even though they would deny it, I know they want to believe that you love them and shed your blood for them!*

Wearing a smile, the pastor resumed, "The winning sums are essentially pledges, with one-twelfth of each pledge due each month to our new church secretary, Miss Mabel Frantz. Now with all the preliminaries taken care of, our first service to be auctioned is from Ma, soon to be Mrs. Bruno Havlecek." The pastor waited for the well-meaning teasing and cooing this occasioned to die down, then continued. "Ma will bake some fortunate soul a pie of his or her choice every month of this coming year. Now what will you bid for this culinary bonanza?"

The bidding started at ten dollars and ended up at fifty-two, bid by Olie Olson. The next service was for free driveway plowing for the rest of the winter and the beginning of the next winter by Harry, the auto repairman. Again bidding went fast, and the final bid came in at one hundred and sixty dollars. Before moving to the next bid, the pastor said, "I'd like to take this opportunity to thank Harry publicly for plowing out the church parking lot for free this winter."

Harry waved the pastor to stop. "My privilege."

Pastor Bruce smiled and moved on. Several more offers of service passed under the minister's gavel. Harlan kept announcing the total money. The figure mounted to just under seven hundred dollars. "Now our next service is a year of two days a month of housecleaning by Mrs. Benser."

As the pastor continued, the basement door opened, and Sage and Trav walked in. Wendy popped up and ran to the back of the room. Sage opened her arms and Wendy hugged her tightly. Missing Sage had been just under the surface throughout Christmas. Now Wendy could only hold Sage close and press back the tears.

Harlan came up behind her and put his arms around both granddaughters. "Welcome home, Sage," Grandfather rumbled close to Wendy's ear. "How is your mother?"

Sage pulled away from Wendy and kissed his cheek. "Mom's great, Gramps. She sends her love."

Harlan offered Trav, standing a little behind Sage, his hand. "Thanks for bringing her home safe, son."

Trav shook Harlan's hand but said nothing.

Wendy became aware of an undercurrent of emotion in Trav. He seemed anxious, jumpy—dark. Had Sage told him something about their mother that Sage didn't want to say in front of Grandfather? Sage glanced at Trav and looked worried about him. Mulling this over, Wendy led them to the table where she and Grandfather had been sitting. Sage took Trav's hand in hers as though he needed her support. Concern creased Wendy's forehead. What was wrong?

The bidding for the year of housecleaning was lively and reaching its end. Wendy looked to their pastor, who was doing a fine job of auctioneering. She knew how much the money would mean to Doc and Dr. Doug.

Clyde Sparrow raised his hand. "Two hundred and fifty dollars!"

Veda spoke up for the first time. "And five dollars."

There was a momentary pause, and then Clyde countered, "Two hundred and sixty!"

"And five," Veda added.

"Two hundred and seventy."

"And five!" Veda grinned for the first time that evening.

Hostile murmuring rustled through the gathering. Clyde looked disgusted.

Wendy didn't blame him. He'd worked up the price and stayed with it until his competitors had dropped out. Now Veda, who hadn't bid earlier, was pushing the price up higher. Was that her game? Did she want to gouge Clyde? Why?

"Three hundred!" Clyde declared and glared at Veda.

"And five!" Veda crowed.

Silence, an uneasy one, fell over everyone. Something beyond the simple bidding was going on. Wendy folded her hands tightly in her lap so she didn't forget and bite her nails. *Lord, whatever her evil intent is, confound it!*

"Well, anybody going to bid against me?" Veda demanded, glee in her voice.

"Would it do any good?" Clyde continued to glare at her.

"No." Veda looked smug.

"Well, I have something to say—"

Everyone turned to eye Mrs. Benser, who had stood up and was visibly bristling. "Veda McCracken, I wouldn't clean for you—"

Pastor Bruce held up both hands. "Please—"

"I'm sorry, Pastor." Mrs. Benser drew herself up. "But I've kept my peace for over fifty years about Veda McCracken's nastiness, and I won't put up with it anymore!"

A bewildered hush fell over the room. The pastor tried to remonstrate with the woman but was ignored.

Wendy's heart turned over; her stomach knotted. Kind Mrs. Benser had been one of her first Sunday school teachers. *Oh no, Lord, don't let evil in.*

In the silent room filled with tense waiting, Mrs. Benser declared, "If I thought all you wanted, Veda, was to help out the clinic fund and have your house cleaned twice a month, I'd keep my mouth shut. But we both know—we all know—that you're doing this out of spite. You found out I was the one who exposed you as the thief."

Veda sprang up onto her feet. "That's a lie!"

People gasped. Pastor Bruce tried to speak.

Ignoring everyone, Mrs. Benser pressed on. "And I know just what kind of mess I'd find at your house to clean up! You have never had a kind thought or done something good once in your whole life! And I'll withdraw my offer before I'll let it go to you." Mrs. Benser's face flushed pink. "You're here doing what comes natural to you—being nasty! You gave yourself over to the devil from the time we were children together. And I for one won't stand for it another minute!"

Spontaneous applause burst over the room.

Pastor Bruce pounded his gavel, but in vain. People stood up and began to berate Veda for past grievances with her. Veda turned red in the face, but she returned fire—blasting long-dead relatives of those who dared confront her and shredding the reputations of the living.

Wendy thought she might be sick. How could evil take over this generous and giving evening and poison it? Trembling, she stood up and shouted, "Stop! Stop it!"

Silence. All eyes turned to her.

"This isn't right. It isn't right." Wendy trembled. "We came here to help get a new doctor, not rip each other apart."

"But, Wendy, she's been mean to you your whole life!" Olie put in.

Wendy faced Veda. "Yes, but I won't hate her. She hasn't won. I don't hate her."

"What's going on here?" Rodd's harsh voice boomed throughout the church basement. Everyone swiveled around. Scanning the gathering sternly, Rodd stood just inside the large room.

"Well, if it isn't our esteemed sheriff!" Veda sneered. "Have you arrested the Snowmobile Burglar yet?"

Rodd made his way toward Wendy. People moved to let him through. "I will when the time is right. The investigation is proceeding."

"Ha!" On that jeering note, Veda grabbed her coat and stalked out of the church.

"Good riddance," Patsy muttered, giving voice to the mood in the room.

Reaching for her, Rodd gripped Wendy's shoulder. "I'm thirsty. Will you help me get something to drink?" He offered her his hand.

Needing to get away, Wendy nodded and led him to the church kitchen. As they left the room, Pastor Bruce quietly awarded Mrs. Benser's housecleaning to Clyde for two hundred and fifty dollars and began the bidding on Trav's offer to cut someone's grass for the coming summer.

Her emotions still in turmoil, Wendy concentrated on pouring Rodd a cup of cinnamon-fragrant spiced cider and cutting him a piece of pumpkin pie. She kept her eyes forward. "Do you want whipped topping?"

Coming up behind Wendy, he took the spoon from her hand and put it back in the open whipped-topping container. "What was that woman doing here?"

Wendy wouldn't meet his eyes. "She was just being Veda."

Turning her toward him, he lifted her chin. "What did she do? Did she hurt you?"

Quivering at his touch, she inhaled deeply to calm her shaking nerves. "She tried to get back at Mrs. Benser."

"I take it that it didn't work." He pulled gently on her hands, tugging her into his arms.

"Rodd, we're at church," she objected, but she didn't pull away from his solid warmth.

"Is that all Veda did, try to intimidate Mrs. Benser? She didn't say anything directly to you, did she?"

His concern filled her with sunshine. She smiled and dipped her chin. "I'm fine."

He started to question her but stopped himself. "I've missed you." Parting her bangs, he kissed her forehead.

She blushed. "Someone might walk in," she whispered.

He shook his head. "Veda left. No one else would be so unkind."

Wendy looked up at him. "Veda didn't bother you with that remark about your investigation, did she?"

A smile lit his eyes. "I bothered her today."

"You did? How?"

He kissed her nose.

At his soft touch, she had trouble paying attention.

He ignored her question. "My deputies are all out. I just checked all the trouble spots, and I think I can see the new year in with you. Let's not spoil what's left of the evening discussing Veda McCracken."

Forcing herself to put Veda's unpleasantness behind her, she smiled. "I'm glad." She wanted to ask him not to show everyone that their relationship had changed over Christmas, but she couldn't do that. He'd kissed her and taken her into his confidence about the past. But what did that mean to him, to her? Was she ready to make a change in the single life she'd planned? Or had the change already taken place and was she just realizing it? She let out a deep sigh. "We'd better go back in before someone comes to get us."

"If you insist." He kissed her cheek and then picked up his pie and cider.

With a silly grin she couldn't wipe off her face, she led him back to the table where she'd been sitting. Her grin withered as she felt the unspoken attention of everyone as she and Rodd sat down together. What would everyone think?

Then she noticed that Bruno and Ma were holding hands as they watched the auction move toward the midnight celebration. Smiling inside, she glanced at her sister and Trav, who were also holding hands.

As she observed the young couple, Trav sent a resentful glare to Rodd. The look was so unexpected and out of character that she couldn't look away. Trav never got upset. In fact, his gentle nature was one of his most endearing traits. Was it just the sheriff or was Trav upset in general? She studied her sister's boyfriend from under her lashes. No, the signs were unmistakable. Trav fidgeted and couldn't keep himself from sending heated glances toward the sheriff. *Lord, what's wrong? It's just one thing after another. Please calm Trav. Bring us healing here tonight.*

⁂

SIPPING HIS CIDER and letting it warm him inside, Rodd scanned the lively excitement of bidders, a complete contrast to his last few tense days—since the anonymous phone call. The caller ID at his home had given him the phone number, but it had led him to a dead end, a pay phone at the truck stop just across the county line. Of course, after a day crowded and busy with stranded truckers and travelers, no one there had any information to give him.

What had the caller meant about checking the snowmobiles? Rodd had scrutinized the machines belonging to the three main suspects—Elroy, Dutch, and Veda—and many more besides. Then he started calling people in for questioning. Nothing. He'd delayed doing any formal questioning before now, preferring to ask questions in passing. But he'd decided leaning on people might shake things up, bring something to light.

It hadn't. He was no further ahead tonight than he'd been before the anonymous phone call. The caller's voice had sounded like a man, but some women, including Veda, had deep voices. And the caller had taken care to disguise and muffle his voice.

A break. One little break was all Rodd needed to catch the thief. His only hope remained that the anonymous caller had been the Weasel himself and that he would become increasingly overconfident and give himself away. Galling as that was, it was all he could hope for now. Rodd glanced around the room, then at his watch. Ten minutes to the new year.

Pastor Bruce turned to Harlan. "How are we doing?"

"Almost one thousand dollars!" Harlan beamed.

"Then let's see how close we can get to twelve hundred by midnight." The pastor's words were greeted with shouts of encouragement.

Pastor Bruce went on. "Our next item is free baby-sitting, not to exceed ten hours a month, for a year from the lovely Carey sisters, Wendy and Sage. Who will open the bidding?"

Rodd sipped the sweet cider and wished he'd had time to take Wendy out this week. But their schedules hadn't coincided in the days after Christmas. Still, she'd popped into his thoughts at will. He'd never thought that in moving back to Steadfast he'd fall in love. Had he found in Wendy his wife? Only time would tell. He glanced at his watch again; the final minutes of this year were ticking away.

Two mothers refused to give up competing for the prize. They bid fast and furiously until one dropped out at seventy-eight dollars. "That's a bargain. Ladies, are the rest of you going to let this go for this price?" Pastor scanned the audience. "Going once, twice, sold!"

"It's New Year's!" Patsy called out.

Shouts of "Happy New Year" broke out all over the room. People stood up and hugged each other. "Auld Lang Syne" was sung. Rodd took Wendy's hand and pulled her close. "Happy New Year, Wendy."

She smiled up at him, filled with such joy. "I wish you the very best in the coming year."

"The same to you." And then he kissed her.

Wendy knew she should pull away, but she found it impossible to do. She clung to him, welcoming the feeling of being wanted by such a fine man. Rodd ended their kiss but kept her tucked close at his side. Wendy felt like she was floating. *Lord, I never felt this way before! Is it possible? Do you have a different plan for my future than I do?*

A storm in her eyes, Sage came around the table as Trav stalked away, giving Wendy and Rodd a wide berth. Sage glared at Rodd. "Wendy, Trav and I are going to the trailer." Over the surrounding gaiety, Sage's harsh voice didn't even sound like her. "He's not in the mood for more festivities tonight. We wouldn't have come, but I wanted to be here when they auctioned off our baby-sitting."

"What's wrong with Trav?" Wendy asked, glancing at Trav, who was waiting by the door.

"Ask your boyfriend," Sage snapped and marched away.

CHAPTER EIGHTEEN

IN THE EARLY frigid hours of the new year, Rodd parked his Jeep outside Wendy's trailer, right beside Trav's battered pickup. He glanced sideways at Wendy sitting in the seat beside him. He couldn't believe the complete turnaround that had taken place between Wendy and him—all in a matter of moments. The joy he'd felt sitting beside Wendy at the auction, kissing her at midnight, letting everyone know he thought Wendy was wonderful—it was all gone. Now the only warmth in the Jeep was coming from the heater vents. "I don't know what to say . . ."

"That's the truth."

He wouldn't have believed that Wendy could sound so stiff, so crushed. *I hurt her. But how?* Even after Veda's disruption of the auction, Wendy hadn't remained distressed. That changed when Sage had told Wendy to ask him why Trav was upset.

"I can't believe you called Trav in and questioned him about the burglaries," Wendy repeated.

Rodd had tried but failed twice to explain his actions and the reasoning behind them. How could he make her understand that part of his job was being unpopular at times? He had to do whatever it took to catch the burglar. He would use any lawful means to achieve that goal, including questioning Sage's boyfriend.

He took a deep breath. "I questioned a lot of people. It's a technique to shake things up—to get people to talk—"

"People will talk all right!" Wendy turned on him. "All his life, Trav's had to live down his family's reputation, which is even worse than my mother's family's! Did you know that Elroy almost forced himself on my mother once? Uncle Dutch came just in time to save her—but everyone knew! That's why they hate each other!"

Rodd tried to sort through the emotions in Wendy's words. Why was she taking this so personally? "But I didn't charge Trav with anything," he explained patiently. "And I thought his uncle might say something if I questioned his nephew, let something slip. If you rattle people, they talk."

"With that line of reasoning, you should have called me in and questioned me. Then Uncle Dutch could have been rattled. You did question my uncle, didn't you?" She gave him a fierce look.

"Yes." How would she react to that? Would this make things even worse?

"So did Elroy say anything? Did he?" Wendy asked, her head turned away from him.

"No." No one had said anything worth listening to.

"Elroy never says anything and he does less," Wendy snapped. "He's been an albatross around Trav's neck his whole life. Poor Trav lost his parents in a drunk-driving accident when he was five. His poor indigent grandmother has struggled to raise him alone. . . ."

Rodd decided to try one more time. "Wendy, I'm sorry. This will all blow over as soon as I've arrested the thief. Everyone knows what a good kid Trav is."

Wendy wiped her eyes with her gloved fingers. "You just don't understand what you've done, do you? You don't know what Trav has had to go through to build his good reputation." She let herself out of the Jeep and ran up the steps into her trailer, the tinny sound of the metal steps ringing in the silent hour.

"She's right," Rodd spoke to his windshield as he drove away. "I don't understand."

❊❊❊

WENDY RUSHED INSIDE, fighting the tears. *Lord, he doesn't understand me at all. He doesn't understand what it's like to work your whole life to establish a good reputation! He doesn't know what it's like for people to look at you as though you're trash—poor white trash! He's a Durand—how could he know how a Rieker or a Dietz feels?*

In the darkened room lit only by the small lights on the Christmas tree, Sage and Trav sat on the sofa.

At the sight of them holding hands and looking so downhearted, Wendy burst into tears. What could she say to them? She'd made no headway with the sheriff at all.

Sage hurried to her side. "Don't cry, Wendy. You haven't done anything wrong."

"I'm just so . . . sorry. . . ." All the turmoil from the long evening finally pushed her over the edge. She couldn't stop the tears.

Trav came beside her and patted her on the back. "Please don't cry, Wendy. It's not your fault. How could the sheriff understand how we feel? He's never had people talking behind his back like the three of us have."

But he has. Cram and Veda have done their best to make his life miserable. Wendy couldn't verbalize these thoughts to Sage or Trav. Rodd wouldn't like it; he didn't want anyone to know that the gossip and rumors bothered him. Wendy sank down into the chair by the couch, next to the small tabletop Christmas tree.

"I should go home. I promised Gram I'd be home by one. She worries." Trav put his arms around Sage. "But I hate to leave you." He brushed away the hair from her face and leaned his cheek against hers.

"It's all right," Sage assured him. "Wendy and I'll be fine. We always have been. Trav, I'm going to tell her. She should know. I told Mom and I've waited too long as it is."

Trav nodded.

Sage moved the few steps to Wendy's chair and knelt in front of her. "Trav and I are getting married right after graduation this spring."

Wendy couldn't find her voice. Get married right out of high school? Just like their mother! No!

* * *

IN THE CHILLY entryway between the outer and inner doors to the clinic's emergency room, Rodd faced Wendy.

"Rodd, I just can't think right now."

Wendy's tired, flat voice made him ache. Two days had passed since New Year's Eve and in those two days, he'd tried to reconnect with her—but in vain. He had to try once more to get her to reveal what was troubling her.

Was it just his questioning Trav or something more? The way she stood there with her arms wrapped defensively around her cut him deep. Was she warding off the cold? or protecting herself from him? His arms ached to pull her close and warm her within his embrace. But her stiffened, wary stance warned him away. "What is it, Wendy?"

She shook her head.

The way she looked at him hurt him. She looked as though she'd given up, as though all the life had gone out of her.

Dr. Doug opened the door from inside the clinic, letting a breath of warmth touch them. "Wendy, I need you."

"Sure. Right away." Wendy turned to go.

"I'm sorry," Rodd said, desperate to get her to look at him the way she had when he'd walked into the auction on New Year's Eve.

She only nodded and walked away.

Rodd's lonely ride home felt like a ride to nowhere he wanted to go. The usual lift he felt when he turned into his snowy lane didn't come. Why was Wendy so upset with him? *I was just doing my job. What does she want from me?* His mind echoed: *What does God want from me?*

Rodd parked his Jeep in the garage and walked into his kitchen. The big old farmhouse that he loved felt cold and empty. He stood at the window over the sink and stared out into the winter gloom, seeing the clear night sky spangled with glittering stars. How could he make

Wendy understand why he'd questioned Trav? How could he make things between them better? Maybe if he talked to Trav himself . . .

The phone rang. Rodd picked it up. "Durand here."

"Hi, Sheriff. Don't you think it's time you caught the Snowmobile Burglar?"

Rodd came alive. The anonymous caller was phoning a second time. "I've been trying to catch him. What do you know that I don't?"

"I know where he's going to hit next. Would you like to know where?" the muffled voice taunted him.

"Are you going to tell me?"

Silence. Would the caller hang up?

"Be at Harlan Carey's tomorrow night." *Click.*

Rodd gripped the receiver, then hung it up. Harlan's? Why would someone target Harlan? But did the Weasel have a conscience? No. Another thought jarred him. Could he trust the caller or was this just another ploy like the call about the snowmobiles?

He'd have to follow this lead just like any other. And he had to keep anything from happening to Harlan. Not only for Harlan's sake, but for Wendy's. Anything that hurt her grandfather hurt her. He'd signed on to protect the county, and so far he hadn't been very successful. He'd have to be at Harlan's tomorrow night—ready for anything. He had no choice. *God, all the doors leading to the Weasel have been locked tight to me. What am I doing wrong?*

⁂

NIGHT HAD DROPPED its inky shade over the sky and landscape. A brave luminescent full moon was rising above the darkened horizon. Rodd eased his snowmobile to the thick line of snow-flocked evergreens behind Harlan's machine shed. He had to have his snowmobile in place near enough to respond if the Weasel really did show up and try to break in to Harlan's. Hampered by deep snow, Rodd crept around in the dim light from the full moon. Right away, he realized that Harlan was at home. Would the Weasel break in to an occupied house?

Who knew? The thief's original pattern had been broken with the kegger. Yes, the Weasel might hit the house with Harlan there. Or Harlan might be scheduled to go somewhere tonight. Just in case this was another ruse, Rodd had all his deputies on alert and patrolling the county, ready for anything, and he'd called to ask Dr. Doug if any rural residents had been brought in for an overnight stay. None had. Rodd took one last look around to see if everything on Harlan's property looked normal; then he retreated to the cover of the trees to wait.

He'd thought about warning Harlan and Wendy about the possibility of the house being hit tonight, but he had decided it was best not to. Either Harlan or Wendy might do something out of the ordinary, which could alert the thief that he was expected. Rodd also knew that Wendy wouldn't be in the picture tonight. She would be working at the care center. Before New Year's Eve, she'd given him her schedule for this week so they could plan a day to go snowmobiling for fun. Well, that probably wouldn't happen now. Would he ever be able to reconnect with Wendy? *How did I misjudge the situation with Trav so completely? Why has something so routine upset her? Do women ever get easier to understand?*

The cold wind rustled the trees around him. Time crawled. He shivered. Even his snowmobile gear couldn't keep out the unrelenting January chill. The weatherman had predicted below-zero temperatures for tonight. Rodd played mind games with himself to stay alert. He counted stars. He named the constellations. Behind his face mask, he yawned.

The sound of a car motor disrupted the night. He was on his feet, working through the knee-high snow to the end of the line of trees where he could see who was coming up the drive without being seen. Wendy's station wagon! He wanted to curse. Then he calmed himself down. That fit. She'd probably come to take her grandfather somewhere, but why now—he checked the luminescent dial of his watch—at almost ten at night? That didn't make sense. What was going on? Was this another Weasel trick? Had he come here for nothing?

Wendy parked her car in Harlan's machine shed and hurried inside the house. Rodd felt like pacing back and forth. Should he go in now and alert them? What if the Weasel arrived when he was inside?

Rodd could lose him, and he couldn't afford to let that happen again. Better to go back to his spot and just wait. What could happen next on this miserable, freezing stakeout?

The minutes on Rodd's watch kept passing. He waited, hoping that Wendy would leave with Harlan. But after a while, the lights in the house started going out—one by one—till the house was nearly dark. Was Wendy staying the night with Harlan? Rodd nearly went to the house to ask but stopped himself. *God, this doesn't feel right. Am I being set up instead of the Weasel?* He looked skyward as though the stars knew the answer. *God, I don't know what has been holding me back from asking you to head up this investigation, and right now I'm too cold for deep thought, but Wendy's right. Send me all the help I need. I mean that! Amen.*

Now in the silence of the winter night, he could do nothing but wait. He waited. The moon rose higher. The icy temperatures dropped lower. He shivered.

The faint buzz of a snowmobile sounded in the distance. He froze in place. As if in a scene from a movie, the snowmobile skirted the moonlight by hugging the shadows beside the fence line as it headed straight toward Harlan's.

His adrenaline pumping, Rodd found it hard to breathe. He stayed well hidden, afraid he might alert the man on the snowmobile that he was waiting for him.

The snowmobile didn't stop until it was right at Harlan's back door. The suited, masked figure threw something at the yard light. The sound of tinkling glass, then darkness. The figure ran up the steps and struck the door with a crowbar.

Rodd slid onto his 'bile, swooped between the trees, and zoomed toward the Weasel. His heart pounded. He felt like shouting, "Got you!" The figure spun around and made a dive for his snowmobile.

Rodd jumped from his snowmobile and lunged for the thief. Their two bodies slammed together and fell to the ground. They twisted and rolled in fervent battle. The crowbar hit Rodd across the shoulders, loosening his grip on the thief.

The Weasel sprung up and raced off! Clambering onto his 'bile, Rodd tore after him. *You won't get away this time!*

❖❖❖

WENDY HEARD THE crowbar hit the back door, the shouts, then snowmobile motors outside. She darted to the window. She knew instantly who drove the two snowmobiles disappearing into the night along her grandfather's fence line. Rodd! And the thief!

She rushed to the back hall, quickly donned her snowmobile suit, and stepped outside into the freezing cold. Racing to the machine shed, she pulled on her mask, helmet, and gloves. She jumped on her grandfather's machine and barreled outside. The whine of the two motors drew her, and she pushed the throttle to the max.

Her mind raced as fast as her snowmobile. Around a bend near the Thorpes' trailer, she caught a glimpse of what must be Rodd's bright red taillight. Her response in following him had been instinctive. Now her conscious fear for Rodd surfaced.

At high speed, he'd be overdriving his headlights. And even with his month of night patrolling, he still didn't know all the traps the Weasel could lead him into. And that was the only way the Weasel would be able to get free of him now. *Rodd, be careful. God, stick with him, with us!*

Snow flew beneath her and flared up behind her. Though she swept on at top speed, the two snowmobiles still loomed far ahead of her. When they turned toward Hunter's Lake, her fears quickened.

Both snowmobiles broke away from the trail. The Weasel was leading Rodd across open country. Any low spot could cause the snowmobiles to flounder and kill the engines. But she kept pace with them, her prayers flying as fast as the wind past her ears.

The first snowmobile turned and headed out onto the frozen surface of Hunter's Lake. Wendy sucked in breath. No! She knew instantly what the Weasel planned to do. *No!*

Even though she knew she wouldn't be heard, she shouted, "Rodd! Stop!" She hunched down and snaked one of her hands to the seat behind her. She found the nylon rope and fumbled, finding its end.

In front of her, it happened exactly as she knew it would. The Weasel sped toward the edge of the lake. Rodd roared after him. The Weasel swung wide. Rodd headed straight for him, cutting across the area the Weasel had avoided. Wendy heard the crack of ice breaking.

Rodd swerved, but too late—the hazard had him.

The thick ice shuddered. Wendy felt it under her as she slowed her machine, skirting around the area of thin ice over the spring that fed the lake. *Craaacckk! Craaaccccckkkkh!*

She cut her motor and sprang off, the rope in her hand. As the front end of Rodd's snowmobile angled up, he slid back toward the opening ice.

"Rodd!" she shouted. "Catch the rope!" She swung the coiled cord like a lariat over her head and sent it sailing toward Rodd as he floundered on the parting ice. "Rodd!" she screamed.

He grabbed the rope.

"Tie it around your waist!" she shouted. "Don't try to walk! I'll tow you out!" She jumped back onto her 'bile, restarted the engine, and slowly moved away from the ice fault. A glance backward told her that Rodd was holding tight. Slowly . . . slowly . . . she inched forward until Rodd's body was on solid ice again with several feet to spare. "You're safe!" she yelled.

A terrible moan rent the air. The ice over the spring opened wide, shuddered, then devoured Rodd's snowmobile as it sank into the lake. The sound sent an aftershock of terror through her. She ran to Rodd and threw her arms around him. "Are you all right?"

"Why did you follow me?" He railed at her. "You could have been hurt, killed!"

She let his angry words fly over her, realizing they were just the reaction to his fear for her, his own fear, and anger at himself for falling into a trap. She clung to him.

Behind them came a hoot of laughter. Rodd went still, the laugh seeming to trigger a memory. He turned in time to see, in the forest beyond the lake, the Weasel pause to perform a distinctive hand-pumping gesture of victory. Again, the unique laugh came. And then he was off.

"He's getting away!" Wendy shouted.

"I know who the Weasel is," Rodd said, half to himself, half aloud. "Let's go!" he shouted and hustled her back onto her snowmobile. "Hold on!"

Wendy clung to Rodd from behind as he barreled back across the firm part of the lake, doggedly pursuing the thief. Wendy didn't bother to look. She'd also recognized the Weasel and guessed where he was headed. All too soon, both her assumptions would be proven true.

Flanagan's green neon shamrock came into view. Rodd slowed the snowmobile and stopped beside the machine the Weasel had been driving. He climbed off and checked the other machine; it was still warm. "It's Elroy! I remembered his laugh from Thanksgiving Day—when we came here to bring your uncle—"

The sound of a loud argument and women's shrieks from inside interrupted him. Rodd rushed into the bar.

Wendy lagged behind him and hung back near the entrance. Elroy and Uncle Dutch were slugging it out. She felt sick.

Elroy shouted, "You lousy double-dealer! You set me up!"

"I don't know what you're talking about!" Dutch swung at Elroy and the smaller man went down.

But Elroy came up swinging. Women screamed. Men shouted encouragement.

Feeling like someone had punched her in the stomach, Wendy stepped outside and made her way to the snowmobile. She started it and turned toward her grandfather's. She'd planned to spend the night with him because he'd come down with the flu. He needed her and by now, he would be frantic with worry.

She knew Rodd would call for backup. In fact, she heard a siren in the distance. She wasn't needed here.

And her heart had been broken—again.

CHAPTER NINETEEN

THREE DAYS LATER Wendy sat on the afghan covering the old, harvest gold sofa and stared out the window of her trailer. The sky was winter drab; it was after ten o'clock in the morning, and she was still in her nightgown. The mug of coffee she held had gone stone cold an hour ago.

She had first awakened in this frozen, depressed, immovable state the day after Elroy had been arrested and Uncle Dutch had been implicated. She closed her eyes, still wrestling with anguish. What were they all saying now at the Black Bear Café every morning about the latest Rieker sin?

Footsteps approached outside. The door opened. Wendy looked up. "Sage! What's wrong? Did school close early?"

Sage let her heavy backpack bump onto the floor and walked to her sister. "Nothing's wrong—with me. Why are *you* sitting here? You're supposed to be at the clinic."

"I just don't feel good." *Go back to school, Sage. Leave me alone.*

Sage tried to put her hand on Wendy's forehead.

Wendy ducked away. "I don't have a fever."

Sage sank onto the end of the sofa. "I know that. Old Doc called the school and talked to me. He's worried about you. This is the third day you've called in sick. And you haven't taken a sick day in two years!"

Wendy folded her legs under her and turned from her sister. "I can't help it if I don't feel good."

"I think it's time we had a talk. A talk I've been thinking for a long time we should have."

"What talk?" *I'll say anything, Sage, if you'll just go away and leave me alone.*

"The talk about Mom, you, me, Uncle Dutch—everything about our lives."

Wendy inched toward the edge of the couch. "Couldn't we do this another day? I just—"

Sage touched Wendy's arm, stopping her retreat. "We're going to do it today and now. I'm not going to let you go into a full-scale depression. This has to stop!"

Sage, I can't talk now! "I'll be fine tom—"

Sage intercepted her, gripping her shoulders. "You won't be fine if we don't face this. So we're going to talk this out. I know I'm just your kid sister, and you don't think I've got it all together. Well, guess what? You don't have it all together, either."

Wendy's eyes filled up and she bit her lower lip. *I don't want to start crying again, Lord. Make Sage stop.*

"Don't get me wrong." Sage let go of her sister's shoulders. "You have most of it together really well, but this idea about going through life avoiding men—and Rodd Durand in particular—has got to stop."

Wendy pulled together her remaining scraps of self-control and pride. "Please, Sage . . . besides, you're mad at him for questioning Trav!"

"I was, but Trav and I talked it over and decided to forgive him. Rodd's been under a lot of pressure and he apologized to Trav. And Trav didn't lose his job like he thought he would."

Wendy pressed one hand on each side of her head. So many words . . .

"Wendy, I know why you decided not to date when you were in high school."

"You what?" Her eyes wide, Wendy sat back, stunned.

"Yes, I asked Mom about it."

"You asked Mom about it?" She stared at Sage. "But you were just a little girl when I was in high school."

Sage gave her an impish grin. "Not so little that I didn't realize that high school girls dated boys."

Shock rippled through Wendy. "What did Mom say?"

"She said that she had loved not wisely, but too well. My words—or Shakespeare's really—not hers. Anyway, she told me all about her and your dad, about how she loved him and he loved her even though she was a Rieker. About how he died and she wanted to die too. Then she told me all about her and my dad. And how guilty she felt for everything she'd put you through with her drinking and her affairs."

This shocked Wendy. She could think of nothing to say.

"We owe a lot to Gramps, don't we? He's the one who made Mom go to AA. She knew she couldn't fight him or he'd call Social Services and she would have lost us for sure."

Wendy sighed. "He took us home with him and said he wouldn't let her have us back until she gave up drinking." Recalling those wretched days pulled Wendy deeper into sadness.

"Was it really that bad?"

Wendy nodded, staring at her hands; after the last few days, all her nails were torn and ragged. "She lost her job at the café. She just hung out at Flanagan's. Grandfather came over and found me home from school trying to take care of you by myself. But I'd run out of formula. . . ." She didn't want to tell Sage everything. Mercifully, her sister had been just a baby and couldn't remember. Wendy choked back a sob, masking it with a fake cough.

"I'm glad God provided Gramps for us then." Sage's tone turned brisk again. "But you've never talked with Mom about it, have you?"

Wendy shook her head. *Dredging up that pain again, no!*

"You and I are wired differently, Wendy. Things that bounce off me cut you to the quick. You realize that, don't you? That's why you always worry about my reputation and I don't. That's why I decided to go out with Trav when everyone said I shouldn't even talk to him. You see?"

Wendy closed her eyes. *How does that help me now, Sage?*

"Trav's grandmother had changed a lot by the time she was left to raise Trav. She kept Elroy away from him. I'm sorry, Sis. This isn't about me." Sage took Wendy's cold hand and squeezed it in her warm one. "This is about you. This latest flap about Uncle Dutch and Trav's Uncle Elroy has brought it all back, hasn't it?"

Wendy felt sick. Elroy had been arrested for the snowmobile burglaries. She'd read all about it in the paper. He implicated Dutch as the one who'd planned the burglaries, including the kegger ruse. He said Dutch had approached him with a foolproof way to get some easy cash for Christmas.

When Elroy had brought up the long-standing feud between them, Dutch had pointed out that no one would suspect enemies like them working together! So even if Uncle Dutch hadn't done the thieving, he might be guilty of planning the burglaries and even arson, then double-crossing his accomplice and exacting revenge. Even worse!

Right now, it was Elroy's word against Dutch's, but in her heart, she suspected it to be true. Uncle Dutch had always wanted to pay Elroy back for forcing himself on Doreen years ago when she'd been a young widow. And Elroy didn't have the brainpower to plan the kegger and pull everything off. But true or not, Wendy couldn't face anyone. Once again, her family's reputation had been marred and broadcast far and near!

With a gentle hand, Sage brushed back Wendy's uncombed hair. "All right. Let's get to the heart of this. The wild life Mom lived after your dad died hurt you a lot. She was young and heartbroken and angry. What she didn't realize then was how she was hurting you. And at the same time, your grandmother and Veda scarred you too. Then Mom got pregnant with me when she wasn't married, and my dad ducked out, never to be seen again. That gave people, especially Veda, another scandal to throw up to you."

"I really don't want to think about all of that." Wendy put her head into her hand.

Sage ignored her. "Now it's Uncle Dutch. Wendy, we don't come from a perfect family, but that's because they're human. But Mom spent years in AA. Then last year she married Jim, and now she seems happy.

"And Trav—who, by the way, isn't thrilled with his uncle either—Trav and I are going to walk the straight and narrow. We're not going to live together. We're going to get married and help each other get an education." Sage paused. "Wendy, you can't let what has happened in the past keep you from having your happy ending. Trav and I aren't! You have an excellent reputation in this town, and it's obvious to everyone that Rodd Durand loves you—"

"No, no . . ." Wendy put her hands over her eyes. *It doesn't matter if he loves me and I love him. Don't you see? I can't face him—not after this!*

Sage tugged Wendy's hands down from her face. "Now you're going to go into the shower. Then you're going to get dressed and head to work to do that blood pressure clinic scheduled for indigent patients this afternoon. Trav's grandmother has been counting off the days to it on her calendar."

Impossible! "I can't—"

"You can. Wendy, you're holding on to the past and it's not even your past. Listen to me—God only holds us accountable for what we do, not for the sins of our fathers or mothers. And besides, God would forgive Mom if she'd repent. I haven't had a chance to tell you, but Mom and Jim found a church to take me to when I was there, and they liked it! They've been going every Sunday since Christmas—sorry, I got carried away again! God doesn't visit the guilt of the mother onto the daughter and you know that, Wendy! So if you hold on to guilt that isn't even yours, you're calling God a liar."

"No, I—"

"If he has erased our sins, why are you holding on to them? Is that what you want to do—deny God's power to forgive and blot out sins?"

Stunned by this truth, Wendy stared at her baby sister. She hadn't thought about this feeling of shame as showing a lack of trust on her part. But her sister was right. She couldn't let the past control her, not when God had wiped her slate clean! If she let this destroy her future, then Veda would win! And Satan and his demons would dance with glee! Wendy swallowed tears of relief. "You're very wise, Sage."

Sage threw her arms around Wendy and hugged her close. "And you have the sweetest, most loving heart in all the world. Now get into that shower. I'm not going back to school until you are at the clinic."

Wendy stood up and walked toward the bathroom. Sage's words played over in her mind. They made perfect sense, but Wendy still wanted to crawl back in bed. She was still afraid to face Rodd. Did he take the same view of this? He was a Durand, the county sheriff. They'd both begun to have deep feelings for one another, but would those feelings last in the face of her uncle's revenge and treachery?

❋❋❋

SNOW WAS FALLING again. Barely aware of it, Rodd drove down Highway 27, sick at heart. He hadn't felt this miserable since he'd lost Uncle George. *I should be as happy as a clam. The burglaries have been solved.* Elroy Dietz was in the county jail. A search warrant for Elroy's home had turned up "souvenirs" from each of the burglaries—nothing valuable, just little things the victims probably never even noticed were missing. He'd hidden them in a box under his bed, which seemed to sum up Elroy's IQ as a thief.

Dutch Rieker had obviously been the brains of the larcenous duo. Elroy had told Rodd how Dutch made him practice how to do the burglaries, how not to leave any evidence, and how to take only cash so nothing could be traced back to either of them. This collusion must have been why Rodd couldn't square some aspects of the crimes with others—he'd wondered why such a careless thief who trashed crime scenes without any respect for valuable items reconciled with a thief capable of planning the kegger ruse and later the explosions to mask stealing the bingo winnings. Elroy as puppet and Dutch as puppet master explained everything.

Except Elroy was clever enough to have kept from leaving any clues and getting caught before now. And he cleverly led Rodd onto the ice.

Dutch Rieker was still under investigation. In the latest *Steadfast*

Times, Cram had headlined the end of the case with "Snowmobile Burglar in Custody!" At the Black Bear Café at breakfast this morning, everyone had congratulated Rodd. *So why don't I feel like I should?*

He knew the answer, though he didn't want to admit it. But Wendy's pretty face surrounded by her tousled golden brown hair popped into his mind again. He gripped the steering wheel, pushing down his pain.

The snow fell faster. Rodd switched on the AM station and listened for the weather report. The words *sleet, stagnating front, slick conditions* rolled over him. On routine patrol, he drove down road after lonely road. As the surfaces grew slicker and the sun rose on the horizon, Rodd kept driving, barely conscious of anything but the road and the sky. Wendy's face hung in his mind. He'd called her every day the past week, and every day she wouldn't answer her phone. *God, what can I do?*

The older sedan in front of him suddenly skidded, its rear end swerving to the right. Shocked, Rodd braked. His Jeep slipped in spite of its antilock brakes. The sedan fishtailed. Spinning off the road, it slammed into an ancient pine. Rodd's Jeep rocked to a stop. After radioing dispatch, he jumped out and ran to the car. The driver and the front-seat passenger were slumped forward but still breathing. A baby wailed in a car seat in the back.

Rodd flung open the door beside the baby and quickly unhooked the child's restraint seat. His Jeep was still running and warm. "I'll be right back, folks. This little one will be better off in my car." He jogged to his Jeep and deposited the baby on his backseat, securing it with the seat belt. He closed the door.

The explosion knocked Rodd to the ground. When he dragged himself to his feet, the sedan was engulfed in flames. "Dear God!" Rodd shouted and ran forward. The heat and flames forced him back. He stood, watching the car burn. *Dear heavenly Father, I didn't guess. I should have gotten them out! Dear Father, forgive me!*

❋❋❋

LATE THAT NIGHT, Rodd lifted the baby out of his Jeep one more time. The events of the day—the car accident with two fatalities, meeting with the coroner and calling county Social Services about placing the baby—still ran through his mind like a disjointed amateur video. He knocked on Pastor Bruce's door. Zak opened it. "The baby's here! Mama, the new baby's here!"

Penny hurried forward with open arms.

Feeling more dead than alive, Rodd let her take the unbelievably light bundle from his arms. "She's asleep."

Zak bounced up and down. "Let me see!"

Penny bent down and opened the pink blanket. "Oh, she's darling."

Rodd winced, pain deep inside. *She's a darling orphan, thanks to me. Dear God. Dear God.*

Zak frowned. "She's awful little."

"How old did Old Doc think she is?" Penny asked.

"Two or three months." Rodd's shoulders ached from the burdens of the day. *I feel ninety years old.*

Bruce walked up and rested a hand on Rodd's shoulder. "Rodd, you look like you've had a rough day. Come on in the kitchen. Penny saved you some supper."

The other man's obvious concern made Rodd feel guiltier. "I'm not—"

"You're not leaving," Penny scolded, "until you've eaten and we've talked. It sounds like you had a hellish day. Zak, say good night to the sheriff. It's your bedtime. Daddy will tuck you in for the night. I have to get the sheriff his supper."

Zak looked like he wanted to argue, but his father swung him up into his arms. "We had a deal, Zak. You could stay up to see the new baby and the sheriff if you went to bed without complaining. You're not going to break your promise, are you?"

"No," Zak admitted with deep regret. The little guy called over his father's shoulder, "Good night, Sheriff! 'Member you promised to take me out to see Mr. Carey and your cows on your day off tomorrow!"

Rodd waved and followed Penny into the kitchen. He tried to think of something to say. Finally he came up with, "Where are the foster brother and sister? In bed?"

"Their grandmother picked them up this morning. That's why Social Services had you bring this little one to me." Cradling the sleeping infant with one arm, Penny took a wrapped dish from the refrigerator, put it in the microwave, and turned it on. The aroma of roast beef soon filled the kitchen. "The father and mother agreed to let the grandmother take them until they have settled their differences over the divorce. So you see, we had room for this little one."

Rodd sat silent while Penny poured him fresh coffee and laid his place setting. Her kitchen was filled with peace. He tried to let it work on him. The edge left his emotions, but deep fatigue, almost shock, remained. When she set his warmed plate in front of him, he bowed his head and said the childhood grace his uncle had taught him long ago. He was prayed out today, asking pardon for his dreadful mistake.

Bruce came in and sat down across from him. "I'll let you two talk while I get this little one settled in the nursery." Penny walked out, cooing to the baby girl.

"We heard all about the explosion," Bruce said. "I know you're feeling guilty because you weren't able to save the mom and dad."

Losing the trace of appetite he'd had, Rodd stared at Bruce. "If I'd thought they were in immediate danger, I would have tried to get them out—"

"And then all three would have died and probably you too. Rodd, you're not God. You did exactly what you were supposed to do, and you saved a baby's life. I call that a pretty good day's work. We can't have you going under. Too much has happened in this town this winter. The burglaries. Veda's larceny. Everyone's worried about Wendy."

Rodd's head jerked up. "Why? What happened to her?"

Bruce gave him a pained look and explained. "She's missed two, almost three, days of work at the clinic. Said she was sick, but she just couldn't leave her trailer. Old Doc was afraid she'd slip into a depression."

Rodd paused to get his voice under control. Wendy didn't deserve to be upset like this. "Did she come out of it?"

"She's back at work." Bruce nodded. "But this thing with her uncle has taken its toll on her. Poor kid. She's had so much to deal with in her life. She's come through it all and turned out to be one of the sweetest people I know. Do you think Dutch did what Elroy has accused him of?"

Worry for Wendy made Rodd a little sick, but he focused on the question about the investigation. "I can't comment—"

"Level with me, Rodd. You know it will go no further."

The dam inside Rodd broke. He put down his fork. "After spending a day questioning Elroy, I think he's too dumb to have planned the burglaries, much less the kegger. I think it's quite logical that Dutch was the one who thought up the MO for the burglaries. It would be easy for him to keep track of his niece, then tell Elroy when and where to strike."

Bruce listened as Rodd continued.

"And Elroy's quite capable of hitting Wendy from behind and blowing up his beater truck to get a new one." Rodd clenched his fist. He'd been tempted to deck Dietz when he'd questioned him about the assault on Wendy at Kainzes'.

Now Rodd sucked in air. "But breaking into my house doesn't fit Elroy. It was just a stunt to show up the sheriff. Ego showing off! That fits Rieker. Cocky. And using that old grudge between them as a cover fits Dutch. He's quite capable of coming up with the idea of forming such a unexpected and short-lived partnership, knowing that no one would suspect the two of them of collusion."

"When did the thieves fall out? Or should I ask why?" Bruce folded his arms.

Rodd took a swallow of coffee. "Dutch probably realized fairly early that he could use the fact that Elroy actually carried out the burglaries to stab Dietz in the back. Then Elroy started seeing Dutch's longtime girlfriend, Carlene. That weakened the partnership. But the assault on Wendy probably sharpened Rieker's craving for revenge. So Dutch set Elroy up to get caught with the anonymous calls."

"Why did Elroy hit Harlan's place when Harlan was home? That didn't fit—"

"I think that was Elroy's revenge for my bringing his nephew Trav in for questioning. And I think Elroy would have enjoyed beating up an old man." Rodd had nicknamed the thief the Weasel and he'd been right. Elroy had enjoyed trashing homes of defenseless seniors. He'd killed Ma's old dog and lured Rodd out onto the ice. If Wendy hadn't been there with her rope, Rodd would have had a time getting safely away from his snowmobile before it went through the cracking ice. He didn't doubt for a moment that Elroy would have left him to his fate. He wasn't the kind who'd face an enemy. Rodd could easily understand the enmity between Elroy and Dutch.

"Didn't Dutch realize that if Elroy was caught, he would spill the beans on Dutch?"

Rodd added silently, *And why didn't Dutch understand how much his actions would hurt his niece?* Rodd shrugged, trying to loosen his tired back muscles. "Elroy can implicate Dutch for the next twenty years. But if there's no evidence and no witnesses to back him up, I can't touch Dutch. Dutch isn't out of the clinic yet. Elroy managed to get the best of him in their fight. I've finally got a search warrant for Dutch's place. I had a hard time convincing the judge that Dutch was implicated since all we had to go on was Elroy's story—evidently no one puts any stock in Elroy's word. Maybe I will find something before Dutch comes home."

Bruce shook his head. "They can't have made much money at this. Why did they even bother?"

Rodd thought of the money Dutch had given Sage at the airport. He hoped the young girl didn't realize where that Christmas money had come from. Rodd had told Wendy he didn't see the thief as Santa Claus—but he'd been wrong. That just showed how twisted some minds were.

Rodd wrapped his fingers around his coffee cup. "Neither of them is working. From talking to the victims, I figure Dutch and Elroy each pulled in about six or seven hundred dollars from all the burglaries."

Bruce made a sound of disgust. "Most of which probably ended up in the till at Flanagan's. Why didn't they steal more than cash?"

Rodd took another swallow of coffee to clear his throat. "Fencing stuff means involving a third party and leaving a trail of evidence. Dutch was evidently too smart to do that."

The thought of how this man could be related to sweet, honest Wendy came to Rodd one more time.

Bruce echoed Rodd's earlier thoughts. "Why didn't he think about how this would affect his nieces?" He looked at Rodd. "It's so sad."

"What's sad is that I'm going to have a hard time proving Rieker's connection without any hard evidence. I just hope I find something."

Bruce nodded. "You'll have to turn this over to God. What we cannot do alone, he can. Now eat your supper. You'll feel better."

Though the sour taste of defeat lingered, Rodd picked up his fork and took a bite of the tender beef.

Penny came in and began unloading onto the counter the bag of diapers and formula Rodd had also brought. "Poor little sweetheart. How long do you think it will take to find this little one's family?"

Rodd answered, "I don't know. The license plate was burned, but the number was still molded into the metal. I pulled it up on the computer."

"Then it shouldn't take long," Bruce said.

Rodd shook his head. "The car was stolen yesterday outside of Milwaukee. And we have no surviving ID like a driver's license from either victim. The coroner will have to try to ID them by dental records. That could take a long time."

❋❋❋

EARLY THE NEXT afternoon Rodd drove into his own drive. The gray sky was heavy with snow waiting to drop on them. Harlan sat beside him and Zak sat in the backseat. Zak had been begging to see Rodd's barn and cows for a long time. With the burglaries solved, Rodd decided the excursion would be a good diversion. And God knew he needed one. Elroy was to be arraigned tomorrow, and Rodd was waiting for the analysis of residue on some clothing from Dutch's trailer. It might match the explosives used in LaFollette and link Dutch to that crime at least.

"Wow!" Zak exclaimed. "It looks just like the barn in my storybook!"

Harlan chuckled. "That's because it's a very old barn."

"You don't have one like that, Mr. Carey!" Zak pointed out.

"No, unfortunately, my old barn fell down before you were born, and I had to put up the machine shed. Besides, I'd given up on raising cattle. If you have stock, Rodd's barn is the best kind."

"Is cattle cows?" Zak asked.

"Yes."

"What's *stock?*"

"Another way to say farm animals."

"Oh."

Rodd listened to the exchange, enjoying Zak's lively interest in everything. He wished some of it would rub off on him. Every morning he woke up with what felt like a two-ton sack of rocks on his back that he was forced to drag around with him all day. He parked outside the barn entrance.

Zak trotted over the packed snow ahead of them into the barn. "What can I do? Can I help?"

Rodd grinned and took Zak's hand. "Here, you can pump the water for the cows. I'll get it started for you."

"Wow!" Zak jumped up and down. Harlan brought over a wooden box for the little guy to stand on so he could handle the old hand pump.

Rodd got the pump working easily and showed Zak how to push down the handle. Every time the water gushed out into the sluice to the trough, Zak shouted with glee.

Rodd walked over to the ladder and climbed up to the loft, where his pitchfork stood against the wall. He picked it up and began to fork down hay to the cattle. Harlan followed him up.

Rodd glanced at him and then down at Zak, still working the pump. "Why do kids get so much fun out of pumping water?"

Harlan smiled. "It's something easy they can do, and it's something they can't break so they don't get yelled at."

"Sounds right," Rodd said.

"Rodd, what are your intentions concerning my granddaughter Wendy?"

The out-of-the-blue question startled Rodd. Pitchfork in his hands, he turned to face Harlan. "I don't know what—"

"I know it's an old-fashioned question. But I'm in my eighties so I remember being asked that question when I was courting. I want to know if you are serious about my Wendy or not."

Rodd's mouth went dry. "Does 'serious' mean marriage?"

Harlan nodded. "I grew up with your great-uncle George, so I am sure that he would ask you the same question. You've found yourself a good woman, and it's obvious to everyone that you have deep feelings for her. So what's happened between you two?"

"She won't return my calls." Rodd cleared his throat.

Harlan walked over and put a hand on Rodd's shoulder. "There's more to this than just you and Wendy."

"What is it then?" Rodd's voice didn't sound normal. It rasped and felt rusty.

"I think it has to do with the fact that a Christian needs to depend on God every day."

"Wendy beat you to it. She already made that point."

"She did?" Harlan said, his eyes sparkling with good humor. "Smart girl."

Rodd smiled. "I finally turned the case over to God while I waited outside your home that night."

"Praise the Lord!" With one of his large, gnarled, work-worn hands, Harlan squeezed Rodd's shoulder. "Don't expect to feel anything and don't expect it to 'take' the first time, son. But from now on, whenever you begin to worry, give it over to God. Just let God in. Okay? Now we'll both have faith that in God's own time, not ours, he'll bring Dutch to justice."

Rodd pulled away and lifted another forkful of hay over the side of the loft. Harlan's counsel made sense, and how many times had Uncle George said, "Lean not on thine own understanding. But in all thy ways, acknowledge the Lord"? *Forgive my hardheadedness, Lord.*

Rodd felt better. Having his uncle's old friend here with him was a true blessing.

"Now, son, what are your intentions toward my Wendy?"

Rodd looked into Harlan's eyes. "I wasn't very nice to Wendy the night I arrested Elroy. I yelled at her, but she scared me so much, coming right out on the ice while it was breaking all around me—"

"You know that's not what Wendy's upset about." Harlan studied him as if he were sifting through Rodd's soul for truth. "Wendy has to learn to see herself as a child of God, separate from her family. After all her mother's problems, she's had trouble trusting men. That's easy to understand. But you have to make her see that she can trust you and that you trust God. If you don't, you're going to wind up a lonely, spiritually stunted man. And that's what your Uncle George would tell you if he were standing here right now." Harlan turned and started down the ladder.

Rodd stood with the pitchfork in his hands. Below, Harlan and Zak exchanged places. Harlan began pumping while Zak splashed his hands in the water going down the sluice. The old pump squeaked. The cold water gushed and the little boy squealed.

Rodd closed his eyes, drinking in the sounds of having others in the barn with him. He watered the cattle and fed them daily—but he worked alone. Always alone. Raised alone by a dad and an uncle. Always alone at his job, even with a partner beside him. His loneliness had prompted him to leave Milwaukee. He'd felt at home here on his family's land. But even here he was alone, holding everyone at arm's length. Did he want to live alone—without Wendy, without a family?

No. He wanted Wendy in his life. *I'm sorry, Lord. I've tried to do everything on my own. Without Wendy, I might have gone into the icy water on Hunter's Lake. I might have died. Elroy might have gotten away.* He paused to draw a deep breath. *I need your help, Lord. I love Wendy. And I want her as my wife. Help me find a way back to her. I don't know how to break through the barrier she's put up between us. Help me persuade her that she stands apart from her family. I'm going to turn this over to you completely. Just remember I love her. Give me the key to her heart, I pray.*

When he opened his eyes, he felt refreshed, hopeful. He finished forking over the hay, then climbed down the ladder.

Zak greeted him at the bottom. "Can I climb up the ladder?"

Rodd smiled at Zak. "Sure. But first we have to give the cows some special feed. They're all going to give birth, starting soon—"

"Now?" Harlan countered. "When did you have them bred?"

"Too early, but I couldn't get on the vet's breeding schedule anytime later in the summer. I shouldn't have any calves until February, but a few of these old girls look like it could happen any day."

"Can I see a calf get borned?" Zak jumped up, grabbing Rodd's outstretched arm, then swinging back and forth on it.

Holding his arm stiff to let the boy play, Rodd said, "If it's all right with your parents. Now let's get the feed. You can measure out each portion."

"Wow! Wait till I tell my dad!"

Rodd's smile broadened. His heart lifted. *Heavenly Father, please prepare Wendy's heart. You've prepared mine.*

CHAPTER TWENTY

TEN DAYS AFTER New Year's Eve, Wendy got out of the pastor's van and walked toward Rodd's barn through the bright but deceiving afternoon sunshine. A call from Rodd, just a half hour ago, that one of his cows was in early labor had brought an instant response from Zak. He was invited to come, and everyone, including Wendy, who was visiting with Penny, had to go and see the birth, too! So now Penny, with the baby in her arms, and Bruce, carrying the pink gingham diaper bag, trailed after Wendy and Zak.

The bright sunshine made Wendy squint and shade her eyes with one hand. Zak tugged her along to hurry her, his small mittened hand gripping her free one. "Come on, Wendy! The calf might get borned before we get there!"

In spite of her reluctance, Wendy picked up her pace. She wouldn't do anything to spoil Zak's delight. Besides, most of her wanted to see Rodd. The past few days had brought healing for her. After Sage had confronted her, Wendy had returned to work. The people of the town wonderfully demonstrated their support for her. And for once, Veda's nastiness had been soundly shouted down wherever she had tried to voice it. Wendy knew about that because her patients all delighted in reporting the facts to her.

And each day, Rodd had called her trailer. She'd listened to his phone messages over and over, needing to hear his voice but unable to return his calls. She couldn't face him. She yearned to see him, but the yearning was too sharp, nearly painful. She'd admitted to herself not only that she wanted to fall in love, but that she had in fact fallen—deeply and truly—in love with Rodd Durand. But she needed time to take it all in. It was all so new, tender, oversensitive like new skin. And maybe she'd realized all this too late.

But Zak's insistent invitation had rushed her ahead. Now, nearing the barn, the little boy dropped her hand, pushed open the door, and charged inside. Still hesitating, Wendy ducked in, then turned back and held the door for Bruce and Penny. "Go ahead," Bruce said.

Wendy turned around and there stood Rodd, looking at her. She lowered her eyes, blushing warmly. *Is it true, Lord? Does Rodd . . . care for me?*

Zak ran back and grabbed her hand, tugging on it. "Come on, Wendy. I know which cow it is. Rodd told me." He pulled her forward right into Rodd. Her breath caught; she couldn't inhale.

Rodd reached down and took Zak's hand from hers. "Don't be in such a hurry, little guy." He chuckled.

His laughter, as he stood so close, vibrated through her. *Rodd, oh, Rodd, you're here beside me.* She remembered the last time they'd been here together—Christmas Day, that crystal morning on their snow-mobiles—and their kiss as they'd gazed at Hunter's Lake—

"Come on!" Zak urged, interrupting.

Wendy moved forward in the dimly lit barn, so cozy after the chill outside.

Rodd took her arm and walked at her side. He murmured, "I'm glad to see you."

His words sent shivers of joy through her. She nodded but couldn't meet his eyes. Hope bubbled in her like the vibration of laughter, spar-kling up from deep inside. She tried to cap it, control it—impossible!

"Zak, I have the cow over here in a birthing stall," Rodd told the little boy. "It shouldn't be long. I called the vet, but he said everything sounded like it was going right." Rodd's excitement colored his voice.

"This is your first calving since you bought stock, isn't it?" Wendy asked, feeling as shy as if they were strangers, yet longing to lean closer to him.

"Yes, I had forgotten how exciting a calving can be."

Her eyes met his silver blue ones and skittered away. There was too much emotion inside her—she couldn't make herself calm down. How could she behave as though nothing had changed? Everything was different—in her heart!

Zak stood on tiptoes and hung over the railing of the stall. "When do I get to see the calf? Is it really in the mama cow's tummy?"

To steady herself, Wendy tried to take a deep breath a little at a time, so no one would notice.

Rodd ruffled the little boy's hair. "That's right, Zak. And remember, some blood will come out with the calf. That's just natural—"

"I know!" Zak interrupted. "We all got blood in us! Old Doc told me that! I'm not scared!"

The cow bawled loudly at them and tossed her head as if they were annoying her. Rodd chuckled again.

And the chuckle danced through Wendy, nearly lifting her off her feet.

Zak laughed and began talking to the cow. "Hi. I'm here to see your baby get borned. We got us a new baby that the sheriff saved from a fire."

Gathering her nerve, Wendy looked up at Rodd, so rugged and handsome, standing so close beside her. He made her feel very feminine. No one else produced that effect. "The story about the baby is the talk of the town. I'm so glad you were there to save her."

Rodd hung his head. "I wish I'd suspected the car might explode. I would have tried to get the parents out—"

Wasn't that just like him? "Harry said it sounded like their gas tank had had a tiny crack in it already, and the impact made it that much worse," she pointed out. "You saved the one you could. That's what counts."

❋❋❋

FOR THE FIRST time since the accident, Rodd felt a beginning of healing. He recalled Wendy's explanation about their making life-and-death calls. Wendy would understand the weight he carried. As a nurse, she'd accepted the same heavy responsibility. His tenderness toward her expanded inside him. *Lord, you've brought her here. Help me find a way to show her how I feel. Please help me. And yes, you heard right. Help me!*

The baby in Penny's arms sneezed. Everyone smiled. The other cattle in their stalls moved restlessly, waiting too. The cow bawled long and hard as a baby calf slid out onto the fresh hay.

"It's the calf! It got borned!" Zak bounced up and down; then he jumped into his father's arms. "We want a baby too. Not this baby." He pointed at the bundle in his mother's arms. "We're just keeping this baby till they find its grandma or aunty. We want another baby in our family. Sheriff, when are you and Wendy going to have a baby?"

A brief silence came. At least, a human one. The new mother cow lowed to her calf as she got up and examined him, nudging him. Zak's words had startled Rodd. What was the right thing to say?

"Zak," Bruce began, "you know we talked about how God's first choice is that every baby have both a mother and a father. We also talked about how it's good for a man and woman who love each other to get married before they have a family. That way, a baby gets love right at the start in a family that has a mother and a father who love each other and the baby."

"But Rodd and Wendy love each other. Don't you, Rodd?" Zak implored.

Wendy turned bright pink. "Zak—"

"Well, you do, Sheriff! You kissed her! I saw you at the auction! When are you going to get married?" Zak demanded as if Rodd were being particularly dense.

Shock rippled through Rodd. *How like God to use a child to give me the push I need.* And he had to confess, God had certainly come up with a novel way of broaching the subject of marriage. Rodd took Wendy's hand in his. He'd thought it might take weeks to win his way back into Wendy's heart. But he'd sensed Wendy's happiness today as soon as she'd entered the barn. Had God whispered to her too? *Okay, Lord, I'll take it from here!* "Excuse us, Zak. This is something Wendy and I should discuss privately. You watch the mama clean up her calf."

❋❋❋

LEAVING BRUCE AND Penny to deal with Zak's questions, Rodd led Wendy to the end of the stalls into a vacant one. The moment had come. He prayed for the right words to say. Inside the stall, he gently cupped her shoulders with his hands. "Wendy, I know this isn't the usual time or place for a proposal, but I love you with my whole heart."

Her breath caught in her throat.

"You are the only woman I've ever wanted to be my wife, the mother of my children. I know this winter has been a tough one, but . . ."

Wendy watched Rodd's intent face as he spoke. His words flowed over her like a soft caress, but his tender expression, tone, and touch told her even more. *Rodd Durand loves me, Lord. And he wants me to be his wife.*

A few weeks ago she would have been upset by Rodd's proposal. In the past, before she'd ever really felt this kind of love for any man, she'd closed the door on romance. All because of what had happened to her mother. *But I'm not my mother, Lord. And Sage is right. I won't let the past destroy my future. You've brought a fine man into my life. Rodd Durand would never betray my trust.* "Yes, Rodd."

He stopped. "You'll marry me?"

She nodded.

Sweeping her into his arms, he kissed her.

And with a full heart, she kissed him back.

❋❋❋

IN THE CHURCH office on the second day of May, Wendy's mother, Doreen, slipped another bobby pin into the crown of Wendy's wedding veil.

"Ouch," Wendy complained. "How many of those things do you need to hold on a veil?"

"That's the last one. It's good you grew your hair out longer or we'd have had to tape it to your head." Mom stepped back and gazed at Wendy, dressed in a white satin wedding gown. "I think you're the first Rieker to be married in white satin in generations."

"And I'll be next," Sage said, picking up her yellow-and-white bridesmaid bouquet from the table.

"Are you sure you want to wear this same gown?" Doreen worried aloud. "We can afford another—"

"Don't worry about it," Sage interrupted. "Since I'm taller than my big sister, Mrs. Benser is going to add another ruffle to the skirt, and she's going to shorten the sleeves for my August wedding."

Wendy had reconciled herself that Sage and Trav should get married. She didn't have the right to tell her very perceptive sister whether or when to marry. And she knew her mother was sad that her brother, Dutch, was in custody and waiting to stand trial for his part in the explosion in LaFollette. But Wendy pushed these thoughts from her mind.

Sage was saying, "And Miss Frantz is going to do something to the veil to make it look different, too."

Much to everyone's surprise, Miss Frantz had insisted on making Wendy's veil for free. Over the past months it had become clear that by stealing the bazaar money and trying to avenge herself on Mrs. Benser, Veda McCracken had alienated herself from her final few cronies.

Doreen took out her handkerchief and dabbed at her eyes. "I don't know what I ever did to deserve two such beautiful, wonderful daughters. I don't deserve you—"

"Don't say that!" Wendy and Sage put their arms around their mother and hugged her as much as they could with all the pearls, lace, and crinoline that surrounded them. Doreen and Jim appeared to be adjusted to their move and were still attending their church in Florida every week.

"I love you, girls."

"We love you too, Mom."

The organ music increased in volume. "That's our cue, Mom," Sage said and walked out into the church entry hall. Standing beside Harlan, Jim waited for Doreen. Jim offered his arm to the mother of the bride and led her proudly into the sanctuary to their seats in the front pew.

A few moments later, Sage leaned over to kiss Harlan. Then holding her bouquet of daisies and baby's breath, she walked down the aisle toward the groom and best man, Rodd and Trav.

Dressed in his new wedding suit, Grandfather offered Wendy his arm. She took it, trembling inside. She smiled at him nervously and clutched her bouquet. As they stepped into the sanctuary, the organ sounded the chord, and everyone rose in her honor. She gazed ahead and saw only Rodd.

Grandfather whispered into her ear, "Your daddy would be so proud of you."

Wendy's joy swelled inside her. "I love you, Grandfather."

He squeezed her arm. "And I'll always love you too, sweetheart. You're marrying a fine man."

Rodd stood proud and tall, waiting for her.

I waited for you too, Rodd. But our waiting is over. Our life together begins today. Thank you, Father!

EPILOGUE

Far from Steadfast . . .

She stood with her head against the cool window, looking outside. How long had it been since she'd walked down a street? *Dear God, how long is he going to keep me here? I'm so sorry for everything. What's going to happen? Why haven't Pete and Lisa come back for me?* A sob caught in her throat. *Will I ever see my baby again?*

A Note from the Author

Dear Reader:

When I married my husband over twenty years ago, I "married" the north woods of Wisconsin too. His family had been vacationing there since the 1920s. I loved going north every year and getting to know his uncles, aunts, and cousins. In the summertime, the north woods is a paradise of spring-fed lakes, tall pines, and sunshine. But after a snowmobiling trip one January, I found winter is completely different. Winter that far north near Canada can be challenging and dangerous. I chose Wisconsin in winter as the setting for my romance/suspense series because it was the perfect place to challenge my characters as they struggled against the elements and elusive evil.

Rodd and Wendy had to learn to trust the Lord before they could accept God's gift of love. As my editor, Diane Eble, said, "Rodd had to learn to trust the Lord in the present, and Wendy had to learn to trust the Lord to clean up the past."

Please let me know if Rodd and Wendy's story touched your heart. Contact me by mail in care of Tyndale House Author Relations, P.O. Box 80, Wheaton, IL 60189; online at l.cote@juno.com; or through my Web site, www.booksbylyncote.com.

About the Author

Born in Texas, raised in Illinois on the shore of Lake Michigan, Lyn now lives in Iowa with her husband, son, and daughter. Lyn has spent her adult life as a teacher, a full-time mom, and now a writer. She enjoys floral crafts, classical music, and traveling. By the way, Lyn's last name is pronounced "Coty."

Lyn's novella "For Varina's Heart" appears in the HeartQuest anthology *Letters of the Heart.* Her other novels are *Hope's Garden, New Man in Town,* and *Never Alone* (Steeple Hill); *Echoes of Mercy, Lost in His Love,* and *Whispers of Love* (Broadman & Holman).

Lyn welcomes letters written to her in care of Tyndale House Author Relations, P.O. Box 80, Wheaton, IL 60189; online at l.cote@juno.com; or through her Web site, www.booksbylyncote.com.

Turn the page for an exciting preview of book 2 in the Northern Intrigue Series

www.HeartQuest.com

AUTUMN'S SHADOW

Excerpt from Chapter One

JUST AS KEELY was about to turn onto Highway 27 to drive to the clinic to check on her injured cheerleader, her cell phone rang. "Keely Turner."

"Ms. Turner—" the young male voice on the line shook—"could you come? Carrie, you know, my girlfriend—"

"Who is this?"

"Ma'am, I volunteer in our high school store—"

She recognized his voice then. "What's wrong?"

"Shane—my friend Shane—gave me your cell phone number and told me to call you. I'm really scared for my girlfriend, Carrie Walachek. Carrie went inside her trailer . . ." The teen was obviously fighting to control his emotions. "There's been a lot of shouting and . . ."

The line clicked.

Her pulse thudding in her head, Keely looked at the phone and then hung up. She stopped on the side of the road. Reaching into her glove compartment, she took out the student directory, located Carrie's name and address, then turned her car back on the road. She sped all the way to the edge of town where a few trailers huddled together.

When she pulled up at Carrie's address, she saw Shane Blackfeather and the teen who'd called her, pounding on the trailer door, shouting Carrie's name.

Dread chilling her, Keely got out and approached the bottom of the metal steps up to the trailer. "What are you two doing?"

Shane's friend knotted his hands into fists. "This is all my fault." He turned back to Shane. "Let's break down the door—"

"Shane!" Keely snapped, trying to keep the two teens from making matters worse. "What's happening?"

Shane, tall and dark, ran down to her. "We're afraid Carrie's dad is beating her. We can't get him to open up—"

She held up her hand. Muffled shouts and groans came from inside the trailer, then a thud like something heavy—like a body—hitting the inside wall. This was more serious than what she could handle. She pulled the cell phone from her purse and speed-dialed the sheriff's department.

The trailer door burst open.

Keely dropped her phone.

"You!" the large man shouted. "Who invited you, Turner?"

"Mr. Walachek—," she began.

"Get out of here!" Alcohol slurred his voice. "Off my property!"

Carrie appeared just behind her father. She tried to squeeze around him. But the big man pinned her under one arm.

"Mr. Walachek," Keely spoke calmly, playing for time. Would the sheriff's dispatcher recognize her cell phone number on the caller ID? Could they do that? "The boys called me. What seems to be the problem? Can I be of any help?"

"I told you! This ain't your business, lady! Just 'cause you're a Turner don't give you the right to meddle! Get off my property—"

Carrie tried to twist out of her father's grip. The man slammed his fist into his daughter's face.

Keely stooped and grabbed up her phone. *Why did I send that deputy away so quickly!*

The teens made a rush for the girl. The father dragged his daughter inside, but he couldn't get the door shut in time. The boys rushed inside—yelling.

"Get her out of there!" Keely screamed.

A police siren drowned out her voice.

Shane and his friend burst out with Carrie between them. They hustled down the steps, half carrying the girl.

"Get her into my car!" Keely shouted.

"Don't move!" the father bellowed at the top of the steps. "Don't move, any of you!" He held a rifle and pointed it deliberately at Keely's head.

The three teens froze halfway down the steps.

Keely couldn't draw breath.

"Mr. Walachek?" a calm voice came from behind Keely. "What seems to be the problem here?"

It was that new deputy, Burke Sloan! Thank God!

"Get off my property!" the man bellowed again, the sound vibrating inside Keely, making her tremble.

"Mr. Walachek, you know I can't do that," Sloan said in a calm tone. "Not when you're pointing a weapon at Ms. Turner. I can't leave until you put that rifle away."

"I didn't ask her to come. She's on my property. I got a right to shoot trespassers!"

"I don't want to argue with you, but if you think you can shoot Ms. Turner as a trespasser, you'll find out it won't hold up in court."

"Yeah, but if she's dead, she won't care. And it would serve her father right!" The man cursed.

"Mr. Walachek," the deputy said in a tone anyone would request a weather report with, "you still haven't told me what the problem is."

"He got my girl pregnant! And he's going to marry her or—"

"This be your first grandchild?" Sloan asked.

The man stared at him. "What?"

"I said, will this be your first grandchild?"

"Yeah! What about it?"

"I just thought you might want to be around when the baby's born." The deputy's tone continued matter-of-factly.

"What's that mean?" Walachek glared and tightened his grip on his deer rifle.

"That means this is no time to be pointing guns at people."

"Get that Turner off my property then! Her father—"

Keely tried to block out the nasty words and the hateful tone. Her father's high-handed reputation was making matters difficult for her once again.

"I don't see how that has anything to do with Ms. Turner. Now, Mr. Walachek, put down your rifle."

The drunken man glared at Keely.

"Mr. Walachek, my weapon's safety is off. I can get several rounds off before you can aim and fire one. This is no time to be firing guns. Your daughter is in the line of fire and she's expecting a child. Now you wouldn't want anything to hurt your little girl, would you?"

Keely held her breath. Walachek stared into her eyes, seeing her fear, feeding on it—she thought. But she couldn't hide it.

"Mr. Walachek, put your gun down." The deputy's easygoing tone hardened to forged steel.

The drunken man's glare turned belligerent.

CURRENT HEARTQUEST RELEASES

- *Magnolia,* Ginny Aiken
- *Lark,* Ginny Aiken
- *Camellia,* Ginny Aiken
- *Letters of the Heart,* Lisa Tawn Bergren, Maureen Pratt, and Lyn Cote
- *Sweet Delights,* Terri Blackstock, Elizabeth White, and Ranee McCollum
- *Awakening Mercy,* Angela Benson
- *Abiding Hope,* Angela Benson
- *Faith,* Lori Copeland
- *Hope,* Lori Copeland
- *June,* Lori Copeland
- *Glory,* Lori Copeland
- *Winter's Secret,* Lyn Cote
- *Freedom's Promise,* Dianna Crawford
- *Freedom's Hope,* Dianna Crawford
- *Freedom's Belle,* Dianna Crawford
- *English Ivy,* Catherine Palmer
- *Finders Keepers,* Catherine Palmer
- *Hide and Seek,* Catherine Palmer
- *Prairie Rose,* Catherine Palmer
- *Prairie Fire,* Catherine Palmer
- *Prairie Storm,* Catherine Palmer
- *Prairie Christmas,* Catherine Palmer, Elizabeth White, and Peggy Stoks
- *A Kiss of Adventure,* Catherine Palmer (original title: *The Treasure of Timbuktu*)
- *A Whisper of Danger,* Catherine Palmer (original title: *The Treasure of Zanzibar*)
- *A Touch of Betrayal,* Catherine Palmer
- *A Victorian Christmas Keepsake,* Catherine Palmer, Kristin Billerbeck, and Ginny Aiken
- *A Victorian Christmas Cottage,* Catherine Palmer, Debra White Smith, Jeri Odell, and Peggy Stoks
- *A Victorian Christmas Quilt,* Catherine Palmer, Peggy Stoks, Debra White Smith, and Ginny Aiken
- *A Victorian Christmas Tea,* Catherine Palmer, Dianna Crawford, Peggy Stoks, and Katherine Chute
- *Olivia's Touch,* Peggy Stoks
- *Romy's Walk,* Peggy Stoks
- *Elena's Song,* Peggy Stoks

COMING SOON (SUMMER 2002)

- *Enduring Love,* Angela Benson
- *Roses Will Bloom Again,* Lori Copeland
- *A Home in the Valley,* Dianna Crawford

HEARTQUEST BOOKS BY LYN COTE

For Varina's Heart—What says romance more than a handwritten letter from the one you love? Suddenly finding herself tied to a man she does not know, Varina treasures her heart's dreams while hanging on to each letter that arrives from Gannon Moore. This historical novella by Lyn Cote appears in the anthology *Letters of the Heart.*

OTHER GREAT TYNDALE HOUSE FICTION

- *Safely Home,* Randy Alcorn
- *Jenny's Story,* Judy Baer
- *Libby's Story,* Judy Baer
- *Tia's Story,* Judy Baer
- *Out of the Shadows,* Sigmund Brouwer
- *Pony Express Christmas,* Sigmund Brouwer
- *Child of Grace,* Lori Copeland
- *Christmas Vows: $5.00 Extra,* Lori Copeland
- *Ribbon of Years,* Robin Lee Hatcher
- *The Price,* Jim and Terri Kraus
- *The Treasure,* Jim and Terri Kraus
- *The Promise,* Jim and Terri Kraus
- *The Quest,* Jim and Terri Kraus
- *Winter Passing,* Cindy McCormick Martinusen
- *Blue Night,* Cindy McCormick Martinusen
- *North of Tomorrow,* Cindy McCormick Martinusen
- *Embrace the Dawn,* Kathleen Morgan
- *Lullaby,* Jane Orcutt
- *The Happy Room,* Catherine Palmer
- *A Dangerous Silence,* Catherine Palmer
- *Unveiled*, Francine Rivers
- *Unashamed*, Francine Rivers
- *Unshaken*, Francine Rivers
- *Unspoken,* Francine Rivers
- *Unafraid,* Francine Rivers
- *A Voice in the Wind*, Francine Rivers
- *An Echo in the Darkness,* Francine Rivers
- *As Sure As the Dawn,* Francine Rivers
- *Leota's Garden,* Francine Rivers